Bay Tree Cottage

Bay Tree Cottage

ANNA JACOBS

Allison & Busby Limited
12 Fitzroy Mews
London W1T 6DW
allisonandbusby.com

First published in Great Britain by Allison & Busby in 2018.
This paperback edition published by Allison & Busby in 2018.

Copyright © 2018 by ANNA JACOBS

A CIP catalogue record for this book is available from
the British Library.

10 9 8 7 6 5 4 3 2 1

ISBN 978-0-7490-2346-1

Typeset in 10.5/15.5 pt Sabon by
Allison & Busby Ltd

The paper used for this Allison & Busby publication
has been produced from trees that have been legally sourced
from well-managed and credibly certified forests.

Printed and bound by
CPI Group (UK) Ltd, Croydon, CR0 4YY

Chapter One

Ginger waited till the café was empty to speak to Joe. She put her tray of dirty dishes down on the counter, took a deep breath and said it. 'I need a week's holiday, urgently.'

As she'd expected, he folded his arms and scowled at her. 'Why?'

'Private business.'

'Can't do it.'

'You could bring Karen in full-time. She'd welcome the extra money.'

'I don't want Karen; I want you, Ginger. And so do the customers.'

'If I'm so popular with them, Joe, why don't you give me the rise I've been asking for? Two years it is, now, since my last rise. Anyway, that's neither here nor there. This is really important. I have to go somewhere.'

'You haven't said what it's about.'

'I already told you: it's private.'

'Well, I can't do it. Even a funeral only takes half a day off usually.'

Suddenly her resentment at the way he treated her boiled over. She'd stayed because there were advantages to working within walking distance of home, not to mention the free food when leftovers couldn't be sold any longer. But this was a once in a lifetime opportunity and she didn't intend to miss it. She folded her arms across her chest. 'Then I quit.'

The words seemed to echo in the air between them. He gaped at her for several seconds, then shook his head slowly. 'You don't mean that! You've been here for nearly ten years. You can have one day off and that's it.' He turned back to his newspaper as if the problem was solved.

It was the final straw. She left the tray on the counter and went into the back room. It only took her two minutes to dump the things from her locker into her shopping bag. When she turned round, he'd brought the tray into the kitchen and was staring at her in shock.

'What are you doing?'

'I just told you: I'm quitting.' She went to stand right in front of him, so close he took an involuntary step backwards, still holding the tray.

'I want my wages and holiday pay before I go.' She told him the amount. She always kept an eye on the money side of things. You had to with Joe.

He shuddered and dumped the tray on the nearest surface. 'It *can't* be that much!'

'It is. You know I'd never cheat you.'

'That's all very well, but I'm short of cash. Just take a

couple of days' leave, if you have to. I'll pay you holiday rates for it after you get back.'

'I'm not coming back to work here. If you don't pay me now, I'll report you to the authorities.' She knew how carefully he avoided anything which gave officials the right to poke their noses into his affairs, so she added, 'That'll bring the VAT man down on you.' She didn't think it had anything to do with VAT, but Joe hated even to say the words and knew even less about it all than she did.

'Take the whole damned week off, then.'

'No. I've had enough of your bad temper and poor pay. I'm ready for a change. I'll not be coming back to work here, so you'd better call Karen and start looking for a replacement for me.'

'But—'

'No.'

Another long silence, then he took out his wallet and counted out the money, slapping it down on the counter in front of her. 'Don't think I'll have you back.'

'I won't even consider asking.'

She took the notes and coins, counted them again, just to be sure, and stuffed them into her purse any old how.

When she was out of sight of the café, she stopped and took a long shuddering breath.

What had she done?

As Ginger walked home, it began to rain and she put up her umbrella. She was, she admitted to herself, feeling more than a bit shaky. She'd well and truly burnt her bridges now, hadn't she? She was a woman who valued security and usually planned every aspect of her life.

She hadn't planned this, let alone thought it through.

'What have you done, girl?' she muttered as she went into the small terraced house. She looked to the right and saw her son sitting in the front room watching TV and smoking. He must have come home from work. Was it that time already?

She'd been smelling cigarettes on him for a week or two but hadn't said anything because she was fed up of quarrels that got you nowhere. Now, the anger that had carried her through against Joe bubbled up again and gave her the courage to stand up to her thirty-year-old son, who seemed to be getting nastier by the month.

'How many times do I have to tell you, Donny? I'm not having smoking in this house. Even your father did his smoking outside. If you want to follow his example and die of lung cancer, you can do it somewhere else. I'm not putting my life at risk with your sidestream smoke, though.'

'Don't nag, Ma. I'm not really smoking. I just need a cigarette every now and then. Anyway, I can't do it outside. It's raining.'

'You're still not smoking in here.'

'Mum, let it drop!'

'No. And while we're at it, I'll give you a week to get out or I'll hire someone to throw you and your things into the street. I've asked you several times to find a place of your own to live and you haven't. This smoking is the final straw.'

'You wouldn't do that.' He sounded amused.

'Oh, wouldn't I?'

'Well, I can't *afford* a place of my own.'

'You could if you stopped smoking and cut back on the boozing.' She plucked the cigarette out of his mouth and threw it into the fireplace.

'I'd only just lit that.' He jumped up and thumped her, sending her crashing into the corner of the fireplace surround.

It was the second time he'd hit her. They both froze in shock.

'You drive me to it,' he muttered. 'You and your nagging.'

She rubbed her arm where it'd hit the fireplace. 'Your father never laid a finger on me in all our years together. You're definitely not staying here, Donny.'

'You needed me to help with the lifting when Dad was dying of cancer, didn't you? And I came for you then. You need me now as well. I pay half the rent and I keep you safe. It's getting a bit rough round here, in case you hadn't noticed.'

She had, but wasn't going to admit it. 'I'll be safe from everyone but you then.' She took out a tissue and blew her nose to prevent herself from crying. Her own son had hit her! Twice now. How could he do that?

'I'm not leaving, Ma, but I'm sorry I thumped you. It won't happen again.' And before she could say anything else, he grabbed his jacket and left the house.

He'd promised that the first time he hit her, too. She didn't believe it any more because he'd just done it again, hadn't he? Sitting down abruptly because she felt wobbly, she let the tears fall. It was going to come to a serious confrontation if she wanted to get rid of him, because why should he move out voluntarily when things were so comfortable here? The trouble was, she couldn't bear to live in a pigsty so she kept on clearing up after him. That meant he had a built-in housekeeper and cook.

Last month she'd caught him raiding her purse. He'd always been lazy and sometimes lied to her but she'd never expected that. He was going from bad to worse. She had to stop it.

She'd threatened to ask for the council's help in getting rid of him. She wasn't even sure that they would help but knew the thought of them butting in would upset Donny. And it had. That was why he'd thumped her the first time.

He'd been very careful since, not a sign of violence, but she'd been shaken to the core by him daring to hit her, so had gone online and read about family members beating others up. She'd found out it didn't just happen to wives, but to parents too, especially elderly ones.

She was only fifty-one, and no way was she elderly, but she was a small, thin woman and he was over six foot tall and burly. Apparently grown-up children, usually the sons, sometimes started thumping their parents. Only occasionally at first and they apologised, but gradually they got a taste for it.

It seemed to her now that Donny was showing the classic start-up symptoms and she hadn't been doing a good job of standing up for herself. After she'd told him to leave last time, she should have followed through. *Dare* she do something about getting him out this time?

Well, she had to or her life would be miserable.

She looked at the town's website and found out that there was a phone number for women in trouble. She studied herself in the mirror and pulled up her sleeve. There was a nasty bruise on her arm now, where she'd hit the fireplace.

She was definitely in trouble.

She got out the cheap smartphone she'd treated herself to last year and took a selfie of her upper body, showing the bruise.

Then she stared in the mirror and nodded, promising herself that things were going to change. She had a chance for a new life now and she intended to seize it with both hands. Giving up her job was the biggest risk she'd ever taken.

When she considered his reaction to a little thing like her throwing away his cigarette, she worried about another thing she'd be risking: him wrecking the house. But perhaps she could do something to protect the things she cared about.

She paced up and down, trying to work out how best to do this. In the end, she decided to write to the council and plead for their help in getting rid of Donny, who had become abusive.

First things first. Before she left for the interview she had to make sure the possessions she cared about were safe. There weren't many: her embroideries, her family photos, a few special books. The only real jewellery she owned was her wedding ring and that never left her finger. Well, she couldn't get it off now, could she? Her knuckles were a bit swollen. Those hands had worked hard.

She looked round and grimaced. The furniture was too shabby to care about. You could pick up better stuff at the tip in the recycling section. It'd be a bit of a nuisance if Donny damaged things, but she didn't care about it.

What else needed adding to her mental list of preparations?

Oh, yes. Get the car ready for the long drive from Newcastle to Wiltshire. She'd already replied to the email from Mrs Denning, agreeing to attend the interview. And if she didn't get the job, she'd have a go at something else.

She should have made some changes after her husband died. She'd stayed on in the house out of habit. Time to change her habits. More than time.

'Just get on with it, girl!' she muttered. 'Do what you have to!'

By the time her son got home from work the following evening, Ginger intended to have everything ready so that she could leave as soon as he went to work the next morning. It was a good thing she didn't have to go into the café today because she was going to be very busy indeed.

She started by going next door and having a chat with Kerry, who was a good neighbour and long-time friend – as much as anyone could be a friend who had six married children and goodness knew how many grandchildren forever needing her help.

Reluctantly she showed Kerry the bruise.

Her friend gave her a big hug. 'You don't deserve that, love. Didn't I tell you to get him out?' She had one son, divorced, who kept getting into trouble, so she knew what she was talking about. She'd been telling Ginger for a while that some folk didn't want to be helped and you just had to give up on them.

'Yes, and you were right. I should have got him out.'

'Anyway, if anyone asks me, I'll tell them what he's like and about those bruises, by heck I will. I've no time for your Donny these days. He's gone to the bad like my George did.'

Ginger couldn't argue with that. But this was her *only* son. Kerry had other sons – and daughters. She wanted the old Donny back, the child she'd loved so much.

The next thing Ginger did was pick up some empty cardboard boxes from the back of the supermarket and load them in her car boot. On the way home, she hired a small storage locker from a place that had opened last year a few streets away in a disused factory.

It took her longer than she'd expected to pack all the things she cared about, but at last it was done and she took them to her storage locker.

The cupboards and drawers in her bedroom were almost empty now, and so were those in the sideboard downstairs, but Donny wouldn't notice that. Apart from his pigsty of a bedroom, he rarely got beyond the kettle, the TV and the fridge.

She felt exhausted, as if she'd been running ever since she got up, but she wasn't going to stop till she'd done everything on her list.

She went to a garage where she wasn't known to fill her car and check the oil and tyres. Donny used the nearby garage and the owner was one of her son's drinking pals. She didn't want him gossiping about seeing her getting the car ready for a trip.

She was now all set for a quick departure in the morning. It was a long way from Tyneside to the south-west, but she'd always enjoyed driving and she thought her old car would manage to get to Wiltshire all right because she looked after it, like she looked after all her possessions, and had it serviced regularly.

The only thing she hadn't done by teatime was write to the council and ask for help.

When Donny came home from work she was pretending to be watching the TV news. She didn't even look round till he said her name a second time. 'Sorry? What did you say?'

'I asked what's for tea.'

'There's nothing much in the fridge because I wasn't at work today. I ate up the odds and ends. You'll have to buy yourself a takeaway.'

To her astonishment he took a step towards her, scowling, fists clenched. 'You should have gone shopping, then.'

Was he going to hit her again? What on earth had got into him lately? Was it the boozing?

She stood up and shouted back. 'If you hit me again, Donald Brunham, I'll go straight to the police and lay a complaint. I won't put up with any more violence.' She rolled up her sleeve and brandished the bruise at him. 'I'll show them this, for a start. You did that to me yesterday.'

The bruise seemed to surprise him. She watched him frown at it as he considered what to do.

After a moment or two, he said, 'Some mother you are, not having my tea ready! No wonder you make me angry.'

'Some son you are, not paying your own way. Anyway, I give you one week to get out, then I'll take action to have you evicted.'

'You wouldn't dare.' He slammed out of the house.

How had her son turned so sexist?

She sat down at the kitchen table and after a moment or two she poured herself a glass of her special occasions amontillado sherry. She only ever had a single glass but it always cheered her up because it tasted so nice.

This time she drank a toast to her interview going well. When she'd finished sipping the sherry delicately, relishing the taste, she washed out the glass and hid the sherry in her bedroom.

'You'll have to do it, Ginger! Stop procrastinating!' She switched on her laptop and wrote an email to the address on the council website. No getting out of it. Donny had nearly hit her again tonight.

She explained that her son was an unwanted lodger whom she'd put up in an emergency, but who now refused to leave. He'd started hitting her and she was frightened to stay here while he was around. She attached the photo of the bruise, feeling ashamed to have to do that.

She paused to think about it. Where had she gone wrong as a mother?

With a sigh she went back to the email, telling them she was going away for a few weeks because she was frightened of her son thumping her again. She would be grateful if they could get Donny out of her house. If they didn't, she was afraid he'd wreck the place in one of his violent tempers.

She finished by saying that she didn't dare come back till someone from the council emailed to let her know her son Donald Brunham was out of the house and it was safe for her to return.

Her neighbour Kerry Smithers at No. 17 could verify everything she'd said about the situation.

If they needed any more information, they had only to ask.

That should make them act, surely? They might not care about her but she'd read in the paper that they were clamping down on people who damaged council property, trying to keep maintenance and repair costs down.

After signing it she reread it and was about to send it off when she realised she'd signed it 'Ginger'. Oops! She deleted it quickly and typed in 'Jean' instead. She'd never liked her real name and had been known as 'Ginger' ever since she started school because of her red hair, but this was an official document and she was Jean Brunham in council records.

She glanced sideways at the mirror and pulled a face. She had to colour her hair now to keep it red, because she'd gone grey early – not grey but pure white. It never came up as nicely as her own colour used to be, though. The last time she'd tried a new colour called 'soft red', but it had come out far too garish. Well, it would fade gradually and she didn't have time to do anything about it now.

She closed her laptop and packed it in its carrying case. She wasn't leaving that behind.

It was only eight o'clock so she switched on the TV, but there was nothing worth watching and anyway, she couldn't settle, because she kept worrying that Donny would come home drunk again.

She had a shower and went to bed to get an early night, but couldn't settle to sleep, either. But she felt safer in her bedroom.

Donny didn't come home till well after the pubs closed. She heard him slamming about downstairs but gave no sign that she was awake. She'd jammed a chair under the door handle, just in case. He didn't usually come in here, but she wasn't risking it.

To her relief, he went straight to bed without trying to speak to her.

Thank goodness, oh, thank goodness!

But even so she didn't sleep well. Donny's snoring woke her several times. He always snored when he got drunk.

She kept dozing off then jerking awake, listening, worrying – was glad when dawn slowly brightened the world.

Ginger used the bathroom and got dressed, but didn't go downstairs. She went back into her bedroom and didn't leave it till after Donny had gone to work. She used the time to pack her final bits and pieces and scribble a note to him, repeating that he had one week to get out. Then she stood staring out of the window, waiting to see him go.

Only then did she leave her room. The kitchen was in a

mess and he'd vomited in the sink last night, the pig. Hadn't even rinsed it away. Ugh!

The smell put her off her breakfast, so she cleared out the fridge, wiped it clean and switched it off. She took some food with her to save buying meals and gave the rest to Kerry.

On the way out with her suitcase, Ginger stopped at the front door and stared back down the narrow hall. She had a sudden feeling she'd not be living in this house again, one of her tingly presentiments that came true, more often than not. Which was strange, because she was planning to return, of course she was, whether she got this wonderful opportunity or not. She hadn't lived anywhere else than this house for over twenty years, had she?

She probably wouldn't succeed at tomorrow's interview, anyway. She'd never been lucky, had had to work damned hard for every single thing she'd got in her life. But she'd give it a good try. It'd be practise at interviews if nothing else.

If she didn't get the job, she'd been thinking she might take an Open University course and gain a qualification of some sort. She'd read avidly all her life and watched current affairs on TV, so considered herself fairly knowledgeable about the world. Only, to get a decent job you needed an actual piece of paper saying you could do it.

Ah, she was silly thinking like that. She should concentrate on what to say at the interview. One step at a time.

Whatever happened, she wasn't going to live with Donny again. No way.

A tear or two escaped as she drove towards the motorway. Raindrops spattered against the windscreen as if the weather was in sympathy with her. She wiped the moisture away from her cheeks with one hand, but more tears followed.

Well, she was only human, wasn't she? When your only son treated you so badly, you had a right to cry.

Chapter Two

Wiltshire

Saffron Lane was bathed in sunshine for most of the morning but during the early afternoon the brightness faded and clouds started to drift across the sky. There were only two houses occupied in the short street. The six 1930s houses had been left untouched for decades because the War Office had commandeered them during the Second World War.

The government had held on to them for a few decades after the fighting ended and the cold war began. When it eventually returned them to the owner, she was so old and frail she hadn't bothered to do anything with them.

Angus Denning had inherited the family property from her, but he'd had enough on his plate renovating the small stately home on two acres tucked away on the edge of the town centre at the top end of Peppercorn Street. Apart from checking that the houses were weatherproof and no danger to anyone, he'd left them alone.

Recently, however, he'd turned his attention to Saffron

Lane again and had renovated the houses in the hopes of generating some ongoing income to help with the maintenance of the big house.

He and his new wife had decided to set up an artists' colony here, offering free start-up residencies to suitable tenants. They were also planning to set up a café/gallery on the ground floor of Number 1 to display the artists' wares. They would, of course, take a percentage of the sales money as well as the profits from the café, and later on rents would be charged for the houses.

The first two artists were now in residence.

At Number 2, Stacy Walsh put down her small electric welder and eased her shoulders as she studied her latest creation. The long-legged, two-foot-high metal bird wasn't finished yet, but it already seemed to be eyeing her cheekily, head on one side. She smiled back at it involuntarily.

It had definitely begun to acquire a personality of its own, as most of her small animal sculptures did. They might be made from odd pieces of scrap metal but somehow she had a gift for seeing what she could bring to life by putting them together. To her delight she had now started to sell the finished pieces.

She also liked to make steam-punk-style installations, the sort of thing her parents called Heath Robinson creations. She loved Heath Robinson's cartoons and valued this compliment, but the installations took a lot longer to make than the little animals. She'd sold the last one to the owner, Angus Denning, when she moved here.

The tenancy of this house was allowing her to work

full-time on her art, which was bliss, especially after the hassles, financial and otherwise, involved in the recent break-up of her marriage.

She'd had enough working for the moment and wondered if Elise next door would fancy a coffee break. On the off chance, she put the kettle on and went out into the long, narrow rear garden that the first four houses shared, peering unashamedly into the next house. She could see her friend sitting at the table in the back room with a sketchbook open in front of her. Elise was staring into space, not working, which usually meant she'd be happy to take a break.

When Stacy rapped on the window, Elise jerked in shock, then smiled and beckoned her inside.

'Do join me. I'll put the kettle on.'

'Mine's about to boil and I've got some chocolate cake left.'

Elise stood up. 'In that case, I'll be happy to help you eat it.'

They left the house the front way, because at nearly seventy-six, Elise preferred the more stable footing of the paved paths to the uneven grass. Strange, Stacy thought, how well the two of them got on, in spite of the fifty or so years between them. And it wasn't as if Elise felt like a grandmother figure – on the contrary, she had a lively enquiring mind and seemed young at heart.

As Stacy was about to open her front door, a car drew up at Number 1 and a man got out. He gave them a cursory nod and frowned as he checked his watch. He must be expecting to meet someone.

When they went inside, Elise gestured towards the street. 'I'm unashamedly nosey. I'll keep an eye on him while you brew a pot of tea, shall I?'

'Yes, please. I'm not ashamed of being nosey when it comes to possible neighbours.'

The older woman went over to the window and kept up a running commentary. 'He's pacing up and down. Now he's peering into the front window of Number 1. He's looking at his watch again. Oh, bother! He's gone round the back. Can you see him?'

Stacy peered out of the kitchen window. 'Yes. He's trying the back door. I think we ought to call Angus. A burglar wouldn't usually try to break in at this time of day, especially when he knows we've seen him, but still, better safe than sorry.'

She picked up the phone and rang their landlord at the big house.

'I'll be down straight away,' Angus said. 'Can't be too careful.'

Stacy put the phone back in its cradle. 'Shall we have our tea in the front room for a change? I'm sure you're as curious as I am to see what's going on.'

'Good idea.' For all her silver hair and wrinkles, Elise had a cheeky urchin's grin, which in some weird way rather reminded Stacy of her bird sculpture.

The stranger was back to pacing up and down in front of the end house by the time Angus arrived. He swung round at the sound of a car then looked disappointed.

'Can I help you?' Angus asked. 'I'm the owner of this estate.'

'Ah, yes. Angus Denning, isn't it? I'm Emil Kinnaird, Jason's son.'

'Pleased to meet you.'

The two men shook hands.

'You and my father have spoken on the phone and emailed, I gather. He was tied up today so he sent me in his place. I'm going to take some photographs for him, at least I am if the local heritage officer turns up as arranged.'

'Who?'

'Charlene Brody.' He looked at his watch again. 'I was expecting her to be here. Do you know her?'

He saw his companion's expression lose its warmth and raised one eyebrow. 'Not a friend of yours from the look on your face, I'd guess?'

'Not exactly. She's employed by the council and she isn't really a heritage officer. There's a regional heritage group that I'm dealing with, who are the real experts, but she's not part of it.'

'That's strange.'

'She's rather annoying, like a wasp that's got into the kitchen and won't be shooed out. She's only supposed to liaise and keep an eye on such matters for the council, but she's overkeen and keeps trying to manage things. As we haven't played her game, she's inundated me and my wife with paperwork about Dennings. I think she's out to make her name and gain a promotion. Her former manager was arrested recently, you see, and she's acting in the job.'

'Ah. I must say, she was very emphatic that I deal only with her.'

'Actually, since I own this property, any visits should

have been referred to me before they were arranged. As far as I know, Ms Brody doesn't even have a key.'

'But she mentioned letting me in, so she must have, surely?'

'If she does have one, I'll be changing the locks.' Angus's mobile rang just then. 'Excuse me a minute. It's my wife and she doesn't ring unless it's important.' He took out his phone and had a brief conversation. 'Send her down, love.'

He turned back to the stranger. 'Ms Brody has turned up at the big house, demanding a key to this place, apparently.'

'*Demanding?*'

'That's how she usually makes requests. She's been trying to get hold of a key ever since we found the secret communications centre from WWII hidden in the roof space.'

'Yes. Dad told me about all that and the secret passages from it underneath the street. He's very excited because he's really into WWII memorabilia. I must say it sounds quite exciting to me, too.'

Angus pointed to a fenced area to the right of the house, where heavy metal sheets were bolted into place across the ground. 'That's where the underground passage was damaged by a lorry and exposed. We had to make sure there was no way anyone could get in, so the barrier is a bit rough and ready, but safety first, eh? We'll make everything look better before the gallery and your father's little museum open. There's a lot of conservation work and cataloguing still to be done by the heritage people inside the building, so there's also the need to protect our history from being tampered with.'

'Well, I'm sorry Ms Brody misled us. I've driven down from Leeds today to look round before I take over the area office in town here. Any chance *you* could let me in just for a quick peep and a few more photos for Dad to gloat over?'

Before Angus could answer, a small red car suddenly turned into the street, going much too fast. It had to brake hard to park next to them without running on to the narrow pavement.

The driver got out quickly, frowning as she approached them and not wasting time on greetings. 'Your wife has once again refused to give the council a key, Mr Denning. I really must protest at the way you're keeping our officials away from this property.'

'It's still not been made safe. And even when it has, I shan't be giving out keys to all and sundry.'

'As I deal with heritage matters on behalf of the town council, I have a *right* to be involved.'

He shrugged. 'I haven't changed my mind from last time we discussed this. The regional heritage people are handling it. They have the necessary expertise and resources.'

Emil noticed she was tapping her foot impatiently and watched with interest to see what she'd do next. He didn't like the sharp tone of her voice or her attitude.

When Angus didn't make any other comment, she said even more sharply, 'Surely you can let us in for a quick inspection now that Mr Kinnaird has come all this way to see the place?'

'Sorry, but I can't. It's not open to the public, hasn't been passed as safe by the heritage people.'

'I just told you: I am *not* the public!'

'You are as far as I'm concerned.'

'I shall complain to a higher authority.'

He shrugged. 'Complain away.'

She turned to Emil. 'I'm sorry to have brought you here today to no purpose, Mr Kinnaird. I hadn't expected Mr Denning to be so intransigent.'

She turned back to Angus and her voice grew even sharper. 'You will definitely be hearing from the council, Mr Denning. This place is of public interest and you have no *right* to deny local people entry. And what's more, it's definitely in *my* remit to ensure that it's *safe* and no one can get into it.'

After glaring at him for a moment or two longer, as if expecting a reply, she muttered something and got into her car.

The two men watched her drive away.

'Phew! You're right. She is rather wasp-like,' Emil commented when the car had disappeared from sight. 'An angry wasp at that.'

'Yes. Um, look, I'm happy to give you a quick informal tour if you'll promise not to tell on me to Ms Brody.'

Emil chuckled. He liked this guy's style. 'I promise.'

'But you must promise not to touch anything, not the objects still lying around nor the furnishings. We've left everything exactly as it was, you see, as did the heritage people in their preliminary inspections. I had the structure of the house checked by experts because the outer wall at that side was damaged by the lorry ramming it, but they think it's safe, because it was heavily reinforced when built.

Only, as you can see, the side of the house still looks a mess as well as the ground nearby.'

'Thanks. I'd appreciate a quick tour. Can I ask what made you offer to do that when you've just refused to let Ms Brody in?'

'You seem a reasonable chap, and your father is going to fund a small museum here, so that gives your family a genuine interest in getting this development right. That woman has no reason to get involved and she doesn't give a toss about the history of the place. I do, the real heritage people do and, of course, your father does. Presumably you share his interest?'

'Not to the same extent but I do think what the British people did to hold off an invasion during the war was incredible. Dad says the terrorists are underestimating them today, as well.'

'Yes. The more I learn about World War II, the more proud I am to be British.'

'My father has been looking to do something to honour his father's memory for a while. He's very proud of my grandfather's secret contribution to the war effort, and now that the authorities are releasing information about Bletchley Park and other formerly hush-hush war projects, the time seems ripe and this is the perfect opportunity to do it in a small way, because he's not a billionaire.'

'There were a lot of unsung heroes at Bletchley Park whose deeds are only just coming to light.'

Both men were silent for a moment or two in respect to those who'd worked without glory or fanfares to protect their country. Then Angus opened the front door of the first house, ushering Emil inside and locking the door behind them.

'Just in case she comes back.' His smile faded as they walked through the ground floor and saw Ms Brody standing outside the rear French windows peering in. 'Talk of the devil. Look at that!'

'You've got to give her marks for persistence,' Emil commented.

'I don't give her marks for anything!'

The heritage officer rapped on the windows and when Angus made no move to let her in, she rapped again.

He went closer to the window and yelled, 'Go away! You're trespassing.'

She folded her arms and glared at him. 'I'm not going anywhere till I've checked the inside of this house.'

Angus turned away. 'She can stand there like patience on a monument, then. If she'd been a reasonable person I'd have let her in as a matter of courtesy. Now, forget about her. Let's get on with our tour. There's nothing to see downstairs. They kept it like a normal house. We're going to turn it into an art gallery and café.'

He gestured to one side of the room. 'The communications room is accessed via a concealed door in the hall. You can also get to it from the cellar via a secret passage, as your father no doubt told you, but we're keeping the entrance closed for the moment so that it doesn't show.'

'Amazing.'

'Yes. If Hitler had managed to invade Britain, certain people would have worked here and in other hidden places to resist them.' He demonstrated the concealed door on the first floor. 'Come in.'

'Wow!' Emil stared round the communications room, which covered one half of the roof space, with a rather low ceiling at one side. There were big sheets of transparent plastic sheeting over the surfaces now. 'I didn't realise it was so well equipped.'

'Yes, and every single piece of paper is as they left it. Incredible, isn't it? I feel honoured to be able to keep it safe. The heritage people have done a preliminary assessment and are now working out how best to display everything so that the public can see but not touch.'

'Yes, they've been in touch with Dad about it. May I take photos, Angus?'

'As long as you promise not to give copies to anyone except your father.'

'I promise.'

When Emil had finished, Angus opened a concealed door in the wood panelling that covered all the walls and revealed a narrow staircase that was hardly more than a ladder. 'Watch how you go.'

They backed down it into the tunnels.

At the bottom Angus said, 'Turn right. The other direction is open now underground at the place where the lorry caused the cave-in, but that passage leads to an electricity substation and that's got a metal grille across it now. I have no right to go into it and someone at the council, probably Madam Wasp, has the key. There isn't anything to see in the tunnels, really, but you'll get a feel for the cellar and passages, at least.'

He switched on some lights. 'Those who built it had to use torches but we put in lights using the electricity supply from Number 6, which is the largest house in Saffron Lane.'

Emil followed him along the tunnel, shivering in the chill air. The ceiling and walls of the passage were shored up with sheets of corrugated iron, held in place by rough wooden posts and joists. As Angus had said, there was nothing to see except a locked door at the other end. But he felt a tension in the air, as if something might happen at any moment.

It was probably his imagination, but it made him glance over his shoulder a couple of times.

Angus grinned. 'Makes me feel like that too, sometimes. I won't take you into Number 6. We'd only tramp in dirt and, actually, the door is so well hidden I don't want to disturb it, because we're going to have artists living there.'

As they started back, he said, 'I wouldn't put it past the Brody woman to be prowling up and down the road and peering through the windows of all the empty houses. I'll check afterwards that she really has left the street, then perhaps you'd like to come up to the big house for a cuppa before you set off back to Leeds?'

Emil smiled. 'Actually, I'm staying in town from now on. Dad has a regional branch office here. Not everyone likes to buy their insurance online and there are claims to deal with, too. I'll take a rain check on the cuppa, if you don't mind. I'm supposed to be meeting the guy who's been running the branch for a briefing. He's taking early retirement and I'm going to pick his brains before he goes, because there isn't a detail he doesn't understand about the insurance industry.'

'Do you have somewhere to stay? We aren't well supplied with hotels and B & Bs here, I'm afraid.'

'I shall be moving into the flat above the office till I see how things stand. It's been empty for years but apparently all the domestic equipment in it is still functional.'

'Welcome to Sexton Bassett, then. We'll maybe get together another time.'

'I'd like that. I've been working frenetically in Australia and am intending to slow down and smell the roses now I'm back, as they say. I'm really looking forward to exploring Wiltshire. It's such a beautiful county. You'll have to tell me the best places to go. I wish it'd warm up a bit, though. I'm still getting used to a cooler climate.'

'Well, it'll be summer soon.'

Emil chuckled. 'The UK summer is quite similar to the West Australian winter.'

Angus locked up Number 1 and waved the visitor goodbye. Ms Brody's small red car might no longer be parked in Saffron Lane, but he could see it in the street outside the entrance to Dennings. She wasn't sitting in it and there was no sign of her anywhere that he could see. What the hell was the devious idiot up to now? He hoped she wasn't going to keep trespassing. He had better things to do than keep an eye out for her.

He went to knock on Stacy's door. He'd better warn her and Elise about Charlene Brody's attempts to interfere and reassure them that she had no authority over Saffron Lane, whatever she said.

When Angus got back to the big house, Nell was working on preparations for the interviews to select artists for Numbers 4 and 5. She'd printed out the emailed photos of the various artists' work and was studying one so intently it took her a minute to realise her husband was back.

She put the papers down. 'How did it go? Did you find a burglar casing the joint?'

He joined her at the table and explained about Emil Kinnaird, then indicated the scatter of folders and paperwork. 'Got any favourites among this new lot of applicants for residencies?'

'These *are* my favourites and they all look quite good. What I'm trying to figure out is how commercial their work is. Look at this embroidery. It's gorgeous, a modern take on seventeenth-century raised stump work. If I have any favourite, it's this artist.'

He let out a low whistle. 'It's lovely, got a rather quirky charm to it.'

'Yes, but how commercial can such work be? We have to be practical about who we allow to set up here. It must take ages to do a piece of embroidery as exquisite as this, so how many will she have available to sell? Even if she has some stored away, I doubt her output will be enough for her to make a living from after those are sold, and therefore not enough to give us a good profit.'

'I see what you mean.'

'We're not setting up an artistic charity, but trying to find a way to turn that row of houses into an asset. An art gallery and café will complement visits to the big house on open day quite nicely, too.'

'If you don't think this work is commercial, why did you ask her to come for an interview?'

'Because it's gorgeous. Her scenes are so lively. Some of

the figures and set-ups make me smile every time I look at them. I wanted her to at least have the satisfaction of having gained an interview. And besides—' She broke off and frowned.

'Besides what?' he prompted.

'I'm not sure about this guy who does woodcarvings. He sounds, well, a bit arrogant. Maybe I'm reading that into his emails unfairly, but his work isn't charming; it seems distinctly spiteful to me. His carvings aren't enjoying or celebrating human and animal frailties; they're caricatures twisting a nasty screw into them. And yet he's a brilliant carver. So I can't make up my mind.'

After a thoughtful pause, she added, 'What I really wanted was to find a potter, and I even found a small kiln that hires out firing time. Pottery would give us lots of smaller pieces to sell, don't you think? But I'm still not sure. It might just add complications, and none of the potters who've applied so far seem special enough. I've got one coming and have asked him to bring a couple of ideas for pieces that aren't just tourist trash.'

She grinned at him. 'I didn't call it "trash" of course, but I think he'll get the idea.'

'Well, you'll not only have me but Elise at the interviews. She's a shrewd old bird. I doubt anyone will be able to pull the wool over her eyes.'

Nell nodded and stretched. 'Let's adjourn to the sitting room and open a bottle of wine.'

'I'm going to be working on a project tonight. It came in just before Stacy rang. So no alcohol for me, I'm afraid. But I'll pour you a glass, if you like.'

'No, don't bother. It's much nicer to share a drink. Do you have to start work straight away?'

'I've time for a coffee.'

'You're on.'

They walked into the kitchen arm in arm, chatted for a few minutes, then he vanished into his office. His IT troubleshooting was in demand and he was charging much more for his time these days, thanks to her business input. But she missed him when they didn't sleep together.

Chapter Three

Emil found the company's branch office in Sexton Bassett deserted, with a 'Closed' sign on the door. He knocked on it good and hard, but there was no answer. This surprised him, because it was only mid afternoon and the office should be open, and anyway, his visit was expected.

He used his master key to get inside and was horrified to find George Turrell lying unconscious on the floor in the back room, sprawled next to a table with an untouched meal set out on it. The poor man must have been lying there for a while as the food looked well dried out.

Emil knelt down quickly beside him, and to his relief found a faint, erratic pulse. There were no signs of violence so he had to assume it was a heart attack or stroke.

He got out his phone and dialled the emergency services, not sure what to do to help George in the meantime. The woman he spoke to said an ambulance would be there in a few minutes.

It was only three minutes before Emil heard the siren, but it felt much longer. He let the paramedics in and they quickly got George on oxygen and whisked him away.

He immediately got in touch with his father, asking him to get hold of George's family. Then he made sure everything was locked up and followed the paramedics' directions to the local hospital. He was annoyed to find he had to pay to park there, even with an emergency to follow up. Still fuming at this, he hurried inside the building.

His phone vibrated and he found a message from his father. *George's daughter is on her way to the hospital. She'll be there in about ten minutes.*

He sent a quick text asking for her name, but received no reply so could only tell the nurse at A & E reception that Mr Turrell's daughter was on the way.

Exactly eleven minutes passed before a woman ran into the A & E, paused for a moment to get her bearings, then rushed across to the desk. 'My father's been brought in – George Turrell.'

Emil went across to join her. 'I'm Emil Kinnaird. I'm the one who found George.'

'Mmm.' All her attention was on the receptionist and she didn't even turn to look at Emil, let alone give him her name.

'Your father's undergoing some tests at the moment, Ms Turrell. Could I please get some details while we're waiting to hear from the doctors?'

'Can I just see him?'

'Not till the doctors say it's all right. They're still working on him.'

The woman, who was about Emil's own age, sagged against the counter, answering the questions and glancing occasionally towards the doors beyond the reception desk, through which people whose clothing identified them as working there were coming and going.

Ms Turrell had such utter concentration on what the receptionist was saying that Emil could only suppose she loved her father dearly. He waited for her attention, studying her. She was tall for a woman, nearly six foot, he'd guess, with a mass of gorgeous chestnut hair, tied back any old how. Her glasses kept slipping down her nose and she kept pushing them back impatiently. Why didn't she have them adjusted, for goodness' sake?

'Thank you, Ms Turrell. That'll be all for now. If you'll just take one of those seats, I'll call you when there's any news.' The receptionist indicated a small group of chairs separate from the rest of the waiting area.

Emil hesitated, then followed her across, ignoring the scowl she gave him as if to tell him to go away. 'I'm Emil Kinnaird. Your father worked for our company.'

'Did he?' She didn't seem interested in a conversation of any sort.

'Can I get you a coffee or something?'

'No, thanks.'

He took a seat beside her. 'Had your father been ill?'

But she was frowning into space, so he had to repeat the question.

'What? How should I know? I haven't seen him for a couple of years.'

'But head office told me you're his next of kin.'

'That doesn't mean we get on, just that we have a blood link.'

'What about your mother?'

'She's overseas and they've been divorced for ages, don't communicate. She's remarried.' She looked at her watch. 'I can't stay much longer. I have to pick up my son from after-school care.'

He was trying to work through these relationships. 'Can't his father do that?'

'He could if he were still around. Look, I don't want to chat *or* give you my life history. I just need to make sure my father's all right. There's simply no one else who can deal with it. Then I'll go and pick up my son.'

Emil held up his hands in a surrendering gesture. 'Only trying to help.'

But she was on her phone, waiting to be connected, foot tapping impatiently.

What an annoying female. He was about to leave her to it when the woman on reception came across. 'The doctor would like a word with you about your father.'

Emil hesitated, but something about the way the woman spoke and looked at his companion sounded ominous so he followed them across.

The doctor looked up as they entered the small room, took a deep breath and said gently, 'Please sit down.'

'Just tell me,' the woman said sharply.

'I'm afraid it's bad news, Ms Turrell. We couldn't save

your father. He had a massive stroke just after he got here and although we have him on life support, he's lost his brain function.'

'You mean, he's dead?'

'Brain dead, I'm afraid.'

'You're sure of that?'

'Yes. Utterly positive.'

Ms Turrell sat there looking stunned, then tears welled in her eyes. 'Oh, hell. What am I going to do?'

The doctor looked at Emil questioningly.

'My company employed her father,' he said quietly. He went across to sit on the chair next to Ms Turrell. 'What can I do to help?'

'I don't know. I've never had anything to do with death before. And there's still Louis to pick up.' She looked at her watch. 'They charge extra if you're late.'

'Shall I pick him up for you or is there a friend who could do that?'

'They won't let him go off with a stranger. I'd better go and fetch him myself.' She looked at the doctor. 'I'll have to come back to deal with whatever has to be done. My son's only seven, so I can't leave him waiting.'

'That's all right. We'll make sure there's a patient affairs officer available to go through what's needed with you when you get back. How long will you be?'

'About an hour.' Ms Turrell left without even a glance in Emil's direction.

He followed her outside, thinking that she had to be one of the rudest people he'd ever met.

Then, even as he watched, she stopped dead and leant

against the nearest car, shaking. Reaction must have set in. Oh, hell! He couldn't leave her like that, however rude she was.

He hurried across to her. 'Where's your car? I'll help you to it.'

She looked at him, still looking wobbly. 'Not a car. It's a bicycle.'

As she spoke it began to rain, a few drops here and there, and suddenly a downpour.

He tugged her arm. 'Come and shelter in my car till you feel steadier.'

And she let him guide her to it, which said something about her present state of mind, given her earlier abruptness.

Abbie wiped the raindrops from her face and took a few deep breaths. 'Sorry. I'll be all right in a minute.'

'No worries. I'm not in a hurry to go anywhere.'

'I am.' She glanced down at her watch, then outside at the weather, bracing herself visibly. 'A bit of rain won't kill me.'

As she was about to get out of the car, he laid a hand on her arm to stop her. 'We could leave your bicycle here, and I could drive you wherever it is, and you could pick up the bike later.'

She looked at him suspiciously. 'Why would you do that?'

'To help a fellow human being. And also because your father worked for us and was well thought of by *my* father, so if we can help you in any way now, we will. Which bike is yours?'

She studied his face, then sagged back and pointed. 'It's the end one in that rack, but we can leave it there, it has a good combination lock.'

He helped her into the front passenger seat and got into the driving seat.

'Thank you.'

'You're welcome. Do you have a first name or do you prefer to be called Ms Turrell?'

'Abbie.'

'And I'm Emil, in case you didn't notice last time I introduced myself.'

She nodded, but clearly she still wasn't interested in making conversation. Well, her father had just died, he had to remember that.

'Where's the school? I'll take you there, then drive you and your son home again. Or back to the hospital. Whichever you prefer.'

'If you could take us home, I'll be able to pick up my own car. It isn't far.'

In spite of the seriousness of the situation, he couldn't help being amused at how grudgingly she had accepted his offer. He hoped he hadn't betrayed this reaction.

When she came out of the school, Abbie was accompanied by a lad wheeling a shabby-looking bike and talking non-stop. Emil got out of the car and let the boy help him stow the bike, then drove them home.

'You'll be all right?' he asked as he pulled up. 'Here. Take my card. If there's anything else we can do to help, you've only to ask.'

'Thank you. You've been very kind.'

But as she wheeled away the bike she didn't turn to wave goodbye. The boy did and Emil returned the gesture.

That was one uptight woman.

But very attractive, or at least she would be if she ever smiled.

Then he got annoyed at himself for thinking that way. She'd just lost her father. Why on earth should he expect her to smile?

Only she said she hadn't seen George for two years. They mustn't have got on. But if that was the case, why was she so upset?

Back at the office, Emil let himself in and locked up again. He went through to the rear room, which was partly kitchen and rest room, partly storage area. He'd better check out where he'd be living. He went up two flights of stairs, as he'd been told, feeling tired now. He still wasn't fully recovered from the operation.

On the way, he passed what looked like an office and a couple of interview rooms. He could check them out later. He needed to see where he'd be living, make sure it was suitable.

They'd moved to this building after he'd gone to work in Australia to broaden his experience, so he'd never been here before. Unfortunately, he might have to spend more time in the office itself than he'd originally planned, now that George was dead, poor chap. He just hoped the woman who also worked here was up to scratch on everything.

At the top of the stairs he looked round. There was

a skylight but it was small and everything was dim because of the weather. Luckily the light switch was where you'd expect it to be, so he turned it on to show a landing with a row of cupboards under the eaves at one side.

At the other end of the landing was the entrance to the flat. He went in but though it had two dormer windows, it wasn't much brighter than the landing. As he looked round the room, he grimaced.

'There's a studio flat, where you can stay whenever you're in the area,' his father had told him. 'Fix it up and charge the company. Come and visit us if you get lonely.'

'Studio flat' was a fancy phrase for what people used to call a bed-sitting room: this one consisted of a large room, old-fashioned and dusty, with a tiny kitchen area to one side. The only internal door was at the far end and presumably led to the bedroom and bathroom. He sighed, wishing he could turn and walk out again. He'd spent two years in places like this when he was at university and hadn't expected to have to live so meanly again.

Especially now, with his own health problems to deal with on top of everything else.

More rain pounded against the dormer windows and the sky outside was charcoal grey, even though it was only late afternoon. 'Welcome to Sexton Bassett!' he muttered, fumbling for the light switch.

The living room looked only marginally better once he'd turned on the central light – he'd have to get a bigger bulb for that. He saw a very ugly lump of a lamp squatting on a side table and turned that on too, nearly tripping over the frayed edge of a rug on his way across to it.

To his relief the door did lead to a bedroom, a bit bigger than he'd expected, and a tiny shower room. Someone must have checked it out because there was a brand-new bed, still with the plastic wrapping on the mattress. There was an unopened packet of sheets and pillow cases on it, sickly cream in colour, and a folded duvet, but no cover for that. The only pillow was a limp thing, well past its use-by date. He definitely wasn't putting his head on that. He tossed it off the bed in disgust.

The shower looked adequate and there was an old-fashioned washing machine in the bathroom. The towels were new, mid-grey of all the boring colours to choose. Whoever had bought the new furnishings had a great sense of colour – not.

He went back into the living room and switched on the fridge. After a few hiccups it condescended to start cooling its contents. Only it didn't have any contents. Nor did the cupboards. Someone had half-heartedly dusted the furniture but dust was thick in the corners. How long was it since anyone had used this flat?

Raindrops hurled themselves against the windows as another heavy shower passed through and he shivered. A quick check showed no sign of a heater of any sort, so he added that to his shopping list.

He had no choice, would have to go out and get some food, as well as some pillows.

He left the flat and ran across to the car. Then he had to run back, because the heavy rain had distracted him and he'd forgotten to lock the office up. Strange how you automatically left a business expecting the door to shut itself.

He remembered seeing a shopping centre on the outskirts of town as he drove in and managed to find his way there.

It was full of bright lights and bedraggled people. He filled a shopping trolley with basic food supplies and a couple of bottles of wine, put everything in the car and then decided to find a duvet cover in some bright colour. And two new pillows. And a heater.

His final purchase was some takeaway food, because he didn't feel like cooking. There wasn't much choice by this time, so he settled on garishly coloured chicken tikka from the food hall. It'd fill the great cavernous hole inside him, even if it wasn't the healthiest-looking dish on the planet.

When he got back, the reception area of the office seemed so unnaturally quiet and shadowy that it felt rather spooky. Shivering, he went up to the flat, glad he'd left the lights on there. Something made him lock the flat door behind him.

He shoved the frozen food into the freezer, and the dry goods into the nearest of the two kitchen wall cupboards, then warmed up the curry in the microwave and opened a bottle of red wine.

Wiltshire on a stormy day was a long way from the warm weather and companionship of Australia. But the county was reasonably close to his parents and sister, who lived in Hampshire, and he'd always meant to come back to England to live, so he wasn't too worried about the weather.

Well, he had a few personal problems, didn't he? And they made weather seem a very minor thing.

He suddenly remembered Abbie Turrell and wondered what she was doing now. She must be feeling sad to have lost her father, even if she'd been estranged from him.

He raised his glass in a silent toast to the dead man. His father had had a lot of respect for George's skills. Without the man to brief him, Emil was going to have to rely on his deputy. He hoped she knew her job. He wasn't the sort to sit all day at a desk.

The TV was working but he didn't have a TV guide, so flicked through the channels and came to the conclusion that there was nothing worth watching. He got out a book that had caught his eye in the supermarket, admiring the cover again. He liked this author's mysteries and he preferred real paper books to ebooks. They felt right in your hands, somehow, as if they truly linked you to the story.

He realised how cold it had grown, so unpacked the new electric heater he'd bought and switched it on. There was a pop and the electricity went off abruptly.

'Hell and damnation!'

He found the fuse box but couldn't get anything working again, so had to phone an emergency electrician. Unfortunately it was midnight before the guy reached him and all that time Emil had to sit in the front office with a blanket round his shoulders waiting to let him in.

The man set up a temporary fix and gave him a lecture about the need to rewire old houses unless you wanted to risk a fire.

Emil needed no prompting to book him to come back and do a complete rewire. He was quite sure his father would approve.

By the time he'd locked the front office up again and trudged back upstairs, he had no trouble whatsoever getting to sleep.

Abbie took Louis to the hospital, explaining what had happened.

'So I don't have a granddad at all now?'

'No. 'Fraid not.'

'But I still have a grandma?'

'Yes.'

'Only she doesn't live nearby, does she?'

'No. Not now.'

He was silent for a while, then said thoughtfully, 'I read this book last term, and the boy in it didn't have a family, so he went round choosing some uncles and aunts and cousins. Can we do that?'

'No. We don't know anyone suitable, so we'll just have to manage on our own.'

He gave her one of his sulky looks that said he didn't agree with her.

The patient affairs officer Abbie saw at the hospital was very reassuring. Her father had, it seemed, worn a medic alert bracelet stating that he had a heart problem and giving the name of his doctor.

'We were able to contact the doctor and check your father's condition. Fortunately, he'd seen your father only a couple of days ago, so establishing the cause of death was very straightforward. A heart attack and massive stroke, as they told you.'

Abbie was relieved that there would be no need for an autopsy, declined to see her father's body and took the official paperwork away with her to complete in the required time.

It wasn't till Louis was fast asleep that she could sit down and try to come to terms with today's events.

Damn her father! Never there when her mother needed help in the house. Never there for Abbie's school functions when she was small. The only thing he'd done steadily was provide money and pay off the mortgage so that her mother would be all right when he walked out on them.

Only her mother had met someone else and left years ago, so his beautiful plans had come to nothing.

Damn! Her father couldn't have picked a worse time to die. Abbie had just started a new job and now she'd have to take time off to make the funeral arrangements and do whatever else was needed. Well, who else was there to do it? She had a list from the patient affairs officer and would check it in the morning.

Great way to make an impression on her new employers, that would be.

She hoped her father had left enough money to cover the costs, because she didn't have anything to spare, was only just managing to get by.

She felt guilty that she was more annoyed than upset by his death but there you were. He hadn't been a particularly lovable person, had he? She'd often envied her friends their close, loving relationships with their fathers.

She could have murdered a glass of wine tonight, but she'd decided after Louis was born that alcohol was an extravagance and had rarely bought any. She was sick and tired of watching every penny, and if she could have traced her ex-partner, she'd have put the hard word on him about maintenance for his son.

Sighing she went through her nightly routine, unfolding the studio couch and making up her bed. She was fed up of sleeping in the living room, too, having to make up her bed every night and put it away in the morning. She could usually settle into a book as she lay in bed, but not tonight. Tonight the book seemed stupid, and she tossed it aside. She lay there for a long time before she could get to sleep, her mind churning over the implications of what had happened.

At last she admitted it to herself: she wished she hadn't quarrelled with her father the last time she'd seen him, wished she hadn't been so stubborn when he tried to make it up.

But she'd seen him let Louis down after promising faithfully to attend his school's grandparents' day in just the same way he had let her down so often when she was a child. She'd heard her son crying about it in bed, so she'd confronted her father and told him to stay away from them until he could absolutely guarantee to keep his promises to his grandson.

He'd said no one could ever guarantee that, in his usual literal way. Why was everything always black or white with him?

And now it was too late to mend matters.

It didn't feel right for someone to die on you without a quarrel being settled, though.

She didn't let herself make a noise as she wept, kept wiping away the tears that would trickle down her cheeks with the corner of the sheet.

Damn her father! He'd done nothing but let people down all his life, and he'd even died in a way that left her with unfinished business.

Chapter Four

Ginger found the journey south more tiring than she'd expected, or perhaps her poor night's sleep was showing. She stopped only twice on the way to Wiltshire, anxious to get there before dark and find a bed and breakfast for the night, preferably a cheap one.

She had an anxious few moments when her car started misfiring but just as she'd decided to turn into the next services and see if someone could look at it, the misfiring stopped and the car began chugging smoothly along again.

'Oh, thank goodness!' She had no one to turn to for help getting to Wiltshire if it broke down.

She let out a groan of relief when she arrived at Sexton Bassett and immediately found a friendly policewoman patrolling the town centre to ask about a bed and breakfast. Perhaps fate was on her side, for once.

In her bedroom she took stock of what food she had left – enough sandwiches to manage for an evening meal with an apple for dessert, which would save spending any money.

She felt stiff after so many hours sitting at the wheel, so took a brisk walk round the town centre. The air felt chilly and damp, and she was caught in a sudden heavy shower. Luckily, she found a shop doorway to shelter in till the rain eased, but she shivered as she looked out through a grey curtain of perpendicular rain. She could have done without this, she really could.

She was so cold she had a quick shower to warm herself up and as she snuggled down in bed, she felt so tired, she was sure she'd sleep well.

To her annoyance she woke abruptly at two o'clock in the morning and couldn't get to sleep again. She felt slightly feverish and tossed off the bedcovers, then had to pull them up again as she began shivering. Perhaps she was starting a cold. Well if so, it'd better hold off till after the interview. She hadn't got *time* to be ill and what sort of impression would it make to be sneezing or blowing your nose all the time?

She wondered what Donny was doing, whether he'd even notice that she was gone. Yes, of course he would. There'd be no one to get him a meal, and to add insult to injury, she'd emptied the fridge and switched it off.

On reflection, she should have simply left it switched on with one or two bits and pieces of food still available.

And maybe her note hadn't been all that tactful, either. But she meant it about him getting out of the house. She hadn't told him where she was going, only that she was visiting a friend and hoped he'd quickly find himself somewhere else to live.

* * *

The following day in Bristol, Michelle Cutler confronted her husband for the umpteenth time, 'You're mad applying for this residency, Warren! Do the sums, damn you! We need your wages to pay the mortgage, you know we do.'

'If I get this, it could lead to better things,' he said soothingly. How many times did he have to tell that to the stupid bitch?

'No one makes a living from art these days. I'm not moving to the back of nowhere with you, even if you do get selected, and you'd better make sure it pays enough to keep up with your share of our mortgage. We worked hard to get the deposit on this house.'

'Yeah, yeah! I know all that.'

He could hardly bear to look at her when she was dressed in her work clothes. Talk about Mrs Ugly! If he didn't need her to look after the house and help pay the mortgage, he'd have left her before now. As it was, he had difficulty finding the money to buy the sort of wood he needed for his sculptures and she was always complaining about the mess he made in what had previously been the conservatory.

It wasn't as if he hadn't sold any of his carvings. He sold them regularly. They were up for sale in a local gallery, and last Christmas he'd sold some smaller ones cheaply from a stall at the market. Market stalls indeed! He was beyond that. The people organising the artists' colony in this Saffron Lane place were going to open a gallery on site to sell the pieces people produced. How convenient was that?

If he got the residency there, it'd be another step up the ladder he was determined to climb, and to hell with mortgages. And double hell to wives!

Warren had a final few sharp words with Michelle when he spilt some coffee on the tablecloth, and was glad to see the back of her as she left for work. Stupid bitch! What had he ever seen in her?

He packed things carefully in his car boot, wrapping each woodcarving in bubble wrap and then putting them into cardboard boxes. He wedged the boxes in a row with his rucksack, then closed the hatch door on them.

He had plenty of time to get from Bristol to Wiltshire but he wasn't leaving anything to chance, so he set off early.

As he drove east along the M4 motorway, he listened to the radio in case there were any hold-ups. It was a talkback show. What idiots people were, spilling out their private information for anyone to listen to. He'd never do that.

The Dennings had sent him clear directions so he found his way across Sexton Basset to Saffron Lane without any difficulty. It didn't look like a thriving artists' colony to him, more like a building site, because there were workmen doing something to the end two houses. Still, at the very least a residency would give him six months' rent-free accommodation – and away from his stupid wife, too. He made a triumphant fist in the air at the thought of that. And even better, it'd be a chance to produce a lot of work.

If this place didn't do well as an artists' colony, he'd find somewhere else to go when his free stay was up. There were a couple of other things he'd been looking into.

His own house had gone up nicely in value. He came to a sudden decision: he wasn't going back to Michelle. She wasn't even good in bed these days, she was always so tired.

And she was putting on weight. What did she look like? He couldn't bear any more of her inane conversation and stodgy cooking. As for the way she economised, agonising over every penny she spent and trying to control what he spent too, it was driving him mad.

They could sell the house and take half of the money each. It'd gone up in value nicely.

What was he doing thinking of *her* at a time like this? He should be preparing cheerful answers to possible questions. It always paid to be cheerful at interviews.

His carvings would speak for themselves. He knew how good he was. But it never hurt to add value.

He took a few deep breaths before getting out of the car and fixed 'the smile' on his face. He could summon it up any time he needed, because he'd practised it in front of a mirror. He intended to make an excellent impression today.

Nell peered out of the window. 'Must be Warren Cutler. He's lifting a box out of his car boot.'

Elise joined her at the window. 'He's a funny-looking little man, isn't he?' She chuckled suddenly. 'He looks just like his carvings, all sharp and ready to claw or bite.'

'He's smiling.'

'That's a very plastic smile, if you ask me. I bet he rehearsed it.' She went back to her chair.

Angus looked at her in surprise. 'I've never heard you speak so negatively about anyone, Elise.'

'Just occasionally you meet someone and take an instant dislike to him.'

'But you haven't actually met the man yet.'

'I don't need to meet him if I can see him and study his face when he doesn't know he's being observed. Life writes lines of character on faces, and people's expressions tell you a lot. If you live long enough, you learn to read them. Oh, not a hundred per cent, I'll grant you, no one can do it that well. But I'm old enough to have had a lot of practice. Of course, some people are born with a gift for acting and they can fool anyone, but I'm usually pretty accurate.'

'They say a person's character shows in their eyes,' Nell said from where she was waiting to open the door. 'That's what I look at.'

Elise nodded vigorously. 'Yes. It's a good place to start, I'll grant you. It's been recognised throughout history that the eyes are the mirror of the soul. I like Cicero's version of it best. He lived in about the first or second century BC, if I remember correctly, but his words are still true: he said the face is the picture of the mind and the eyes are its interpreter.'

Someone knocked on the door and Nell moved to open it. 'Here goes! We're about to get our first chance to interpret Warren Cutler, eyes and all. It'll be interesting to compare notes afterwards.'

Angus winked at Elise as Nell went out into the hall and made a thumbs-down sign, whispering, 'I didn't like the looks of him, either, I don't know why.' He turned back to watch the newcomer.

'Ah, Mr Cutler? Do come in. I'm Nell Denning, manager of this project.' She introduced the others then looked at the box he was holding. 'Why don't you put that down on this side table? We'll have a little chat first then you can show us your other piece.'

'Certainly.'

He sat down opposite the three of them, looking bright and alert. He answered all the questions without hesitation, sometimes offering what Elise felt were politically correct answers without any real passion behind them. But she couldn't help noticing that most of his answers were directed towards Angus and only one towards her, when she asked him a question directly. His smile seemed painted on his face and hardly slipped for a second, hardly changed either.

'Would you like to show us your other carving now?' Nell asked once the panel members had gone through the agreed questions.

Cutler opened the box and took out the piece, a wickedly clever old woman with everything about her slightly exaggerated.

You had to admit he was good, she thought. More than good.

Cutler's eyes flickered towards Elise as he took the carving out and a slight frown crossed his face. Perhaps he was regretting his choice of other piece of work now he'd seen an old woman on the panel.

Was it her imagination or had he paused for a few seconds to reinstate the smile. Oh, she definitely hadn't changed her mind about her first impression of him.

'The carving is clever,' Angus said. 'You're very skilful.'

Cutler took out some photos. 'I thought you might like to look at some of my other work as well.'

Once again, it was Angus he was addressing, and Angus to whom he handed the photos first.

Elise watched Nell frown at that, but the younger woman didn't comment, just let Cutler go through his photos with Angus, who passed each one to his wife and stopped the artist explaining the next till she and Elise had had time to see it.

And still, Cutler continued to pass them to Angus first. He wasn't very good at picking up clues about the people he was interacting with, however good he was with wood.

His photos showed excellent carvings, but all seemed to emphasise people's and animals' weaknesses or vanities.

After they'd handed back the photos, Nell said briskly, 'Do you have any questions, Mr Cutler?'

'Warren, please. You made all the terms of the residency clear in the material you sent me, but I wondered when you expect to make a decision.'

'Within a couple of days. We'll be in touch. Email all right?'

'Yes, of course.'

She walked him to the door.

Elise sighed in relief as the air in the room seemed to brighten and grow fresher.

When he'd driven away, Nell came to sit down again. It was a moment or two before she asked, 'Well, what do you think?'

'He's a brilliant carver,' Angus said. 'There's no doubt about that.'

'But all his carvings seem cruel,' Elise said. 'I couldn't live with any of them. And he only addressed me once, very briefly. I think he's ageist underneath all that smiling.'

'He certainly focused on Angus,' Nell said thoughtfully. 'He ought to have paid more attention to you and me, Elise. Perhaps he's sexist as well.'

'Do you think people are stupid enough to be overtly ageist or sexist these days?' Angus asked. 'It can be the other way round, in my experience, with people being too politically correct.'

Elise scowled. 'Well, you're still young. In *my* experience, they aren't as politically correct with older people as they are with people your age. My own niece used to be ageist, tried to lock me away to keep me safe because she didn't think I could look after myself. Ha! Who wants to live in a cosy little prison and be so safe that you're bored to tears?'

'Ah. Right. I'm sorry to hear that.'

Her scowl deepened. 'And it'll be easier for you as you grow older, Angus, simply because you're a man. Being an old woman is far more difficult than being an old man. I was out with my friend Victor before he died, looking at new computers. We went into a shop and the young man there asked him what he wanted, didn't even look at me after the first glance.

'When Victor said it was me who needed a new computer, the man still spoke to him. He actually asked, "And what sort of computer does your wife want?" as if I couldn't speak for myself.' She let out a little huff of annoyance at the memory.

'He really said that about you?'

'Yes. I gave him a piece of my mind and walked out. When I buy my new computer, I shan't do it from any shop where I'm treated like that, I can tell you.'

'Where did you get your new computer in the end?'

'I haven't bought one yet. My old one still works. Victor died suddenly, you see, and I lost heart for a while.' She blinked away a tear. She still missed him.

'If you tell me what sort of computer you want, I'll get you a good price,' Angus said. '*And* help set it up, if you like.'

'That'd be great. I can afford a good one now I've sold my house.'

After a moment's silence, Nell brought them back to the point. 'So do we cross Cutler off our list?'

'I don't know. My heart is warring with my head here. You can't deny that he's a truly brilliant woodcarver.'

'Well, we'll have to see what this Jean Brunham is like, then. Let's grab a cup of tea while we're waiting for her. I'm parched.'

Chapter Five

Ginger got ready for her interview in plenty of time, but however much she fiddled with her hair and make-up, she wasn't happy with her appearance. It showed in her face how deep-down weary she was. There were not only dark circles under her eyes but her face was drawn and her whole body looked tense. She felt tired out. It must be the long drive.

Worst of all was her hair colour, which was far too garish. She hoped to do something to fade the colour, but didn't dare experiment just before an interview.

In the end, she scrubbed her face clean of make-up, which she rarely wore anyway. They could take her or leave her as she was. This wasn't a beauty contest, after all. It was her work that was being judged, not her appearance.

She took the bags of embroideries and other needlework with her because she didn't like to leave them in the room at the B & B, even though the owner seemed a nice woman. They were too precious.

Most of her work was in storage back in Newcastle, years of work that had filled the empty hours of her life with Alan, with beauty at small cost. Her favourite embroideries, including the ones she'd sent photos of, were all in the old carpet bag she'd brought with her because she couldn't bear to leave them in the storage locker she'd hired.

She patted the bag as she put it on the front passenger seat next to her.

Now all she had to do was find the place where the interview was being held. *Dennings is at 1 Peppercorn Street*, it said on the email she'd printed out. *Drive past the main house and down the slope to Saffron Lane, which is on the left at the bottom. We'll be using Number 1 for the interviews.*

She asked directions from her landlady and set off in plenty of time. She really liked this little town. The centre was so pretty, with hanging baskets of flowers everywhere, looking glorious against the golden-grey stone. She might put one in her next embroidery.

She let out a scornful sniff. You could hang a dozen baskets in the street where she lived and it'd still look a mess, besides which kids would probably nick them to sell if you even tried.

Peppercorn Street was easy to find and her spirits lifted a little. Her head was still aching but it'd just have to ache. She'd stop to buy some aspirins on the way back from the interview. She hadn't thought to bring any with her because she didn't usually get headaches.

She followed the long street up a gentle slope. There were small blocks of flats at the lower end, houses and a retirement development in the middle stretch, and huge, old-fashioned three-storey houses at the top. Imagine living in one of those!

She stopped in the turning circle, which seemed at first like a dead end, and looked for Number 1, nearly panicking when she couldn't find it. Then she realised that the drive which led off the top of the street had a sign to one side saying '*Dennings, 1 Peppercorn Street*' half-covered by a drooping tree branch. No wonder she'd missed it at first.

There weren't any gates so she turned into the drive. Strangely, as she passed through the entrance, she felt a sense of welcome. It felt as if she were coming home. And why she should feel that so strongly when she'd never been here before, she couldn't understand.

Perhaps it was a good sign. Or perhaps she was just imagining it. Who knew?

She braked when she saw a small manor house set a little way back to the right. It was such an elegant building! Eighteenth century, from what she'd read about architecture in her library books, symmetrical and balanced, built of the same beautiful stone as the main buildings in the town centre.

It couldn't be more unlike the modern monstrosity of corrugated iron with garish red and yellow panels they'd built near her home to rehouse the library. That looked more like a couple of egg boxes, plonked together by a child. This house was not only beautiful but had a well-loved air, or was she imagining that as well?

She shrugged. Imagination was free. She could imagine anything she wanted, and often did.

She'd seen photos of stately homes in books but had never visited one in real life. She'd been ill when they'd taken her class at school to see one. She'd mostly been bored by school and the only thing she'd enjoyed had been the sewing classes. Well, she'd needed them, hadn't she, to learn how to mend her own clothes because her mother didn't do mending or sewing of any sort.

Most of Ginger's general knowledge and education had been acquired as she grew older and life served her a few sharp lessons in reality on the way. With a husband more interested in drinking with his mates at the pub than in spending time with her, she'd stayed with him mainly so that her son could have a decent home.

And look at the thanks she'd got for that!

She'd turned to books because they were free from the library. Even her passion for raised stump work embroidery had come from a book she'd read as a young mother, and then the librarian had got her more books on the same subject. Without their silent companionship, she'd have been lost over the years.

It hurt her to see on the news that libraries were being closed down all over the country. The barbarians weren't just at the gates, it seemed to her, they'd got right through them. Didn't they realise how much children and older folk needed libraries, not just to borrow books, though that was important, but to have somewhere safe to go and meet people?

She'd learnt a lot from TV, too, then a few years ago she'd taken an evening class and saved up to buy a computer. Going on the Internet had expanded her world even further.

Realising she was still parked near the big house, lost in thought, she shot a panicky glance at her ten-pound cheapie wristwatch, terrified of being late. No. She was all right. She had time to linger by the gardens, which were as pretty as the house they surrounded.

How lucky the occupants were to live in such a beautiful place! Did they appreciate that? She'd love to have a garden full of flowers. She'd had to make do with pot plants. Donny would probably let them die of thirst.

Still, the owners of this house must be kind, civilised people if they were setting up a small artists' colony and giving six lucky artists such a wonderful gift: time to pursue their dreams and hone their artistic skills without worrying about rent.

Oh, please let me win a place here! She crossed her fingers for luck at the mere thought. But her common sense reminded her that she mustn't let herself feel too optimistic because she wasn't the only person applying for one of these six-month residencies.

The organisers must have liked her embroideries, though, or they'd not have asked to see photos of more. And those had won her an interview with all travel and accommodation expenses paid. So surely that was a hopeful sign?

As she let her car roll forward, her mobile phone tinkled and she stopped in the shade of a huge old tree to see who it was – then promptly wished she hadn't. Her son. She switched off the phone without reading the message.

Donny might know her phone number but he couldn't trace where she was from that. She couldn't afford to buy a new mobile phone or change providers, and probably didn't have the skill to do it efficiently. She'd needed his help to learn how to use this phone and hadn't he rubbed that in! She'd just have to ignore his messages. She didn't need to open them to know what was in them, after all.

She stared down the last part of the gentle slope through gardens filled with flowering bushes and bees buzzing gently as they foraged among them. She wished she could go and bury her face in the flowers to clear away all the petrol fumes she'd breathed in on the journey here. That must be why her head felt rather muzzy today.

Something drew her eyes to the bottom of the slope. A shaft of sunlight was shining down on what looked like a very short street set behind a grove of small trees and shrubs. That had to be Saffron Lane and the houses where the artists would live. They looked charming, with those dormer windows.

The sunlight flickered and she blinked her eyes, not sure whether she was seeing clearly because the house at the end, which was set at a right angle to the others, seemed to be in a spotlight, with all the windows twinkling a welcome. There were men working on it and vans parked outside.

She'd love to do an embroidery of that house, with people at the windows and in the garden, a dog playing with a child outside, maybe. If she got this residency, she would do.

Parking in front of Number 1, she stretched her body and eased her shoulders, then waggled her hands about to get rid of the stiffness. She must have been clutching the car wheel too tightly.

Time to face the interview. 'Best foot forward, Ginger!' she muttered aloud as she got out of the car and bent down to take out the bag of embroideries, before locking the vehicle.

Please let this work out for me, she prayed as she moved towards the front door.

It didn't seem too much to ask.

Nell peeped out of the window when they heard a car draw up. 'She's here.'

Her husband joined her. 'She looks older than fifty and utterly exhausted. Has she driven down from Newcastle today, do you think?'

'She said she was coming down yesterday. Maybe she was too nervous to sleep properly. Oh dear, look at her hair. That colour of red's far too garish for someone with such a pale complexion. And her clothes aren't very smart. How can she produce such beautiful embroideries and not know to dress better than that?'

'She said she was a widow, so perhaps her husband didn't leave her comfortably set up.'

'We aren't choosing someone because they look needy, Angus. We're setting up an artists' colony and if we're to attract visitors and earn money from our gallery, they must produce very special work that people will want to buy. I still worry that we're not the best people to judge their quality as artists.'

He put his arm round her shoulders. 'Of course we are. We want to attract ordinary people to visit Saffron Lane, not precious posers who talk up rubbish and call it art, so we're exactly the sort of people to select who moves in. You found several applicants who may be suitable for this slot at Number 4 and we couldn't choose between today's three from the photos of their work. Let's see if we can make a decision when we've seen all their pieces properly, and met them in person.'

'Definitely the latter. They have to be able to deal with visitors, so they need to be presentable and good with people as well.'

He moved away. 'She's coming up the path. I'll let her in.'

The door opened before Ginger got there and she at once felt a little easier because the man who stood there had such a nice, kind smile.

'You must be Jean Brunham,' he said. 'I'm Angus Denning.'

'Pleased to meet you, but do call me Ginger. No one ever uses my real name. Well, it's so plain, isn't it, Jean? And I don't even have a middle name.'

She sounds as nervous as she looks, poor thing, Angus thought as he ushered her in. 'This is my wife, Nell, and this is one of our resident artists, Elise Carlton. Ladies, our visitor prefers to be called Ginger.'

'Lovely to meet you, Ginger,' Elise said with one of her lovely smiles.

'Nice to meet you, too. What sort of art do *you* do?' Ginger asked.

'Paintings. Yours is more unusual these days. I loved your stump work pieces.'

Their visitor blushed. 'Oh. Well, thank you.' She

turned to Nell, holding out her hand. 'Pleased to meet you, Mrs Denning.'

'Nell.'

'Nell, it is. How lucky you are to live in such a beautiful house. And the gardens – well, I had to stop the car to admire the flowers. I love flowers.'

Angus indicated a chair and she stopped talking to sit down and look at them like an inquisitive robin wondering if you were going to throw it some breadcrumbs.

When they went through the interview questions, it took longer than it had with Warren Cutler, because she not only talked more, she asked them questions about how they did things, too. That was a point in her favour as far as Angus was concerned.

Ginger showed them her work and Elise asked if she could hold it. 'It makes me want to touch it. Do you mind? This is beautiful. You have such talent in your choice of subject matter. I've never seen modern people shown in quite this way in embroideries and it really works. Do you have other pieces in your bag? May I see them as well?'

In the end, Angus saw Nell looking at her watch and wasn't surprised when she brought things to a close. The third applicant was expected shortly, he knew. But he'd enjoyed talking to Ginger. And he hadn't enjoyed talking to Cutler.

How important was that in making their choice? The artists would have to talk to visitors, after all.

'That's all we need to know for now, thank you, Ginger. We'll let you know who is selected within two days. Will email be all right for that?'

'It'll be better if you use my mobile phone, Nell. I'm, um, taking a little holiday before I go home, so it won't be as easy to get online. I've never been to the south of England before, you see, and Wiltshire looked so beautiful when I checked it online that now I'm here, I'm going to make the most of this trip.'

Chapter Six

As Ginger stood up, Angus saw her sway and clutch the arm of her chair. If possible, she had gone even paler.

'Are you all right?' he asked.

'Just a bit dizzy. I think I'm starting flu or something. I hope I haven't shared it with you.'

'I'll walk out to your car with you. Here, let me carry your bag.'

He put it in the boot, closed it and waited for her to leave, but when she turned the key in the ignition, all that happened was a brief cough of sound.

He heard her groan and say, 'Oh, no! Please, no!'

He waited as she tried again to start the car. It didn't even cough this time, just clicked.

'Perhaps one of your leads has come loose,' he suggested. 'If you open your bonnet I'll check it.'

The car was quite old but it had clearly been well cared for. Unfortunately, he could find nothing obviously wrong.

'Sorry. I can't think what's wrong. Are you in a motoring organisation?'

Tears filled her eyes. 'No. I don't usually drive far from home and I have to be careful with money, so I didn't bother to join. Oh dear! I don't know what to do.'

He watched her rub her forehead as if she had a headache. The poor woman definitely wasn't well. 'I'll call my local garage and then find you somewhere to wait for them. We have another interview coming up, so I can't stay with you, I'm afraid.'

She sniffed, but a couple more tears escaped and rolled down her cheeks. 'Thanks. I do hope it won't be expensive. I have to—'

She gasped and crumpled suddenly, falling to the ground right at his feet. It was so unexpected, he didn't even realise what was happening in time to catch her.

Nell must have been watching from the house, because she came running out to join them. She knelt beside him to help Ginger, who was recovering slowly but wasn't yet fully alert.

Elise had followed her out and when Angus explained about the car, she said, 'I can put Ginger up for a night or two. She shouldn't be left alone if she's not well.'

'Is that wise? She may not get the residency.'

'Never mind that, Angus. I can recognise a woman in trouble when I see one. Didn't you notice the bruise on her arm when her sleeve rode up? Looks to me as if someone hit her recently.'

'She could have bumped into something.'

'I think someone must have been holding her

too tightly as well. You can see the fingermarks. I'm absolutely certain she needs help and I'm certainly not going to abandon her.'

'Well, if you're sure about putting her up . . .'

'I'm very sure.'

Ginger opened her eyes and blinked at the three people surrounding her. It took her a few seconds to realise where she was. Oh, no! She must have fainted. What would they think of her? She tried to get up but everything wavered around her as she moved.

'Let me help you sit in your car.' Angus helped her to her feet, steadying her as he eased her to sit sideways in the rear passenger seat of her car, feet on the ground.

'Thank you. I'm so sorry to be such a nuisance.'

Elise moved closer and said gently, 'You're not doing it on purpose. Just give yourself time to recover.'

Ginger turned her head towards Elise and everything spun round her again, so she had to clutch the car door frame. 'Sorry. Still feeling dizzy. Could you call your garage, please, Angus? I'll just sit here quietly till they come. I'm sure I'll be better by then.'

'You shouldn't be left on your own if you're unwell enough to faint,' Elise said. 'And you certainly shouldn't be driving, even if they can fix your car. Look, I have a spare bedroom and you're more than welcome to use it.'

'I can't ask you to do that.'

'You didn't ask. I volunteered.'

'Thank you but I'll be all right soon.' Only things were still spinning and the sun was too bright, hurting her eyes.

Ginger closed them. All she wanted to do was lie down.

'You may have flu or some sort of virus,' Elise said. 'I don't think they'll look after you properly in a B & B. Do stay here with me.'

That kindness was too much. Ginger burst into tears and it was a few moments before she could stop sobbing.

'You don't want to catch flu if that's what she's got,' Nell whispered to Elise.

'I can't remember the last time I caught anything. And I had my flu shots last winter. This woman needs help.' She raised her voice. 'Angus, will you help me get Ginger upstairs to my spare bedroom?'

'Yes, of course. Come on, Ginger. Lean on me. After we've interviewed the final person, I'll drive over to your B & B and pick up your things, if you like.'

'Thank you. That'd be so kind.'

A car turned into Saffron Lane.

'Oh, heavens, that must be the third applicant,' Nell exclaimed.

'Take him into the house,' said Angus. 'I'll help get Ginger upstairs, then I'll call the garage before I join you.'

Nell stepped aside to let Elise move past and lead the way into her house. 'We'll wait for you before we start the interview.'

'I'll settle Ginger in my spare bedroom, then join you. But I'm coming back to her as soon as I feel I've got the measure of the third applicant. I wasn't all that fussed about his pottery, anyway.'

'He's won prizes for it.'

'Ha! Experimental twiddly bits, I call it.'

Nell didn't let herself smile, but she loved some of Elise's vivid descriptions of modern trends.

Angus helped Ginger up to the second bedroom, where Elise quickly removed a laundry basket from the bed and turned down the covers. 'Go and phone the garage, Angus. I'll follow you down in a minute.'

She turned back to Ginger, who was shading her eyes, so she went across and pulled the curtains closed.

'Sorry to be such trouble, Elise.'

'You're no trouble, dear. I shall enjoy the company. And the bed is ready made up. The bathroom is next door if you need it.'

Ginger slid down. 'I think what I need most is a nap.'

'Don't go to sleep until I've got you some aspirins. I have some in the bathroom.'

She had to nudge Ginger awake when she got back and after the pills had been swallowed, her visitor's eyes were closed again before Elise reached the door on her way to the interview. Frowning, she stared back at the bed. If this wasn't a woman in desperate need of help, she'd never met one.

As she went downstairs, she thought suddenly, *I hope they don't appoint that Cutler fellow. I shan't vote for him whatever the others say.*

Nell was left with a scruffy-looking young man. 'Rick Tyler?'

'Yes. You must be Mrs Denning.'

'Do come in.'

He followed her inside and she explained quickly what had happened. 'To make matters worse, her car won't start.

If you don't mind waiting for a few moments, we'll start the interview when the others join us. My husband is calling the garage.'

'That's rotten luck for the artist. I'm not in a hurry to get anywhere else, so I'm happy to wait.'

At least this one seemed kind, Nell thought. But was he talented enough?

Angus joined them soon afterwards but it was a few minutes more before Elise came in from Number 3.

'Sorry to keep you all waiting. She's asleep now.'

Angus introduced her to Rick then glanced through the window. 'They can't send anyone from the garage to fetch Ginger's car for an hour or so as their tow van is out on another call. Shall we get on with the interview?'

All three turned to Rick, who answered their questions cheerfully. But his conversation was without sparkle when he spoke about pottery and his own work. Indeed, he seemed far too laid-back about everything. And the plate he'd brought to show his latest piece was again 'experimental', with some bizarre fragments of pattern and texture scattered here and there across it.

They studied it and he did too, head on one side. 'I like to try different techniques but I don't think this one came off as I'd hoped.' He shrugged as if it didn't matter.

'No one can be perfect every time,' Elise agreed.

They were able to get rid of him quite quickly, then Nell asked, 'How's Ginger?'

'Sleeping rather heavily. I think she's got a virus of some sort and she'd run herself ragged getting ready to leave. I gave her a couple of aspirins and left her in my spare bed.'

'We should discuss the applicants while we can.' Nell looked from one to the other and when neither said anything, she started the ball rolling. 'I think Mr Cutler is the most talented of the three.'

'I suppose so. If you like nasty stuff.' Elise sighed. 'I couldn't live with his carvings, though. They're spiteful and I bet he is too.'

Angus whistled softly. 'You've taken a major dislike to him, haven't you?'

'I have, rather.'

'What about Rick?'

'He's a nice young chap, but he and his work don't have any pizazz,' Nell said. 'I doubt he'll ever be more than a hobby potter. He hasn't got the passion.'

'The other pieces he sent were quite good,' Angus said.

'Yes, technically, but he didn't have an individual style, did he? He was hopping from one technique to another.' Elise looked from one to the other. 'What about Ginger? Her work is exquisite.'

'But is it commercial?' Nell asked. 'Even if people love her embroideries, how will she ever do enough of them to make a living? We have to be practical about this.'

Silence fell, broken by the sound of a vehicle drawing up outside.

Angus looked out of the window. 'The guy from the garage is here. We'd better get Ginger to come out and talk to him.'

But when Elise and Angus went into Number 3, they found Ginger still fast asleep looking flushed, and she only murmured and turned away when Elise laid a hand on her shoulder and said her name.

Elise felt her forehead. 'She's got a temperature. I think we should let her sleep. You talk to the garage people, Angus. If they need a deposit I'll give it to them.'

'Leave that to me.'

He came back a short time later. 'They think it's the carburettor. Not an expensive repair but this isn't a modern car, so it'll take a couple of days to get the part. I told him to go ahead and do it and I've guaranteed the payment.'

'We'd better get Ginger's things out of her car, then, and bring them in here,' Elise said.

'You're sure about her staying with you?'

'Of course I am.'

They went to look in the car. 'Did she say which B & B she was staying at?' Nell asked. 'There are only her embroideries here.'

Angus gave her a resigned look. 'No, she didn't say, but there are only two places in town that are cheap B & Bs. I'll ring them and find out which she's at. Can you pick up her things from there? I don't think a man should do that.'

'Yes, I'll see to it.' Nell turned to the older woman. 'If Ginger is going to be too much trouble, we can take her to the big house, Elise.'

'No need. Putting her up will be a sort of payback for the help I got from a friend after I broke my hip.' She looked from one to the other. 'So you both think Cutler should have the residency?'

'I'm afraid so.'

'I shall have to record a dissenting vote, then. I don't think he'll deal well with the public. But it's your decision, so I'll get back to Ginger.'

When Elise had gone, Angus said quietly, 'I'm not sure we're doing the right thing, love. I have to confess that I didn't like Cutler either.'

'It's his talent that counts and whether he'll make money for us, not whether we'd want him as a friend. We agreed to be practical about this.'

'I've never been happy with pure bean counting as the reason for doing something. But still, his work *is* superb. You're right about that. You'll get in touch with him, then, let him know he's got the residency?'

'He'd rather you did it.'

'He's not that bad a chauvinist!'

'Oh, yes, he is!'

As Angus got out his phone, Nell decided that he hadn't experienced the sort of subtle discrimination most women would have, so it was no use arguing. Were they doing the right thing here? She thought so, hoped so. She realised Angus was watching her, waiting for her to bring her attention back to him. 'Sorry. Just thinking about it all.'

'Let's find out where Ginger is staying, then I'll check how the work's going on in the end houses while you pick her things up. The guys have almost finished there now. There will just be the gardens to sort out. I forgot to tell you that they found a nameplate for Number 6 when they cleared the years of weeds and growth from the front garden: Bay Tree Cottage.'

'Is there really a bay tree there?'

'They haven't touched the back garden yet. There may be. I'll have to look bay trees up online. I don't think I'd recognise one.'

'It's a nice name for a house. Let's keep it whether we find one or not.'

It was three hours before Elise heard someone using the bathroom upstairs, so she switched the kettle on and when she heard a door open, called out, 'Want a cup of tea, Ginger?'

'I'd kill for one.'

'Do you want to come down or shall I bring it up?'

'I'll come down. I've given you enough trouble.'

Elise watched Ginger come slowly down the stairs, still looking rather unsteady. 'How are you feeling?'

'A bit better.'

'I don't think so. You look flushed and yet you're shivering. Come into the kitchen.' She grabbed a shawl from a hook in the hall and flung it round her visitor's shoulders. 'Here. It's my comfort shawl.'

Ginger snuggled it round her neck. 'I messed up at the interview, didn't I?'

'No. They chose a man who does woodcarvings because they thought his work was more commercial. I was the dissenting vote for that. He's a brilliant carver but I didn't take to him and unfortunately he'll be my neighbour at Number 4.' She shrugged. 'Oh well. It's done now. Angus and Nell have to do what they think best. Come and sit down on my rocking chair.'

She waited till her guest was clutching a mug of tea to say, 'Nell brought your things across from the B & B. We thought you might like to stay with me till your car's repaired.'

'Are you sure?'

'Of course I am. It was my suggestion.'

'But you don't need the trouble and I might pass whatever this is on to you.'

'You might, but I'm probably old enough to have had everything twice already and therefore be resistant.' She reached out to clasp Ginger's hand. 'Don't reject an offer of help when it's freely made.'

'But—'

'But nothing. I have a spare bedroom and I think you need a breathing space.'

A pause, then Ginger nodded. 'I do. But don't Mr and Mrs Denning mind?'

'Not at all. They loved your work, you know. They just thought it wasn't commercial enough to bring them the return they need. They have a big old house eating money for its renovation needs and they have to be practical.'

'Oh. I see.'

She didn't sound totally convinced, so Elise added casually, 'Before you leave, I'd like to buy one of your embroideries.'

'*What*?' Ginger gaped at her, then flushed. 'You don't have to feel that sorry for me. I do have some savings to tide me over till I find another job. There are always jobs to be found waitressing.'

'I'm not doing this out of pity. I meant what I said. I absolutely love your work.'

'Oh. Which one do you want?'

'That's the trouble. I like all that I've seen and I can't decide which I like best. Tomorrow, or whenever you're feeling better, you could show me all the ones you've brought with you and I'll choose one. Is that all right?'

'Fine by me. I've never sold one before. I don't usually even show them to people. I wouldn't know what to charge.'

Elise shrugged. 'We'll work something out. We can look online.'

Ginger looked at her. 'I think this must be my lucky day, meeting you. Thank you.'

'My pleasure. Now, how about something light to eat? I'm not a very good cook, I'm afraid, but I have a packet of pancake mix that works pretty well, and we can open a tin of fruit to go with the results.'

'I'm happy to eat anything.'

'That's settled, then.'

Ginger stayed up long enough to eat one small pancake, then said she wasn't really hungry. She failed to stop herself yawning.

'Go to bed, dear. If you wake in the night and want something else to eat, there's bread and cheese in the fridge, or biscuits in that tin.'

'Thank you . . . for everything.'

'You're very welcome.'

'You really mean that, don't you?'

'I wouldn't have said it if I didn't.'

Ginger gave her a quick hug and darted away before Elise could say anything.

She listened to her visitor go upstairs, smiling slightly. Such a nice woman. She switched on the television to catch up with the national news, watched a couple of programmes, yawned and decided to go to bed.

Tomorrow she intended to find out more about Ginger's problems.

Victor had helped her when she was in trouble. And now Elise intended to help someone else – 'pay it forward', as her great-niece said.

Chapter Seven

Abbie slept through the alarm clock the day following her father's death and Louis had to wake her up. 'Mum! Mum!'

She blinked and stared at him fuzzily for a moment, then came suddenly wide awake as she caught sight of the time. 'Oh, my goodness! I forgot to set the alarm.' She was about to start rushing round trying to catch up when she realised she had too much to do sorting out her father's affairs to go into work. It was just a question of getting her son to school on time.

She settled Louis quickly with a bowl of instant porridge and a banana, then rang the office. 'I'm sorry to let you down today, but my father died suddenly yesterday. I didn't hear till after I left work. There's a lot to do today so I'll not be in. I don't know about tomorrow yet.'

Her new boss instantly put on his smarmy, sympathetic voice, which she already knew to be as false as the way he smiled at customers. 'I'm so sorry. Is there, um, no one to help you?'

'No.'

'Um, anything we can do?'

As if! 'Thank you, but I can manage. I have to make the funeral arrangements and do the paperwork today. I'll let you know this afternoon whether I'll be at work tomorrow.'

'Yes, yes. Of course. Um, take all the time off you need, but it would help if you could let us know in advance if you have to take tomorrow off as well.'

His tone sounded distinctly unenthusiastic about that and she wanted to bang the phone down on his 'um', which she already knew was when he was likely to be telling a lie. She forced herself to set the phone carefully back on its stand, however. Venting her anger was a luxury she hadn't been able to afford for a long time.

She went to have a quick shower while Louis packed his school bag. By ignoring her own need for breakfast and going by car, even though the weather was fine and her petrol was running low, she managed to get him to school just as the morning bell was ringing. She also snatched a quick word with his teacher, who offered genuine condolences on her loss and promised to keep an eye on Louis today.

'Thank you.' She drove home again, stopping to refill her car. At last she was able to have her coffee and toast. While she ate, she studied the printed list of possible jobs needed after a death that the patient affairs officer had given her. From it she made her own list.

She guessed that since he knew his health was in a fragile

state, her father would have prepared for it in his usual thorough way. He was—no, she corrected herself mentally, *had been* good at paperwork.

She had her father's keys from the possessions they'd given her at the hospital, so tackled the next job on her own list: his flat.

Perhaps she'd be able to have his car. Hers was a very elderly and temperamental vehicle.

It felt wrong to go into the flat without him, but she'd have to check through his papers for his will and the name of his lawyer. She was quite sure he'd have left lists to cover all eventualities.

To her amazement, when Abbie opened the front door of the luxury flat, a voice called, 'Who's that?'

A woman of about her own age poked her head out of the kitchen and stared at her in shock. 'Who are you?'

'I might ask the same thing.'

They both spoke at once. 'I'm George's daughter.'

They broke off at the same time with identical gasps.

Abbie couldn't believe what she had heard. 'I beg your pardon? How can that be possible?'

The other woman bit her lip. 'Oh dear. He hasn't told you about me yet, has he?'

A little girl ran up behind the stranger and clung to her legs. 'Mummy! Mummy! Want a d'ink o' milk.'

'This is my daughter, Susie. She's three.'

'Oh. Right.'

'D'ink o' milk,' the little girl repeated.

'You'd better come in and I'll explain, though Dad

should be doing this.' She froze as she stared down at the keys in her visitor's hand. 'What are you doing with those?'

Abbie ignored that and concentrated on the main point. 'Why did you say you were his daughter?'

'Because I am.'

'But he never remarried after my mother left him.'

'No. Look, come inside and I'll make us a cup of coffee and tell you about it. Pity it's so early in the day. Brandy might be more bracing. I'm Keziah, by the way. And you must be Abbie.'

'Yes.'

'Did Dad get called away? He said that happened sometimes and it did a couple of weeks ago, so I didn't worry when he didn't come home last night.' She gestured to a chair. 'How do you take your coffee?'

She went to put the kettle on and settled the child at the kitchen table with some crayons, a piece of paper to draw on and a plastic mug of milk.

When they were sitting in the living room, Abbie got her news in first. 'Could you put your mug down for a moment, please.' She waited till this was done, then said, 'There's some bad news. Dad died yesterday, suddenly.'

'What?' Tears welled in Keziah's eyes. 'Oh, no!' She fumbled for a handkerchief. 'I don't know what to say.'

Abbie watched her. There was no doubt the tears were genuine. She felt angry at that. Keziah must have got on much better with their father than she had. Maybe he'd always preferred her. There couldn't be much difference in their ages.

How had she not known about her sister?

She waited till Keziah had calmed down a little, then asked, 'What are you doing here today?'

'Dad's let me and Susie stay for a while till I get over the break-up of my marriage. My husband ran off with another woman and cleaned out our bank account, the rat.'

'Oh. Sorry about that. Only . . . how do I know you really are my father's daughter?'

'You're a suspicious type, aren't you?'

'You'd be suspicious if you were suddenly confronted with someone claiming to be your sister.'

'Half-sister.'

'Whatever.'

They glared at one another for a moment or two, then Keziah said, 'I can show you the paperwork. My mother died a couple of years ago and I decided to trace my father. If she'd known she was going to be involved in an accident, she'd have burnt it all, I'm sure, because she always refused to tell me who my father was. She was very manipulative about some things.'

'I'm surprised he let her do that.'

'He didn't know anything about me, though she must have been pregnant when they split up, given my date of birth.'

'Why would she keep your existence secret? You'd think she'd want maintenance, at the very least.'

'How should I know why? She always went her own sweet way. But she didn't have time to destroy anything, thank goodness. And he just accepted me, once he'd checked the paperwork. That meant a lot to me.'

She took a long, wobbly breath. 'I wanted Susie to know

her grandfather because we don't have any other close relatives now.'

Abbie could feel sympathy beginning to grow. She was a single mother too and it could be damned hard going at times. And lonely. 'But now Dad's dead, you're alone again.'

'Yes. My mother was very stubborn about not getting in touch with her own family, and I think she must have upset them big time. She was good at upsetting people.'

'So was Dad.'

'He's not good with people, is he? But he means well, I think, and she didn't always,' Keziah said.

Another silence fell, but this one didn't feel as fraught. Or was that her imagination? 'I don't know what to say or do,' Abbie confessed.

'I don't, either.'

Abbie saw more tears trembling in Keziah's eyes. 'You must have got on well with Dad to be so upset. My mother and I had stopped trying to deal with him, he was so uncommunicative. I texted her and she said to do what I wanted about the funeral. She's not coming back for it.'

'He wasn't easy, but when he found out I'd just lost my job as well as my savings, he offered straight away to let me and Susie come and stay here for a while. I used to see him watching her intently, as if he was looking for something in the way she behaved. But he spent most evenings in his home office after she went to bed and he was never very communicative.'

'Tell me about it. A clam would be talkative compared to him.'

'He didn't tell me much about you, except that you existed, how old you were and that you had a son called Louis. When I asked to see a photo, he said he didn't keep photos. They only made you sad for the people you'd lost.'

'Strange thing to say when it was his own fault he lost people.'

'I was used to that sort of attitude. My mother also had difficulties communicating. None of her other relationships lasted, either.'

After another short silence, Keziah said suddenly, 'I suppose I'd better move out of here. Dad will likely have left this place to you, because you're his only legitimate child, and you'll want to sell it. I'd be grateful if you'd give me a few days to find somewhere else, though. I had to pay off the debts my husband left me with so I haven't managed to save any money yet.'

Her voice grew lower, as if she was talking to herself. 'I may even have to declare myself homeless and rely on the council for help with housing.'

Abbie looked round the spacious flat. Didn't she wish it would be left to her! It'd be wonderful not to have to pay rent.

Then she caught her sister wiping away more tears and felt guilty for thinking like that before her father was even buried. 'I don't know how things stand, so you don't need to rush to leave. He didn't tell me anything about . . . you know, his financial situation. I came to see if I could find out the name of his lawyer. I can't imagine him not leaving a will.'

The little girl had come up to her mother and held out

her arms to be lifted up. Keziah did this automatically, wiped off the milky moustache with a tissue and planted a kiss on her child's cheek. 'How old is your son?'

'Louis is seven. And there's no father around. He fled when I found out I was expecting, said he didn't believe in marriage, so he's never even seen his son.'

'Mine stayed around for three years then took off into the wide blue yonder. He left a note saying he couldn't hack being a father and was tired of being woken in the night. When I got home from work after picking Susie up from childcare, not only was he gone but so were our savings, all except a couple of hundred pounds, which he said he'd left to pay off his debts. Only the debts were much bigger than that, and he must have known it. I haven't heard from him since and nor have his family. They don't want to know me. They've other grandchildren who aren't illegitimate, they told me.'

'That's cruel. And who cares about that sort of thing these days?'

Keziah shrugged, then changed the subject. 'Do you want me to help you look for the will?'

It felt like a big step to take in trusting her sister, but something made Abbie say, 'Yes, please.'

'Thanks for that.'

'Actually, Keziah, Dad may have left you something – or everything, for all I know.'

'I can't see why he would. I've only known him for a few weeks. Oh dear, this is an awkward situation for us both, isn't it? But I've been wanting to meet you ever since he told me about you. I would have looked for your address, but he keeps—I mean, *kept* his papers in his office and there's a lock on the door. Do you have a key to it?'

'I have a whole bunch of keys.' She held them out and shook them.

'You won't regret trusting me, I promise. About the flat or anything else.'

Abbie didn't know what to say to that, was still in a state of shock at even having a sister, hadn't got her thoughts together about it.

'You haven't asked for any proof of who I am, but if the papers I've got aren't enough, I suppose we could take a DNA test. Only I can't afford to pay for it.'

'I don't need to ask for DNA proof of the relationship. Look.' She pulled Keziah across to the mirror and gestured towards their reflections.

It was as if she was seeing a smaller version of herself. Keziah had the same colour of hair and even tied it back carelessly like she did, probably for the same reason, to save money. She didn't wear glasses, though.

'It feels strange, doesn't it? I've never met anyone I resembled before.' Keziah blinked her eyes but one tear escaped and she brushed it away with her fingers. 'Sorry. I'm at the emotional time of month.'

'No worries. Come on, then. Let's look in his office.'

'I'll just get Susie settled with her teddy. If we're lucky, she may have a nap.'

Abbie tried the keys till she found the one that opened the door of her father's office. She was surprised by how much like a commercial office it was. No home comforts here, just an office chair, two metal filing cabinets, a tall metal store cupboard and shelves of box files on the wall above the desks, all neatly labelled.

And there was a state-of-the-art computer, very new-looking. She hungered after it instantly, hoped that hadn't shown.

She studied the other keys. 'I wonder what these open?'

Keziah shrugged and made no attempt to come further inside than the doorway. 'I've never been in here before, but you'd think he'd have something more comfortable to sit on than an upright office chair, wouldn't you?'

Abbie sat down on the office chair. 'It's good ergonomically. He wouldn't have been uncomfortable, just rather upright.' She hesitated. 'I don't like to open the drawers.'

'I know what you mean.'

In the next room, the little girl began to sing 'Baa, Baa, Black Sheep' in a surprisingly tuneful voice for one so young, and somehow it broke the spell.

'Just do it!' Keziah said firmly.

So, Abbie opened the top drawer of the four at the left-hand side of the desk. An envelope lay there, and written on it in big black capitals was:

IN CASE OF MY SUDDEN DEATH

'Look at this!'

Keziah came to stand behind her. 'Wow!'

Abbie hesitated to pick it up. 'I'm being stupid.' She grabbed it and used the paper knife from the desk stand to slit it, saying apologetically, 'He was always very neat in his ways, so I don't like to tear it open, even now.'

She pulled out the piece of paper, read it through and gasped, then passed it to Keziah, who looked equally astonished by what it said.

Chapter Eight

Warren looked at his emails and let out a yell of triumph. 'Yeah! Gotcha!'

He read it again, taking in the details this time. Angus Denning's wife, who did the dogsbody work for the project, said he could move into Number 4 Saffron Lane any time. So, this was it: freedom, escape.

'What are you shouting about now?' Michelle asked from the doorway of the conservatory.

'I got the residency.'

'What does it pay?'

'Nothing. It only covers the rent, service charges and a small living allowance.'

'How can you go, then? You'll lose your job and then what will happen to the mortgage and the other payments here?'

'Doesn't your tiny brain ever get beyond that damned mortgage or the cost of sausages?'

She scowled at him. 'Someone in this family has to be practical.'

'Well, I'm going to accept their offer and that's that.'

'Without even discussing it with me?'

'Yep.'

'If you do go, you're not coming back.'

It took a moment for that to sink in. She'd surprised him big time. He'd have expected her to cling to him. 'I wouldn't want to come back to *you*.'

'My brother was right. I've served my purpose, haven't I? Paid more than my share of living costs while you were getting established as an artist, done most of the household chores and now you don't need me any more, so you're off.'

He shrugged. Their marriage hadn't started out quite that blatantly but he'd gone cold on her within a few months. She was such a fusspot to live with, always wanting him to do work on improving the house. 'It was a bit more than that between us to start with, don't you think?'

'I'm not at all sure about that. If it was, the bloom soon wore off. On my side as well as yours. Don't think you're anything special, Warren Cutler. You're no good in bed, for a start. I'd have put up with that if you'd been loving, but you weren't.'

She suddenly swiped at the shelf of in-progress figurines and sent them flying. 'These damned bits of wood are the only thing you really love.'

As she raised her hand for another swipe, he shoved her hastily back into the living room. 'What the hell do you think you're doing? If you've broken anything, I'll—'

'You'll what? Hit me? I'm as big as you are and I'm a hell of a lot fitter. I'll hit you right back if you lay one finger on me, then I'll go and lay a complaint at the police station. If I cry all over them, who do you think they'll believe?'

'I wouldn't waste my energy on you.' He began picking up the figurines, cursing when he found one had been damaged.

When he turned round, cradling it against him, she was still standing there. But she must have nipped out into the hall because she was holding her old rounders bat in her hand, tapping it gently against one hand.

'Just try it, Warren Cutler.'

'Are you deaf, daft or useless? I told you I wouldn't bother to touch you, you old sow.' He turned away.

'Wait.'

'What?'

'It's only fair to warn you that anything you leave behind when you go off for your precious residency will be chucked away, because you're *not* coming crawling back here.'

'I own half the house till we sell it so why should I have to clear my stuff out?'

She gave him a nasty smile. 'Because you won't be here to protect your little wooden darlings, will you?' She mimed striking a match.

He gasped. 'You'd burn them?'

'Without hesitation. I hate them. They're nasty things, just like you. I'm surprised people buy them.'

She'd do it, too, the bitch, he thought angrily. She

always kept her threats. 'Remember that two can play at that game.'

She glared at him. 'You're not coming back to live here, whatever you say or do.'

'I don't want to but I can't move my things instantly. I'll need to borrow a van to take everything away. Do you think you can rein in your temper for a day or two till I sort something out?'

'As long as you don't take too long about it. I'll move your clothes into the spare bedroom while you're out.'

'Good. I prefer sleeping alone. But I'm taking some of the furniture.'

'We'll discuss that when you get back.'

She'd surprised him with her ultimatum, but it didn't matter because he'd been planning to leave her anyway. He looked round. He'd miss this conservatory, though, had spent a lot of happy hours working in here. The rest of the house was yawningly ordinary, a typically bijou semi-detached residence. A rabbit hutch, in his opinion, with small rooms to suit small minds.

As for Michelle, he'd not miss her in the slightest. *Au contraire.*

It was two days before Ginger started to regain some of her usual energy. She did a lot of sleeping and was grateful that her kind hostess left her to it.

When she came down for a meal or cup of tea, she brought some sewing, because she didn't like to sit idle, but not one of her pictures, which took a lot more effort.

'What's that you're making?' Elise asked.

'Just a patchwork apron. I buy oddments of material from the charity shop. They keep good bits from worn-out clothes specially for me and charge me a pound per bag. I put them together in my spare moments and sell the results at the markets now and then.'

Elise went across to look at it. Bright colours in a pleasing arrangement. This was more than 'just' an apron. 'Why didn't you mention these when you applied for the residency?'

Ginger looked at her in surprise. 'These aren't art; they're only – you know, sewing: make do and mend, my gran used to call it.'

Elise picked up the apron and held it against her. 'It's pretty. I'd like to buy a couple of aprons as well as one of your pictures. They'll make great birthday presents. Really useful as well as pretty.'

'That's what people always say: *useful*.'

'Useful stuff can be artistic as well.'

It was too late now to add Ginger's other skill to the mix, she thought regretfully. Nell had told her that Cutler had accepted the residency within minutes of receiving the emailed offer. Well, why wouldn't he?

She wasn't looking forward to having him as a neighbour. There was something . . . she sought in vain for a defining word and could only come up with 'nasty' about him.

Nell called in at Number 3 that afternoon while Ginger was having another little nap. 'Hi, Elise. I thought I'd better let you know that Cutler will be moving in today or tomorrow, I don't know which.'

'He's not wasting any time.'

'No. He and his wife are splitting up, apparently, so he wants to get away from her as quickly as possible.'

'She'll be well shot of him.'

'Unfortunately, he'll soon be your neighbour, so maybe you should suspend judgement.'

Elise knew she'd never get on with him. 'Don't worry. I can paste a smile on my face that's as false as his, and he can take it or leave it. He'll not get any closer to me than a nod as we pass one another, though.'

'You're not even giving him a chance?'

'I gave him a chance at the interview and he ignored me.'

Nell couldn't deny that. 'Hmm. What about Ginger? How is she?'

'A bit better, but she has nowhere to go. You're not going to ask me to turn her out, surely?'

'Of course not! You should know me better than that.'

'Yes, well, I prefer to be sure. I'm taking her to pick up her car tomorrow, so she'll be able to start looking for a job. Only . . .'

'Only what?'

'I've been wondering. You're thinking of opening a café in Number 1. She's used to working in cafés. How about offering her the job of helping you set it up then running it? She could even sleep there. It wouldn't be fancy accommodation, but there's that room on the upper floor that would make a reasonably sized bedsitter and she can do her cooking in the café. From what she's let drop so far, she's never had anywhere fancy to live, so I think she'd snap it up.'

'Hmm. I'll think about it. You haven't found out what's wrong?'

'Not yet. But there is definitely something worrying her. I'm thinking of tackling that head on tonight.'

After tea, Elise cleared the table, loaded the dishwasher and sat down again. Ginger had switched on the TV but was staring into space, not watching the news, so Elise switched off the sound.

'Isn't it about time you told me what was wrong, Ginger?'

'Is it that obvious?'

'It is to me.'

The younger woman shrugged. 'I'm not sure what to do now. I can't continue to take advantage of you.'

'Oh, I'm not fed up of you yet.'

Ginger gave her one of those delightfully sunny smiles. 'Thanks.' Her smile faded quickly, though. 'But I've always prided myself on standing on my own feet.'

'Tell me what's really wrong, what's behind your homelessness, then maybe I can help you work something out.' Elise left the words hanging in the air between them and the silence went on for so long she was about to give up hope of finding out. She couldn't force a confidence, after all.

'It's my son,' Ginger blurted out abruptly.

'Is he in trouble?'

Ginger flushed. 'Not exactly. He came to live with me a couple of years ago when my husband was dying, to help with the lifting, you see. Alan was quite a big man. And Donny did help, I'll give him that. But after his father died, he refused to move out again and then, well, he got into a fight at work and was sacked.'

She fell silent again, then continued, 'Afterwards he had to take a lower-paid job and that upset him. He made new friends and started drinking with them and . . . well, things went from bad to worse. He . . . he hit me.'

'No!'

'He's hit me twice now and he nearly hit me again just before I left.'

'Hitting his own mother. That's despicable.'

Ginger was staring at the ground as if ashamed of something *she* had done and her voice was low as she added, 'And lately, well, he's cheating. Won't hand over rent money or money for food. I never thought I'd be afraid of my own son. He's a big lad, these days. He's put a lot of weight on. I think that's the drinking. I wouldn't stand a chance if I tried to throw him out.'

She sobbed suddenly and pressed one hand across her mouth, struggling desperately for control, then wailed, 'I'm afraid of him, afraid of my own son!'

When Ginger had calmed down again, Elise got her to explain what steps she had taken before she left for the interview. They didn't sound very effective, but then it wasn't easy to deal with domestic violence, which came in many forms. Even Elise had experienced bullying as her nieces had tried to force her to go into a care home. That was a form of violence as far as she was concerned.

'I've got an idea about a job for you, complete with accommodation,' she said at last. 'If you can bear to stay here for a few more days, I'll see if I can work something out.'

'Can I ask what it is?'

'I'd rather not say in case nothing comes of it. There are other people involved, you see.'

'Oh. Right. If you're sure you don't mind me staying a bit longer?'

'I'm enjoying your company. Tomorrow we'll pick up your car and visit your bank – which one is it? Oh, no! They closed the branch of that bank in Sexton Bassett.'

'They want you to do everything online these days, don't they? If there's a cash machine somewhere I'll manage with that for the time being.'

'All right. Now, there's a TV programme I want to watch tonight, if you don't mind. It's about health and ageing.' She looked at Ginger ruefully. 'I'm trying to keep up with the latest developments. At my age, you need all the help you can get. They're talking about trying to keep older people in decent health for longer – prolonging the healthspan, they call it. I'm doing pretty well since I had my hip replacement, but I do get a bit stiff and achy, so I'm trying to see what else I can do to help myself.'

It was Ginger's turn to pat her hand. 'You seem to be doing really well for your age, Elise. I'd like to see the programme too, if you don't mind company. Donny won't watch things like that and though he makes a joke of it, I can't get the remote off him.'

'He sounds like a bully in more ways than one, then.'

'Yes. I don't know where I went wrong with him. I tried

so hard to be a good mother. Oh, Elise, I reckon he's turning into an alcoholic on top of everything else.'

'If he's drinking heavily, he *is* an alcoholic already. No one forces him to drink. He *chooses* to do it. Not your fault, dear. We can't control the next generation's lives, let alone the generation after that.'

'They have names for each generation now, but I can never remember which is which.'

Elise grimaced. 'It seems like another sort of ageism to me. Generation XYZ and so on. Some people make it sound as if we can't speak to people from different generations or even live near them. That's so ridiculous. In the past, the generations have helped one another, with raising children, in sickness, with old age. Turn and turn about throughout life.'

They sat quietly for a few moments as the opening credits came on, then watched the programme together, after which Ginger went to bed. But though she felt somewhat comforted by her chat with Elise, she lay awake for a long time worrying about what to do next if what her new friend was planning didn't work out – not to mention worrying about what Donny was doing to her little house and remaining possessions.

How could you not worry when you were to all intents and purposes homeless – and had lost your son?

She shed a few silent tears into her pillow. Donny had been such a loving little boy, and bonny too. Now, with his fat face and shaven head, he looked brutal. And acted brutally too.

* * *

Just as Elise was getting ready for bed, headlights raked across her living room window and a big van drew up. Of course, she had to peep through the window to see who it was.

Him!

She watched from the darkened room, surprised that Warren Cutler was moving in so late at night. Normally she'd have offered a new neighbour a cup of tea and a piece of cake, but not him. She didn't know why she'd taken such a dislike to him, but she had.

There was a tap on the kitchen window at the rear of the house and she slipped through to answer it without putting any of the lights on. Stacy, of course. Who else could it be? And she knew why.

'Come in. Let's keep our voices down and spy on our new neighbour.'

'I was up late, burnishing a piece,' Stacy said. 'Couldn't resist watching him. Shall I go and offer him a cup of tea or something?'

'If so, don't include me in the tea party.'

Stacy looked at her in surprise. 'There's an edge to your voice when you talk about him that I've never heard before.'

Elise shrugged. 'I told you: I didn't take to him at the interview. He ignored me, treated me as if I didn't exist. And what's he doing arriving so late? That's suspicious, in my not-so-humble opinion.'

'It's a strange time to move in. Perhaps he had a breakdown on the way here.'

'Nell told me he and his wife were splitting up. Maybe she threw him out.'

'At this hour?'

Elise shrugged again, trying not to be too unfair. After all, she had only her feelings to go by, not any real facts. And he *was* a skilled woodcarver. She tried to keep reminding herself of that.

Ginger came downstairs to join them and the three women stood in the shadows of the darkened living room watching and whispering comments on what he was doing.

Cutler was on his own. He carried quite a lot of what they presumed were woodworking equipment and supplies into the house. Next came a single bed, some boxes that rattled or clanked, a plastic garden table and chairs, and one threadbare armchair, which he struggled with.

Then he closed the back doors of the combi-van.

'Is that all the furniture he's bringing?' Stacy whispered. 'He hasn't got much, has he? What about food? I haven't seen any signs of that. And he hasn't got a fridge, either.'

'Well, I'm not offering to lend him anything.' Elise could hear the sharpness in her voice but couldn't help it. 'He'll probably go out shopping tomorrow for what he needs.'

'He's done nothing but scowl as he's carried the stuff in,' Ginger said suddenly. 'Perhaps she threw him out before he was ready to leave.'

To their surprise, after their new neighbour had unloaded his van, it was only a few minutes before he locked up the house and drove off again.

'How strange!' Elise said. 'Anyway, I'm going to turn you out now, Stacy. I need some sleep and so does Ginger.'

The three women separated.

Ginger lay awake for a while, wondering about the man next door. She'd like to see his art works, to find out what was so special about them. It wasn't just curiosity. It could be useful to find out what he was doing right, why the Dennings considered him more likely to be more commercially successful than her.

She'd decided this morning, lying in bed, just coming awake, that she had to make a huge effort to focus on her embroidery and sewing, really make it her life. She didn't know what Elise was planning or hoping for as a way of her earning a living, but if it gave her the opportunity to stay on here, she'd do it, whatever it was. And she'd be more focused on her sewing from now on, too.

That wouldn't be a hardship. When had she ever been able to concentrate solely on her own needs and wishes? Never, that she could remember. She'd looked after Alan all their married life, raised Donny, worked in cafés, then found herself looking after her son all over again as an adult. And he wasn't easy these days!

Now was her time. She sucked in her breath as she saw how she could do an embroidery about a woman's role over the years. Suddenly she was dying to get to work on it.

She'd started to feel so much better, so much more ready to fight for the life she longed to lead. From what she'd read, artists and writers rarely had it easy.

One author had written a blog about what she called the PS factor, to which she ascribed her own success:

Persistence and Stubbornness – always with capital letters.

And a big dash of Selfishness, too, Ginger added mentally. She smiled as she snuggled down. PSS, that would be her own motto from now on.

Chapter Nine

The two sisters went and sat at the kitchen table and Abbie spread out the papers that had been in the envelope. They were neatly typed, so her father had probably done them on his computer. His handwriting always looked angry, as if he had slashed the marks down on the page in a temper.

She wondered suddenly what other information his computer would hold and if they'd be able to get into it.

Keziah leant forward, trying to see better, so she changed how she was sitting and held the papers so they could both read them.

She unfolded the top sheet of paper and spread it out on top of the others. It had been crumpled up, then smoothed out again, as if someone had nearly thrown it away. She read it aloud.

To my daughters, Keziah Geddes and Abbie Turrell.

'Geddes?' Abbie looked at her sister. 'Isn't that your maiden name? Perhaps this was written a few years ago.'

'Not necessarily. I kept that name even after I was married,' Keziah said. 'My husband hated that. And I registered Susie as a Geddes too, so that's one thing I haven't had to change since the rat scuttled away.'

'Right. I see.' She continued to read the letter.

If the relationship between you is news, I'm sorry that you're finding it out via a letter, but on the other hand, I've never been good with the spoken word, so maybe I can do it better this way.

I gather that I am borderline autistic, so I hope you'll have your children tested for that. Psychologists can help people with autism or Asperger's adjust to society much better these days if they start when the children are young.

I'm writing this in case I drop dead suddenly, and because I don't have long to live whether I die suddenly or not. I've been diagnosed with heart trouble and things are getting worse rapidly. But I expect and hope that I'll still have time to introduce the two of you properly before I die.

My lawyer has my will, so you'll need to see him as your first port of call. His details are listed in these papers.

What my will amounts to is that I'm dividing everything I own into two, half for each of you. That seems the fairest way to do it. I think you'll both find your inheritance more than adequate for your needs. I'm much better at making money than I am at dealing with people.

I wish you well in your lives and hope you will do better with your personal relationships from now on. You've both had the chance to make one big mistake. Please don't rush into anything from now on. I made two big mistakes and couldn't find it in me to try again. I often wished that I had because life can be lonely.

But still, this gave me two daughters in the end, not just the one I've always been glad of.

All my love,

George Turrell

'How sad!' Keziah said softly. 'He didn't even sign it "Dad"!'

Abbie let out a snort of anger. 'How like him!'

'He couldn't help it.'

'If he couldn't say it to our faces, he could have written before now to tell us about one another, don't you think? This is a very lucid communication. Why didn't he try writing to tell us earlier, for heaven's sake?'

And suddenly she was sobbing, rocking to and fro with the intensity of her feelings. 'He should have tried, damn him! I didn't get a chance to make it up before he died.' She would always regret that.

It was a while before Abbie realised someone was holding her close.

Her sister.

She had a sister now!

She pulled back a little and they looked at one another.

Keziah brushed wisps of damp hair from Abbie's forehead. 'He gave us one very important gift. I hope that you value it as highly as I do.'

'Oh? And what's that?' But she knew really, just needed to hear the words before she accepted the gift, she didn't know why.

Keziah's voice was gentle. 'He gave us each a sister. Don't pretend you aren't as glad about that as I am.'

'Oh, I am. You know I am.'

And then they were both crying again, but this time these were healing tears and hugs.

'Oh, what fools we are!' Abbie said at last, blowing her nose and grabbing another tissue from the box to clean the smears from her glasses.

'I won't tell anyone if you don't.'

'There's nothing to tell about you. I'm the one who fell apart. Anyway, let's carry on with this stuff. What does the next paper say?'

'It's a list. The heading is: Things you need to deal with after I die.'

Abbie covered it with her hand. 'Let's have a cup of coffee to help us go through it. I think I need a caffeine jolt to the brain to help me concentrate.'

'I agree. I'll put the kettle on. While it's boiling, why don't you phone the lawyer for an appointment? We need to see him as soon as possible.'

'I have to register Dad's death, too. Within five days, the woman at the hospital said.' Abbie phoned the lawyer and when the receptionist realised what this was about, she was able to offer them a preliminary appointment the following afternoon.

Keziah brought the coffee in. 'Here. It's only a cheap sort. That's all I can afford.'

'I can't afford the fancy sorts either.'

They sat and sipped, then Keziah asked abruptly, 'Do you like your job, Abbie?'

'No. I hate it. If Dad has left us anything worthwhile, I'm giving that job up and buying a B & B in the country, or whatever else I can find that will give me a more peaceful life.'

'What exactly do you do that's so bad?'

'I'm a general office dogsbody because I can't work full-time on account of Louis, so I do whatever they consider necessary, like the minor computing stuff entering the accounts, filing papers – there are still a lot of papers to deal with even in a digital age – not to mention going to the post office, relieving the receptionist, picking up the lunch orders and so on. Boring, but at least it's still necessary to have a human to do those things. And of course, whatever we do today, I have to pick up Louis from after-school care at four-thirty.'

Her phone rang just then and she frowned as she answered it, not recognising the number.

'Abbie Turrell.'

A man's deep voice said, 'Emil here.'

'Emil?' For a moment she couldn't think who that was.

'Emil Kinnaird. We met yesterday when I took you to pick up your son.'

'Oh, yes. I'm sorry. Things didn't register very well yesterday, given the circumstances. I think I was in shock.'

'Perfectly understandable. I'm glad I've caught you. We have some of your father's things at the office, and of course, we owe some money for his unpaid wages and holiday pay. Are you the heir?'

'My sister and I are joint heirs.'

'Sister? George didn't list anyone but you as his next of kin when he started working for us.'

'It's a long story, but I have a sister I didn't know about because he didn't know about her either until recently. We are, apparently, joint inheritors.'

'Is this causing you trouble?'

'No. She's great. And it's nice not to have to cope alone.' She realised she was confiding too much and was surprised at herself, but he was so easy to talk to.

'Then it might be useful for you to have the money owing to your father now.'

'Yes, I suppose it might.' It'd be a godsend but she wasn't going to admit that.

'OK. I could drop it off with your father's possessions later today or in a day or two, whenever best suits you both. You must have a lot to do, so I'll fit in with you. And I meant what I said: if I or anyone from our company can help with anything at all, you only have to ask.'

'I'm fine, but thanks for the offer. I'll take your phone number and let you know when it'll be convenient to bring everything round. Just a minute.' She entered his phone number, said, 'Thank you for your call,' not waiting for his response.

She explained to Keziah who had just phoned and what he'd offered, then looked round. 'I haven't been here before. I gather Dad only moved in a few months ago. He let Mum know his new address and she told me. But I was stupidly angry because he didn't contact me directly. Um, how many bedrooms are there?'

'Three, four if you count the office. It's quite big for a flat.' She cocked her head on one side. 'Are you thinking what I am?'

'Yes. Would you mind me moving in with you?'

'Not at all. I'd like it.'

'Could you show me round?'

But before they could make a start, Abbie's phone rang again. Due to a cancellation, her father's lawyer could fit them in for half an hour at twelve o'clock if they could get to his office on time.

'We'll be there. Thanks.' Abbie looked at Keziah. 'Oh, sorry. I'm so used to doing things on my own, I didn't think to check that with you. Are you all right to go round to Mr Corshaw's rooms at noon? There's a cancellation. I know Dad said we inherit jointly, but the sooner we confirm that officially the better, don't you think? We're going to need some money to pay for everything.'

'Yes, I can come. I'll have to take Susie with us but she's usually good when we're out, especially if she can have her crayons. I'll give her a quick snack, then it'll only take me a few minutes to get ready. If we go in my car, I'll have her child seat.'

She looked at Abbie. 'Oh. There's Dad's car to deal with too. Why didn't we remember that? Perhaps your Mr Kinnaird could have it brought round?'

'Yes. Good idea. We'll phone him after we get back.' She frowned. 'And why didn't he mention it?'

* * *

After Emil put the phone down he looked round the office and grimaced. It was a dingy place. They really needed better premises than these to make it the regional headquarters. He was surprised that business was increasing but apparently some people preferred to arrange their insurance face-to-face and lots of customers were just walking through the door.

He didn't intend to spend another night in that horrible little bedsitter, either. He'd go and look for a hotel.

With a feeling of relief, he locked up and went out to explore the town.

He found a small hotel, lugged his things upstairs and lay down on the bed for a rest. He didn't wake for a couple of hours. He grabbed something to eat and went back to the office, feeling guilty to have left it shut without an explanatory sign.

Fortunately, only a couple of people popped in and he found brochures for them to take away and study.

It was a relief when the afternoon ended, and he could go back to the hotel.

The following morning, Emil felt a lot better after a good night's sleep and a hearty breakfast. He opened up the office and it wasn't long before the doorbell tinkled.

A woman came in and looked at him. 'You must be Emil. I'm Jenny Dalby!'

'Oh! Sorry. We've spoken on the phone a few times. Am I glad to see you!'

She gave him a sad smile. 'I heard about George's death and thought I might be needed.'

'You are. What about your holidays, though? You're not due back for another week, according to the records.'

'My husband is ill so we couldn't go to Cyprus as we'd planned. After what's happened with poor George, I thought I might as well come into work and see if you needed a hand. I can take the rest of my holidays another time, if that's all right with you. I know "staycations" are becoming popular but I'm not one to spend my holidays at home.'

'That'll be such a help! I can't thank you enough. You couldn't come full-time, could you?'

'Happy to. I've been wanting to work full-time since my youngest son left home and George promised I could do that as soon as the office was reorganised.'

'Yes. My father mentioned that too. If you're still interested, you can start full-time from now onwards. Would you be all right to manage the office? I don't know enough about it yet and I have other things to do, like finding somewhere more permanent to live.'

'Happy to. I've been working here for years and I know the job backwards.'

'That's great. And since you'll be managing the office, we'll pay you at a higher level, of course.'

She looked delighted, flushing slightly. 'Thank you. You don't often get rises without applying for them.'

'I'm sure you'll earn it. Turrell always spoke well of you. I wonder . . .' He hesitated, then beckoned to her to follow him and went into the manager's office. 'Look, can you hold the fort from now on, do you think? Hire a temp to help you, if you need one. I'm still recovering from a major operation and I need to take it easy sometimes.'

'Yes, of course. I'll be fine. I've taken over before when Mr Turrell was away.'

'Thank goodness! Now, I was going to use the bedsitter on the top floor but it's a miserable place and I'm not even sure it's safe. I spent half last night waiting for an emergency electrician after the power cut out, and he said the place needed rewiring.'

'Mr Turrell was actually looking round for new premises. I can give you the name of the estate agent he was dealing with, if you would like to look that over at the same time as hunting for a place to live.'

'Good thinking. If I can't find myself a flat straight away, I'll stay on at the hotel. I'd go mad in that nasty little bedsitter, anyway.'

'You'll probably have to sign a lease for several months to get a flat.'

'Doesn't matter. I'm planning to stay in the area for a while. I really like Wiltshire.' A quiet year or two was what the doctor had ordered. Emil had only told his parents why and they'd promised to keep it to themselves.

The estate agent was all over him when he found out Emil wanted a good-quality flat as well as new and bigger business premises.

'There is, as you must know, Mr Kinnaird, a general shortage of rental accommodation, but if you're prepared to pay a higher-than-average rent, I'm sure I can find you something suitable.'

A woman at the next desk called across, 'There's The Quartet. Two of the flats have just been refurbished and are ready to rent. I was going to list them this weekend.'

'How soon can I see them?' Emil asked at once.

'I'll contact the owner as soon as I can get hold of him, then get back to you. All right?'

'Yes, please.' He turned back to the man he was dealing with about new business premises.

'I can show you one place this afternoon, and another next week.'

'Good.'

Emil smiled as he walked out. Life seemed to move at a slower pace here and he liked that. He wanted a place of his own more quickly than he needed the new business premises, but the hotel was comfortable. He could wait.

Chapter Ten

Warren got back to Saffron Lane just before dawn the next morning and didn't wake up till nearly noon. Even then he didn't feel like getting out of bed. He yawned and stretched. It was nice and quiet here. He'd enjoy that.

Then he realised that what had woken him was someone knocking at the front door. 'Damn!' He was tempted to leave it unanswered, but it might be Angus Denning come to see how he was settling in, and he didn't want to offend the man whose largesse was going to support him for the next few months.

He went across to the window and yelled, 'Coming!'

It was only when he looked round for his dressing gown that he realised he'd slept in his clothes. He remembered falling into bed and nothing till now. He rolled his eyes at his dishevelled reflection in the bathroom mirror, then shrugged and ran lightly down the stairs.

To his disappointment it was Mrs Denning at the door.

He didn't like being fobbed off with underlings, hoped that hadn't shown in his face. He tried to summon up his smile, but it never worked until he was fully awake. 'Sorry to keep you waiting. I was asleep. Did you need something?'

'I'm so sorry. I didn't realise you'd still be in bed.'

'I had the chance to borrow a friend's van overnight so I didn't get much sleep. But using that to move meant it only cost me the petrol.'

'I see. Well, I thought I should check that everything is all right in the house, all the kitchen equipment working and so on.'

'I'll have to let you know about that once I've used it.' He couldn't stop himself yawning. 'Sorry. I think I'll go back to bed for another snooze. I'm knackered.'

He left her standing at the door, couldn't be bothered to chat, was never at his best till he'd had at least two cups of coffee.

Nell was amazed when Cutler closed the door in her face. Frowning, she stepped back from it. How rude! When she looked sideways, she saw Elise beckoning from the next house.

'Fancy a cup of tea or coffee, dear?'

'I'd love a cup of tea. You make particularly good tea.'

'I never buy the cheap brands, that's part of the secret.'

Nell followed Elise into the house and found Ginger sitting in the kitchen. The genuine smile she received was such a huge contrast to the scowl with which Cutler had greeted her that she suddenly wished they'd chosen this woman. Which was silly because they had to be strictly commercial about this whole project. But each time she reminded herself of that, she felt less convinced than before that they'd made the right decision.

'You look a bit upset, dear.'

Elise looked concerned rather than nosey so Nell didn't try to hide why. 'I went next door to welcome Cutler to Saffron Lane but I woke him up and he wasn't in the best of moods.'

She explained about having the door shut in her face, feeling indignant all over again. They both looked shocked.

'I told you I didn't like him,' Elise said. 'I haven't spoken to him since he moved in. He arrived late last night, didn't even give us the courtesy of a quick knock when he arrived to say he was here and drove off again after he'd unloaded.'

'I heard him return about five o'clock this morning,' Ginger said. 'He seemed to trip over something and cursed rather loudly.'

'Well, he definitely doesn't improve on acquaintance, does he?' Nell studied Ginger covertly as she sipped her tea. Elise's idea about an alternative offer of a job for her lodger might be worth following up on.

'I'm having a quick check of Number 1 before I go back to the big house. Do you want to come and see the house, Ginger? It's very interesting. There's a secret room that was set up for communications backup during World War II in case the Germans invaded. I think its records must have got lost because it was unknown and untouched until an expert we were using to check the houses found it.'

Elise gave Nell a quick look as if she was guessing why this offer of a tour was being made. She nodded slightly.

'I'd love to see it,' Ginger said instantly. 'I've never been inside a secret room.'

'Maybe I can pick your brain while we're going round the gallery and café. Elise said you'd worked in cafés and we're thinking of setting one up there, just a small place offering snacks, because most of the ground floor is earmarked for a gallery to sell our artists' work.'

'I'm happy to help in any way I can. I know all sorts of small details that will make it easier for the people running it, but the overall setup will depend on the shape of the rooms, won't it?'

'There might be a bit of leeway for making changes.'

'Can I come too?' Elise asked.

'Of course.'

Warren heard voices outside and muttered, 'Shut up, you twittering bitches!' But he couldn't resist sneaking a look out of the window. It would be easier to get what he wanted from this residency if he kept an eye on what his rivals were doing.

He rolled his eyes as he saw the old biddy who'd interviewed him cosying up to Mrs Denning. And who was the other one? My goodness she looked a scruffy tart with that bright red hair, dyed of course, you could see that a mile off.

He watched them go into Number 1, wondering what they were doing, then turned back towards the bed. To his annoyance, after lying on it for a moment or two trying to relax, he had to admit to himself that it was no use. He was wide awake now and wouldn't be able to get back to sleep till nightfall probably. What he needed was a cup of strong coffee.

He went downstairs and looked for a kettle. There wasn't one provided. He'd have to buy his own, dammit. He found one of the dented old saucepans Michelle had given him, put some water in and set it on the gas cooker to boil.

But, of course, he hadn't done any shopping and there was no jar of coffee among the things he'd flung into a carrier bag. Cursing under his breath he took a quick look at what he'd brought and began making a list. He'd have to go out straight away. He couldn't function without coffee.

Getting into his car, he headed out for the big supermarket he'd passed on his way into town yesterday. It had been lit up, must have been open. If only he'd thought of kitchen supplies as well as snack food for the journey, he could have stopped there to buy a few essentials.

He went into the café attached to it and ordered a coffee and a toasted cheese sandwich, eating the latter ravenously. He debated ordering something else to eat because he was still hungry, but after looking at the prices, he decided it'd be cheaper to buy loaves at the supermarket and make his own sandwiches. He had to watch every penny from now on. But he might buy a toasted sandwich-maker. That would save time on cooking.

With that in mind, he walked round the food aisles studying what was on special offer, something he hadn't done very often. He was horrified at how much it was going to cost him to stock up. He should have taken more things off the pantry shelves before he left home, because he'd paid for half of them, after all. No, that wasn't home, now. He'd got to stop thinking about it that way. After he left *the house*, he amended mentally.

He bought a kettle, a toaster and a toasted sandwich-maker, annoyed all over again at the necessity to do that.

When he got back to Saffron Lane two hours later, there was no sign of the other occupants or of Mrs Denning's car. He'd have to find out what they'd been doing in Number 1. He was good at finding things out. Now that he came to think of it, that first house was where the art gallery was going to be.

Well, if the other artists thought they could steal a march on him when it came to placing things in good selling positions, they could think again.

He carted in the bags of food and opened the boxes with the kitchen equipment in them, filling the kettle with water to rinse it out, then filling it again and putting it on to boil.

The fridge-freezer seemed to be working, thank goodness, but his few items looked very lonely sitting on the shelves.

He should have got some fruit, he realised, and went to hunt for a piece of scrap paper to start a list for his next shopping trip. And he'd buy some frozen ready meals because he didn't want to waste his creative time cooking. He didn't care what he ate, just needed to fill his belly regularly. And drink plenty of coffee.

Ginger was excited to be seeing the inside of Number 1, which Elise said was different from her house, so when her friend stood back and flapped one hand to tell her to go ahead and follow Nell inside, she didn't need prompting.

On the ground floor there was a large room with a big window at the front, as there was in Elise's house. Had all these houses started out as shops? she wondered.

At the other side of the room there was a short corridor passing what looked like a storeroom on the right behind the shop, with a barred window at the far end.

This must be intended as a storeroom, she thought, smiling because it was bigger than her front room at home.

At the rear, as in Elise's house, there was a neat little kitchen to the left with a larger living area on the right. However, this house was bigger than Number 3 and so was the rear garden. There was a whole wing behind the living area, containing a large airy room which would make a perfect artist's studio, she thought wistfully, and a bedroom and small shower room behind that.

She stared across the back of the house. 'It'd be nice to pave the outside area,' she said without thinking. 'You already have an L-shaped house. It wouldn't take much to make a lovely patio for sitting out.'

Nell stared outside thoughtfully. 'Good idea. With outdoor tables and chairs. I'll bear that in mind. There's nothing else to see outside, so let's go upstairs now.'

At the top of the stairs was a huge room, absolutely bare, covering the whole of the top floor.

'What's this for?' Ginger asked.

'We can use this space for whatever we like, probably as an extension of the downstairs gallery. We haven't decided yet. This will be the second stage.'

'Why didn't they put a dormer window at the front

side as well as the rear? It'd make it much lighter.'

'There's a good reason for that: the attic's where the secret communications room is.'

'Really? Where's the entrance to it?' Ginger turned round on the spot, frowning slightly, then moved forward to where the secret door was.

Nell exchanged surprised glances with Elise, because most people didn't guess where the entrance lay, it was so well hidden.

'It can only be here,' Ginger said, 'if you look at the rest of the layout.'

'You're right. There are several entrances, actually.' She showed Ginger the hidden catch. 'Before we go in, I need to warn you not to touch anything. It's all under polythene sheeting till Mr Kinnaird brings in some specialists to lay it out properly, so that people can walk round. I think he's going to have glass cases put over the exhibits. At the moment, it's still exactly as Angus and I found it.'

Ginger went inside and walked slowly round, not saying much but studying the table and its contents so carefully she seemed unaware of her companions for a while. Then she looked up and drew in a deep, happy breath. 'I'm so glad I've seen it before it was changed. It makes you feel as if you've touched history, doesn't it?'

'Yes. That's how I feel. Let's go down again. I want to ask you something.'

'Come back to my place and you two can discuss it while I make some more tea,' Elise suggested.

* * *

As they were going back, Stacy waved to them from Number 2 and Elise beckoned to her to join them.

How wonderful it would be to be a permanent part of this friendly group! Ginger thought enviously. She'd got on all right with her old neighbours but these women seemed as if they were close friends, even though they hadn't known each other for long.

'Why don't you discuss your idea with Ginger in the front room, Nell, while Stacy and I make some tea in the kitchen?' Elise suggested.

Ginger looked at her uncertainly, worried that Nell was going to ask her when she was leaving. But Elise winked at her and she took heart from that.

Once the two of them were alone, Nell didn't waste time. 'We're going to open a café on the ground floor of Number 1 and I wondered if you'd like the job of running it? Given your experience, you should be ideal for it. It'll only be part-time but there is accommodation with it, as you saw, and that'll be free, in return for acting as caretaker and helping in the art gallery, if needed. What do you think? You can sell your own things in the gallery as well.'

Ginger could only stare at her, then say in a choky voice, 'I think it sounds wonderful, ab-so-lutely wonderful.'

'The only problem is your council house. How will you deal with that? Will coming here deprive you of somewhere permanent to live? Obviously, no one can guarantee a job will go on for ever. My husband and I have given ourselves three years to find out whether this project is worthwhile, so that long I can just about guarantee you, because I'm sure we'll work well together.'

Ginger didn't hesitate to accept the offer. 'I was wondering whether to return to my old home or not. I can't decide. Sometimes I think I will go back for a while, as long as my son moves out; other times I think I should start again somewhere else and make this a clean break. My life was going nowhere and the suburb is going downhill rapidly. If I have the promise of a part-time job and free accommodation here, I'll simply give my notice to quit the council house.'

'And your son? What will he do? Elise seemed to think he might be a problem for you, might try to move in with you again. There isn't room for him here.'

'I'd not want him to come with me. I'm sick of being responsible for a lazy thirty-year-old. He can deal with his own problems from now on. I asked him to leave and he wouldn't, so I did.'

'Ah. That must have upset you.'

Ginger shrugged. 'My son has chosen his path and I can only leave him to follow it. The council will probably throw him out of the house if he hasn't left already, and unless he can see a way of sponging off me again, I doubt he'll care what happens to me. I desperately needed some breathing time away from him, Nell, to get my head straight about the situation. I left without telling him where I was going or why, because he'd have tried to stop me.'

'I'm sorry.'

'Yes. So am I. But it was the only way I could get away. You can't force another person to do as you want, can you? Even when it's your son. All I can do now is hope that one day things will change and he'll get his act together.' She didn't feel optimistic, though.

Taking out a tissue, she blew her nose. 'Let's not talk about that any more, Nell. Let's talk about my new job instead. How soon do you want me to start? When can I move in?'

'Well, if it's at all possible, I'd like you to start at once. I can let you have basic furniture from our attics at Dennings. I don't think Angus's ancestors ever threw anything away.'

'Yes, please.'

'We'll open the café and part of the art gallery before we open the museum. I thought you could help us plan how to set up the café.'

And Ginger couldn't help it. She flung her arms round Nell and danced her round the room. 'That's wonderful. Just perfect! Oh, I'm so *happy*!'

Elise came to the doorway, smiling to see such exuberance. 'Is this what I hope it is?'

Nell disentangled herself, chuckling. 'I now have no doubt whatsoever that Ginger wants to work in our café. And she's going to occupy the bedsitter at the rear of Number 1, so you'll have a new neighbour.'

'I shall enjoy that.'

Before Nell left, she gave Ginger a key. 'Don't give a copy to anyone else, or let anyone into Number 1 without my say-so, except for your own visitors, of course. We're going to set up a locking system for access to the upper floor before we open the café.'

'I'll be very careful who comes in for my own sake, too.'

'Then I'll get on with my day. Come up to the big house tomorrow morning if you need some furniture.'

Ginger looked down at the key she was holding. 'If you

don't mind, I'd like to go and look at the bedsitter again straight away. I do have some furniture. If I can get what I want to keep sent down here, I'll get rid of the rest. It's nothing special but it'll do.'

'Don't you want to pack up your house yourself?'

Ginger hesitated, then admitted, 'I'm a bit nervous of confronting my son. I'll have to see what I can work out.'

There was silence, then Nell said it again, 'I'm sorry.'

But her companion shrugged. 'These things happen. You have to carry on, whatever.'

Chapter Eleven

When Abbie and Keziah were shown into the lawyer's office, Susie settled down on the floor at her mother's feet clutching her teddy and looking sleepy, with one thumb firmly lodged in her mouth.

Mr Corshaw was younger than they'd expected, not much older than them, and very smartly dressed.

'I'm sorry about your father,' he said. 'You must be Abbie and you're Keziah. He told me about you both when he made his will, so you don't need to explain the general situation to me.'

Abbie nodded. Good. She wasn't sure whether she was comfortable with how to tell people yet. It was such a big change to her to have a sister. Keziah had had time to get used to the idea, but Abbie still felt she was in a state of shock.

He leant forward. 'Basically, your father left you equal shares in his estate. That will amount to several million pounds when everything is sorted out and death duties paid.'

'*What*?'

The two women spoke at the same time, then broke off and exchanged startled glances.

'Am I dreaming?' Abbie asked her sister.

'If you are, I am too.'

'Are you sure about that?' Abbie said to the lawyer at last, seeing that Keziah was still struggling for words.

'Yes. Very sure.' He smiled. 'You had no idea how much?'

'Until today, I had no idea that I had a sister, let alone that I'd inherit anything so substantial when Dad died,' Abbie confessed.

'Does that include his flat?' Keziah asked.

'Yes. And the other three flats in that building. He owned them all and now you will. One is already tenanted, he was occupying the one you're living in, Keziah, and the other two have just been refurbished and are about to be let.'

'How big are they?' Abbie asked.

'All the flats are roughly the same size as his own. He didn't want bedsitters; he was more concerned with getting good tenants who paid regularly, so he bought quality accommodation that didn't need a lot of upkeep.'

She closed her eyes and leant back for a moment, taking a deep breath to calm herself, then looked at him. 'I don't want to sound mercenary, but my son and I are living in a tiny bedsitter at the moment and I'd like to move into the empty flat as soon as possible, if Keziah agrees.'

They both looked at Keziah, who said faintly, 'Go for it. It'd be wonderful to live next to one another.'

The lawyer had a distinctly sympathetic expression on

his face. 'Your father said you were both struggling to raise children on your own. I'm sure it'd be all right for you to move in now, even before you have probate, because who's to complain about it? Certainly not me.'

Once again, Abbie was struggling not to cry and Keziah had an arm round her shoulders.

Mr Corshaw allowed her a few moments to pull herself together, then said, 'Your father had already planned his funeral and arranged it with an undertaker. I have the details and I will, unless you object, carry out his wishes and set the necessary arrangements in motion.'

Abbie felt nothing but relief about that. She hadn't been looking forward to arranging a funeral.

The lawyer caught sight of the time and said apologetically, 'Look, I'm afraid I have another client coming soon. Can I leave you in the hands of my clerk? He'll arrange a time for you to go round the two vacant flats with him and make your choice. He'll need to check that they've been fully finished before you can do that, Abbie. We'll get my secretary to make another appointment with me for you both to continue sorting out the business side of things.'

'Thank you.' She turned to Keziah. 'Will you look at the flats with me and help me choose one, as well? I still can't believe this is happening.'

Keziah nodded, picked up her daughter, then stopped and turned back to the lawyer. 'I'm sorry to ask another mercenary question, but what about Dad's car?'

'Do either of you want it or shall I sell it?'

'We both need a new car.'

'You can toss for that one, or each buy a new one as soon as probate comes through, which will probably be a few weeks.'

'I'm not sure my car will manage even a few more weeks.' Keziah looked questioningly at her sister.

'Mine probably will. You take Dad's.'

They made arrangements to meet the clerk at the building and look over the two vacant flats, then walked towards Keziah's car.

'I can't believe this is happening,' Abbie confessed. 'Can you?'

'No. I thought it only happened in fairy tales.' She fastened Susie into her seat and they set off back.

Neither felt like chatting. What did you say when the world had turned upside down? When you'd struggled to manage on a meagre amount of money for years and suddenly didn't need to struggle? When you could have anything you needed, within reason, for yourself and your child?

Except for your own father, the children's only grandfather, who was lost to you all for good.

Except for a husband and father for your child, something neither of them had.

It was true what people said: fate gives with one hand and takes away with the other. For them, it had been the other way round, things taken away then others given to them.

Ginger went into Number 1 and spent some time studying the whole of the ground floor. If there was going to be a café as well as a small art gallery/shop, it'd need planning carefully. Well, she had lots of ideas about how cafés ought to be set out after working in them for so many years, only she'd never had the power to change things before.

She'd worked for some right old eejits, like Joe, who'd done things in stupid ways. She smiled. She always thought of the word 'idiot' with an Irish accent as her mother had said it.

She drew in a deep breath of sheer satisfaction and twirled round again, but that stirred up the dust and made her sneeze. After another walk round her little flat, she decided to get a breath of fresh air and think about how to furnish her new home, which items she'd need to bring down from Newcastle.

Locking the door carefully behind her, she turned to study the street, her street now. As had happened before, her eyes turned instinctively towards Number 6, the largest of the houses. Elise had told her it might once have been called Bay Tree Cottage because the renovators had found what looked like a house name sign in the garden with that written on it. Nice name for a house. Was there really a bay tree there? If so, it'd be in the back garden.

She strolled along the street, hesitated, then walked up the front path of Number 6 and stopped for another moment at the corner of the house. Nell and Angus wouldn't mind if she walked round the garden and looked for a bay tree, surely? The workmen had gone and cleared up after themselves, more or less. There was no vehicle parked in front of the house, so she doubted anyone would even know she'd been into the garden.

The mess might have been cleared up but the ground had been trampled by feet going to and fro many times, and there were flattened patches where heavy things like skips must have stood. But even so, there was a feel of peace to it – well, that might be her imagination but that was how it seemed to her.

Leaning against the wall just round the corner was a piece of wood. It looked like . . . yes, it was the old sign Elise had told her about. She admired the neat writing on it and the painted edging of green leaves arranged in a sort of wreath: *Bay Tree Cottage.* That last word made her smile. This house seemed much larger than a cottage to her.

She walked round the side of the building eager to see the back garden, but as she turned the rear corner, she bumped into someone. She couldn't help calling out in shock because she hadn't heard any footsteps on the soft grass.

The man clasped her arm lightly for a moment to steady her but he let go quickly, so she relaxed a little.

He studied her anxiously. 'Are you all right?'

'Yes. Sorry. It was my fault. I wasn't looking where I was going because I didn't think anyone was around.'

He let go of her, smiling. 'We were both at fault then, because I wasn't looking where I was going, either. I'm sorry if I gave you a fright. No harm done, I hope?'

She shook her head and couldn't help returning his smile.

'Were you looking for someone?'

Ginger could feel her cheeks growing warm. 'Um, no. I

was just being nosey. I'm going to be living in Number 1, you see, so I was exploring the street.'

'Are you one of the resident artists?'

'No. I'll be running the café in the art gallery. This house looked so pretty I couldn't resist coming to explore. Are you working on something here?'

'I'm going to be doing the gardens of the houses, not that there's a lot of garden to the first four. I parked my car in the street outside the back wall and walked round to get a better feel for the place without a clutter of cars blocking the view, because there's a bit of front garden as well as the bigger patch of garden here at the back. Like you, I'm exploring.'

'I should leave you to it.'

'No, don't do that. Let's explore together and see what hidden plants we can find under all these weeds.'

'I won't be much use. I don't know anything about gardening. I wish I did, because I love flowers. I was going to see if I could find something that looked like a bay tree.'

He smiled again, and she thought what a delightful smile he had. It crinkled up his face and made it seem youthful, even though his hair was grey.

'Please stay, anyway. Obviously, you wanted to explore and you won't be in my way, I promise you. In fact, I can tell you what the plants are, if you're interested.'

She hesitated but he seemed to be part of the magic of the day, a peaceful sort of man with a slow way of speaking, that lovely smile and hands that worked hard outdoors, if she was any judge.

She always looked at people's hands. You could tell a lot

from them. She hadn't much time for soft, useless, droopy hands. And smiles said so much about people. This man's smile was warm and gentle. That Cutler fellow's smile was more like a sneer.

She seized the opportunity to learn something. 'If I'm not going to be in your way, I'd love to stay and find out more about the plants. I always wanted a garden but I've never lived in a house with one.'

'You definitely won't be in my way and I'll enjoy some company,' he said simply. 'My wife died a few years ago and I live alone, so I've no one to chat to after my day's work. I miss that.'

'My husband died too. Cancer, it was.'

'Do you miss him?'

She hesitated but for some reason she didn't want to lie to this man. 'Not really. We didn't *not* get on, but we weren't particularly close, either.'

'I see. Well, I'm Iain – Iain Darling.'

She couldn't hold back a gurgle of laughter. 'Is Darling really your surname?'

'It is. It comes from Durling in the early Middle Ages. It's a bit awkward sometimes. At school, the teacher called everyone by their surname, but he couldn't call me "Darling", now could he, so it had to be Iain D.'

She laughed. 'My name's Jean but no one ever calls me that. My hair used to be red, so I got the nickname Ginger. And I feel more of a Ginger than a Jean, too.' She touched her hair self-consciously. She'd have to do something about that horrible dye.

'And your surname?'

'Brunham. I've never bothered to find out where it comes from.'

'I'll find out for you. I've got a book of English surnames. It sounds like a place name to me.'

'I'd like to know.'

Silence fell but it was a comfortable one. She lifted her face to the sun. 'There's a nice feel to this garden.'

'That's what I think. They talk about feng shui inside houses, but I think it's there in gardens too if you tread quietly and see how it feels. I looked it up online, out of sheer curiosity. If I've understood correctly, for best feng shui, there should be an open front to a house and a square garden at the rear is the best shape.'

'I don't know anything about that but I do like the feel of this one.'

'Then how about we search for that bay tree? There ought to be one, given the house's name.'

He studied the shrubs and trees, then moved forward, fingers gently separating the tangles till he revealed a small tree. 'Aha! Here we are. *Laurus nobilis* is its Latin name, but some call it sweet bay.' He plucked a leaf and held it out to her. 'Smell that.'

She took it and rubbed it between her fingers. 'I've used the leaves in cooking but they were always dried ones and came in a packet. I shall take this home with me and find a use for it.'

'To Number 1?'

'Not yet. I'm staying with Elise in Number 3. She's one of the artists. She does really pretty paintings.'

'And when will you be moving into your house?'

'I don't have the whole house, just a bedsitter at the rear of Number 1. I'm going to need my furniture and other stuff, so I have to go home to Newcastle to get them before I can move in.' She fell silent, frowning as that inevitably brought to mind facing Donny.

'What brought that cloud to your face?'

'Nothing.'

He cocked his head to one side, as if challenging her.

'Oh, all right. Since you asked. My son is living in my house there and he won't get out. He's thirty and he's been sponging off me. In the end I left him to it to come here for an interview for one of the artists' positions, but I didn't get it. Donny doesn't even know where I am at the moment and I don't want him to know.'

Iain took her hand and held it between his. 'I can see that's upsetting you.'

She nodded, near to tears. She found it hard to talk about Donny and hadn't told anyone except Elise that he'd thumped her, couldn't for shame.

'Would you let me help you move?'

She looked at him in puzzlement. 'But why should you? You hardly know me. We've only just met.'

'I like to help people. As I said, I live on my own. I live by the rule that you can't have too many friends, and I feel that you and I are going to become good friends, Ginger Brunham. Would you mind?'

She didn't know what to say to that till she saw him smile again. And that lovely smile gave her the courage to be as open as he had. 'I'd truly like that.'

'Good. We'll have a poke round in the garden here, then

I'll take you out to tea and we'll discuss how to solve your moving problem.'

She could only nod. It sounded so right.

Did Saffron Lane attract kind people? First Elise helping her, then Nell offering her a job, and now Iain. If this was sheer chance, she hoped it'd continue. She'd felt so worn down by the Donny problem when she arrived here.

Chapter Twelve

Warren looked out of the window, trying to see where that red-haired old tart had got to. Why was she still hanging around? What was a woman like her doing in an artists' colony, for heaven's sake? He took the risk of going out of the front door of his house and could just see her down the side of Number 6.

She was talking to a fellow who was even older than her, then they disappeared round the rear of the house. They hadn't noticed him, so he decided to push his luck a little further. He went out of the back of his house and strolled casually out on to the narrow strip of lawn that made up the shared back garden of all four houses in the row. His house was at the end of the row of four, and he knew no one was living in Number 5, the nearest of the pair at the end, so he took the opportunity to peer through its ground-floor windows.

Empty but bigger than his house. He wondered if he

could arrange a swap. Why should he live in one of the smaller houses? He was undoubtedly superior to the other two artists.

He called this 'getting familiar with his territory'. It could come in useful to know all the details about where you lived, something most people didn't bother with.

There wasn't a solid fence between the last two houses and the row, just hedges. He stopped as it occurred to him that if he went into the back garden of Number 5 he'd be able to look into the back of Number 6 and perhaps see what those two were doing, even hear what they were saying. Strangers didn't usually hang around empty houses for no reason.

It was a tight squeeze to get through the untidy hedge but Warren managed it, betrayed into a hiss of breath as a sharp twig scratched his forearm. Standing still, he listened but couldn't hear exactly what those two were saying, just the odd word here and there. He managed to move a little closer to them but it didn't help.

Then the old man suddenly poked his head through the hedge, damn him.

'Ah! I thought I heard someone trampling around here. This is private property, I'm afraid, not open to the public.'

'I'm not the public. I live in Saffron Lane.'

'You don't live in this house, so you've no reason to be in its garden.'

'Well, neither have you.'

'Actually, I do have a reason: I'm in charge of the gardening for all these houses.'

Warren let out a puff of disbelief. 'Pull my other leg; it's got bells on it. No one's touched these gardens for years. You're trespassing too, so it's the pot calling the kettle black. Bugger off and mind your own business.'

The old man looked down his nose at him. It annoyed Warren to be shorter than most other people. Good thing he was smarter.

'You need to learn a few manners, young fellow. Go away and stay out of these two gardens or I'll inform the owners that you're interfering in what I'm doing.' He folded his arms and waited.

With some difficulty, Warren controlled his anger at being spoken to like that, especially in front of the tart. Unfortunately, this chap seemed very sure of himself about calling the owners.

Perhaps he'd jumped to the wrong conclusion and this really was the new gardener. The place certainly needed attention.

As he started pushing aside the hedge to go back to his new home, Warren heard them start talking again, so lingered to see what he could learn.

Iain brushed some leaves off himself and smiled at Ginger. 'Do you know that guy?'

'He's called Warren Cutler and he's one of the artists. He's newly arrived, so no one knows much about him.'

'He doesn't look like an artist.'

'What does an artist look like?'

'More open to the world. What kind of art is he into?'

'Woodcarving. Figurines and animals. I haven't seen them but Elise says they're more caricatures than real-life figures and there's something nasty about them. She wouldn't like to live with one and she doesn't like Mr Cutler either.'

'What about you? How do you feel about him?'

'I don't know because I've never spoken to him. I was interviewed for the same residency as him, but he got it. Still, they did offer me a job at the café and use of the flat behind it, so I didn't lose out completely.'

'You're going to be living here? That's great. I'll be using the café regularly while I'm working here.' He suddenly looked towards the hedge and put one finger to his lips, before whispering, 'I think he's still there, eavesdropping.'

She spun round but couldn't see or hear anything. 'That's not very nice.'

'No, it isn't.' He raised his voice. 'Let's leave the rest of the garden till another day and I'll buy you that coffee I promised.'

She looked at him uncertainly and whispered, 'You don't have to. We can just creep away.'

'I want to.' He offered her his arm.

She took it, enjoying this old-fashioned gesture, and let him escort her round the house and out on to the street.

She stopped at Number 3. 'I'll just tell Elise where I'm going.'

She was back in a couple of minutes, looking a trifle flushed, and carrying a shoulder bag.

'Our eavesdropper has gone back into his house now,' Iain whispered. 'I saw him come to the front window, then step back. I expect he's still there, watching us.'

'How strange. Hasn't he anything better to do?'

'Apparently not. Now, let's forget about him. I know a nice little café in town. Come and see what your opposition is like.'

The café Iain took her to was in the main street of Sexton Bassett. After sitting there for a while, watching, Ginger decided it was efficiently run but it had a limited menu, not even attempting to offer anything gluten-free or give information dealing with allergies. She always felt sorry for people with food problems and had nagged Joe into providing for them.

This place was there for rapid convenience, not to encourage people to linger. The coffee wasn't bad, though.

In her café, she'd somehow have to charm people so that they wanted to come back again, because it wouldn't have a lot of passing trade. She'd need to find some good suppliers and choose what she served with great care.

'Now, about your house move from Newcastle,' Iain said when he'd drunk his coffee, eaten a lavishly buttered scone and ordered a second mug of flat white. 'How much furniture will you be bringing? I have a large van, which I use for carrying stock around, and if you don't need to bring too much, I could probably fit it all in.'

'Carrying what sort of stock?'

'I'm not just into gardening; I run a landscaping business. I can clean our biggest van out and bring your furniture here in it.'

'Why are you offering to do this when you barely know me?'

'As I said, I try to put back good karma into the

universe by helping others. There are enough people in the world doing harm, so I try to do the opposite. As to knowing you, I intend to change that. We've already discussed becoming friends. You haven't changed your mind about that, have you?' He looked at her, head on one side, waiting for her answer.

'Of course not.'

'Good. Then tell me what sort of an artist you are. You must be one if you applied for a residency.'

She tried to tell him but could see he hadn't heard of raised stump work – well, not a lot of people had. It had been at its most popular in the seventeenth century, after all. She'd found out about it in a book, then seen some examples on an antiques show on the telly. In the end she offered to show him a couple of her pieces and he agreed enthusiastically. She hoped he wouldn't be disappointed.

When he dropped her back at Saffron Lane, she ran into the house, grabbed the bag of embroideries and took it out to the car.

She gave one to him to look at, almost holding her breath as she watched him study it for quite a long time. She relaxed a little as he ran one fingertip over some of the little animals sitting around the edges. People who liked her work often did that, touched them. She loved putting in those animals, imagining them watching the scene from the corners of her embroidery canvas.

He looked up. 'This is utterly charming, Ginger, and it shows how much you like people. I absolutely love it. Can I see some others?'

'Oh. Right. If you like.' She was annoyed with herself

for stuttering like a fool and clamped her mouth shut.

When she pulled out the others she could see by his smile that he understood what she was trying to show: scenes from the world around her; not cartoons exactly, but not realism, either. The essence of what people were doing with their lives, she hoped.

'I'd like to buy one,' he said suddenly.

She could feel herself blushing. First Elise wanting one, then him. 'You don't have to.'

'I'm not lying to you, Ginger, and I never will. I know perfectly well that I don't have to buy one, but I *want* to. Very much, actually. I even know exactly where I'll hang it on my living room wall.'

'Oh.' She could feel herself blushing hotly at this compliment, then something occurred to her. 'How about I give you one in return for you bringing my furniture to Wiltshire for me?'

'Done!' He stuck out one big, rough hand and they shook solemnly.

'I have an important appointment tomorrow, but we could go up to Newcastle the day after, if that suits you, Ginger. What do you think?'

'I think that'll suit me just fine. It'll give me time to work out what stuff I'll need to bring and what can be given to the charity shop.'

'Would you mind starting off really early, like four o'clock in the morning? Then we can do it all in one day.'

'I don't mind at all. I'm an early morning person, anyway, and I'm always awake by six, so four o'clock won't be hard to do.'

He pulled out a business card. 'I'll pick you up the day after tomorrow, then. If you need to contact me about anything in the meantime, here are my details. Could I have your phone number, too, please?'

That done, she said firmly, 'I'll bring some food.'

'Good. But we'll buy one meal out. It'll make a nice break, because it'll be a long day. That meal will be my treat.'

She agreed, watched him walk away, then went inside to face some gentle teasing from Elise about 'picking up a clue', which turned out to mean finding a boyfriend.

She didn't mind. It had been a long time since a man had shown an interest in her.

She'd thought her own interest in men had died.

Wrong! It had just woken up again.

What unattached woman of her age wouldn't be interested in Iain Darling with his lovely, friendly smile? It touched something in her, that smile did, warmed something that had been cold for a long time.

The two sisters met at what they now called Keziah's flat a couple of days later and waited for the lawyer's clerk to arrive. He was late and Abbie couldn't sit still, but paced up and down. She was dying to move out of the small flat and had everything packed in boxes, ready to go.

'I can't tell you what this means to me, the chance for Louis to have a decent home,' she told her sister. 'He never complains about our cramped conditions, but we can't have his friends round to play, let alone to stay for sleepovers. And it's hard keeping him entertained quietly, so as not to disturb the other tenants.'

'I know what you mean. I've spent a lot of time trying to keep Susie quiet since we moved in here. Dad didn't like noise and I could see him wince now and then, because she has a really piercing voice when she's upset.'

'Don't they all at that age? Did you hear a car?'

They both rushed to the window.

'Yes, that's Mr Paxley.'

The clerk, who was far from the fussy stereotype of a lawyer's clerk, strode into the building.

When the doorbell rang, Keziah went to answer it and Mr Paxley took them across the inner entrance hall from her flat to the nearer of the two vacant ones.

'It'd be nice if we both occupied this floor,' Abbie said before they even went inside.

'Nice for the children, too, to have those courtyards to play out in. I'd not trust Susie on her own with a balcony for ten seconds.'

The other flat on the ground floor smelt of new paint and Abbie would have liked to throw open the windows, but decided she'd better not do anything except look today. She stood in the middle of the open-plan living area and sighed happily. This space was bigger than the whole of her present place.

'The bedrooms and bathrooms are that way,' Mr Paxley pointed.

'Bathrooms? There's more than one?'

'An en suite in the master bedroom and a shared family bathroom between the other two bedrooms.' He waved one hand. 'Go and check them out. You won't want me breathing down your neck. Take your time. I have my iPad with me and can get on with some work.'

Keziah took a firm hold of her daughter's hand and followed her sister round.

'I can't believe it,' Abbie said when they'd checked out all the bedrooms. 'I think I'll take this flat.'

'You haven't even looked at the other!'

'The clerk says the layout is very similar, but I meant what I said: it'd be good to be on the ground floor together. We can help one another out with babysitting, and stuff like that, by just nipping across the shared hall.'

'Yes. Oh, yes.' They hugged one another spontaneously, then went back to Mr Paxley.

'I like this one,' Abbie said.

'Don't you want to even see the other?'

'No, thanks. I'd like to be on the ground floor near my sister. And this rear shared hall makes it much more private, with just the two of us using it. If we got a lock made for that door, we could use it to store bicycles and big toys in.'

'Well, if that's what you want, we'll go for it. Once probate is obtained, you'll be able to rearrange things to suit your own needs. We have a tenant waiting to take the other flat, so I'll send a message to him that he's got the first-floor flat, which he preferred anyway.'

Without more ado, he unthreaded a small bunch of keys and handed them to her. 'There won't be any rent to pay, of course, and by the time the rates come due, you'll probably have probate and can sort that out for yourselves.'

'Thank you.' Abbie swallowed hard as she looked at the key to her new life. She'd felt so depressed and lonely at times in that bedsitter, and now the future seemed full of promise. And money. She knew money wasn't everything but when you were permanently short, daily expenses loomed large in your life.

Keziah gave her a hug. 'I'll take Susie for a lie-down and put the kettle on. You can join me when you've had another private gloat.'

What Abbie did was stand in the middle of the big living area and cry for joy, just a few happy tears. Then she pulled herself together and walked round again, checking every cupboard and drawer. They were empty, of course, and she didn't have nearly enough possessions to fill them, but they were hers now. She was dying to show the flat to Louis.

When she went across to Keziah's flat, her sister was speaking on the phone.

'Emil Kinnaird,' she mouthed, nodding into the phone. 'Thank you. I'll pick the car up as soon as I've arranged insurance, Emil.'

Abbie could hear his voice, faint and tinny.

'Actually, our company does insurance of various types. I can get you the best deal.'

'Yes, please.'

'Come round to the office, and we'll arrange cover for you on the spot.'

Abbie wished they didn't have to keep dealing with him. He was too good-looking and she couldn't help feeling a tug of attraction every time she saw him. And she didn't want that, wasn't ready for another relationship, perhaps never would be again. She had a son to raise.

But she didn't say anything to Keziah, who was looking delighted.

Later that afternoon, Abbie waited impatiently for school to end and was there in her car to collect Louis when he came out of the building, greeting him with, 'Hurry up. I've got a wonderful surprise for you.'

'What?'

She saw the anxiety on his face. She'd had to pretend over the years that some situations were good when they weren't really, such as moving to a new flat unexpectedly. When would he ever trust that a surprise could be a good one? 'We've got the new flat, one with proper bedrooms. We're moving in as soon as I can arrange it.'

'Bedrooms? More than one.'

She knew how he felt. 'It's not a bedsitter this time, darling.' Once they were in the car, she explained the details and had the joy of watching his face brighten with hope.

'I'll have a bedroom of my own?' he asked for the third time.

'Yes. And a bathroom of your own, too.'

He stared at her, open-mouthed. 'Really?'

'Really and truly.'

'I can't *wait* to see it.'

At the flat she watched, enjoying the sight of her son running to and fro from room to room. He chose which of the two bedrooms he wanted, shouted 'Yippee!' several times and then turned cartwheels across the living area. In fact, he generally acted like a carefree child, a state of mind she hadn't always been able to give him.

'Can we move in here tonight, Mum?'

'I'm afraid not. I have to find someone to move our furniture and finish off the packing.'

'We could camp out here and get our furniture tomorrow.'

'I'm too old to sleep on the floor, darling.' She held up one hand. 'No, Louis. It wouldn't work. A few more nights in the old place and then we'll be ready to move. It's not just packing. I have to leave the place sparkling clean or they'll charge me to have more cleaning done.' She'd been caught that way before when changing places to live and now she not only left a place perfect but took photos to prove it.

Louis heaved a sigh but stopped arguing.

Of course, they had to bump into Emil Kinnaird in the supermarket and he immediately came across to chat to them. She didn't want to encourage his interest, had enough on her plate, but somehow they got talking and she mentioned her coming move.

'It occurred to me: you'll need someone to move you. We signed up a client today who's just setting up the insurance for a new delivery service. He said he was going to do small-scale house removals mainly, because there's apparently a lot of call for it and he doesn't need to invest in a big pantechnicon—'

'What's a pantechnicon?' Louis asked at once.

'A big van for transporting housefuls of furniture.'

'How do you spell it?'

'I'll tell you later, Louis. Let Mr Kinnaird speak.' She

loved her son's enthusiasm about learning new words but sometimes she had to rein it back.

'Shall I give you the removal man's name? He seems a decent fellow.'

'Oh. Yes. Thank you.'

He fumbled for his smartphone and she took down the details. By that time Louis was fidgeting impatiently.

'Sorry to delay you and your mum,' Emil said to the boy. 'When are you moving house?'

'Mum says we can't do it till tomorrow, or even later.' Louis gave an aggrieved sigh. 'Only I'll be at school tomorrow.'

'And we can only do it when this man can fit us in,' Abbie said firmly. 'I'm not a worker of miracles, Louis.'

Emil smiled. 'Well, if you ring him tonight you stand a good chance for getting it done this week. He's only just starting up.' He glanced at his watch. 'I have to go. I'm about to go flat-hunting myself, but I shan't need a removal van because I have to buy all the furniture from scratch. The flat I was supposed to live in over the shop is only a grotty bedsitter and the electric wiring is dodgy, so I moved into a hotel.'

'I can relate to that. Our place is very dingy.'

'Oh. Sorry. I didn't mean to upset you.'

'It's all right. We're moving out to a bigger place soon.'

As she walked back to her car with a trolley full of empty cardboard boxes, it occurred to her that for once, Emil hadn't irritated her. For once, she and he seemed to have been on the same wavelength, to use one of her father's favourite expressions.

And she liked the way he was so patient with Louis, who was at a questioning age and didn't think before interrupting.

Maybe she'd been a bit hasty in judging him.

Chapter Thirteen

The following day Nell turned up at Saffron Lane mid morning and asked if Ginger could spare an hour.

'Of course.'

'I want to introduce you to a neighbour and friend who lives near the top end of Peppercorn Street. Winifred is a friend of Elise's, but she's a little older. I've been wondering how to find really special cakes for the café and I suddenly remembered Winifred. If she has the time and energy, maybe we could get her to bake cakes for the café? At the beginning anyway, perhaps not once things get busy. She's in her eighties, after all. But she bakes far too many cakes now and is always giving them away, so why not sell some of them to us instead?'

Elise had been listening and joined in. 'That's a great idea, Nell.' She turned to Ginger. 'I'm sure you'll like Winifred *and* her cakes. They're the most delicious ones I've ever tasted. Baking is her passion. She doesn't need the money, but she'll enjoy having a reason to bake more.'

'I hope you don't mind, but I took it for granted that you'd come, Ginger, and phoned her, so she's expecting us,' Nell said. 'You're sure you have the time?'

'Of course I do. I shan't be available tomorrow, though.' She took a deep breath and said it out loud. 'Iain Darling is taking me to Newcastle in his van to collect my furniture.'

'Ah, you've met him, have you? Such a clever man with gardens. He's helped me a lot with the one at the big house, which had been let go to seed and needed a lot of attention when I moved in. Angus was too busy with his work and modernising the interior of the house to do much outside, you see. I'm particularly glad that Iain's sorting out the gardens behind the end two houses for us. It'll make such a difference to them.'

'He and I found a bay tree at the back of Number 6 yesterday.'

'Ah. I thought there must be one, given the house name. You must show it to me when you come back. Iain's a careful driver. I'm sure you'll have a safe trip with him.'

The words tumbled out before Ginger could stop them. 'I took to him at once.'

'People do.'

'He's so kind.'

'Very. He helps a lot of people in his quiet way. Just a thought about furniture for the café. I don't think we should try for the modern sterile look, but look for an eclectic collection of furniture and a couple of small sofas, with comfort being more important than style – a lot of modern furniture is too stark for my taste, anyway, and hard on the backside, or too low for older people. As for colours, I'm not turned on by shades of grey and brown and mud.'

Ginger wasn't so sure about that but now wasn't the time to disagree. 'You'll need some outdoor furniture as well for the fine days. If you can afford to pave the outside area it'll be easy to keep it all nice.'

'Yes, I was wondering about that. I think those white plastic tables and chairs that are quite cheap will do out there. All white can look quite nice with greenery and flowers in pots dotted around. We'll get Iain to look at organising the patio. He knows all sorts of handy people. A covered roof would be necessary, given our rainy English climate. As you said, we've got two sides of that area already formed by the building – if you don't mind having people sitting right outside your bedroom. We'll put up net curtains or something so that they can't see in.'

'I don't mind at all. I'll just get my bag.' She never went anywhere without the capacious shoulder bag. People teased her about it, but she could pull all sorts of things out in an emergency, and often had done when others were struggling for lack of scissors or other small items.

'We'll walk up to Winifred's, if you don't mind,' Nell said when Ginger came back with the bag slung over her shoulder. 'It's not far.'

'I'm a good walker.' She'd had to be.

Winifred was another person Ginger liked on sight. She had lovely silver hair and was elegantly dressed, not looking anything like a 'little old lady'.

Not for the first time, Ginger wondered about leaving

her own hair uncoloured. It had started going silver soon after she turned forty and she'd hated that, so had started dyeing it. The women who'd been her neighbours in Newcastle had all dyed their hair as they grew older, so she had too. But Nell's hair was unashamedly streaked with grey and she made no effort to hide it, while Winifred's hair was pure silver and looked lovely. Hmm. Something else to think about.

Winifred made them a cup of tea and produced some home-made cherry and almond cake, which was delicious.

Nell asked their hostess whether she would like to bake a couple of cakes every week for the café, ones that would last or could be frozen perhaps, not cream cakes. They'd pay her, of course.

Winifred went bright pink, seeming delighted and confiding that she'd never earned money by her own efforts because she'd stayed at home to look after her elderly mother.

Just as they were about to leave, a car drew up outside and a young woman came into the house to join them.

Ginger saw her hostess's face light up at the sight of her. You could tell she loved the newcomer.

Nell introduced the newcomer as Janey Redman.

'Janey is my adopted grand-niece.' Winifred hugged the girl again. 'She lives here with her daughter, Millie.' Then she frowned. 'Are you all right, dear? You don't usually come home from college during the day.'

'I came to bring a bit of shopping back and ask if you'd mind my mother coming round to look after Millie this afternoon and evening. I've, um, been invited out by a guy at college.' Janey flushed as she said this.

'Oh, that's lovely for you. And of course I don't mind Hope coming here. Your mother and I get on very well and we both love that child.'

'I'll whizz Mum and Millie back here after my afternoon classes and change my clothes then. It's marvellous having a car. Finding my birth father has been good in so many ways. Wasn't it kind of him to see how much I needed my own transport? I can do so much more these days. I'll just put away the shopping, then go back to college. I wouldn't mind a piece of cake first, though. It's one of my favourites.'

Ginger watched Winifred blush with pleasure, but there was no pretence. Janey was definitely enjoying the cake.

When the young woman had left, Nell asked, 'Are things still going well with Janey and her birth father?'

'Yes. And with her half-sister. They all get on like a house on fire. It's lovely to see.' She chuckled and looked at Ginger. 'Before Janey, I used to feel lonely and few people ever came here. A car would have made so much difference to me. Now, I may be too old to learn to drive but people are coming and going all the time and I absolutely love it.'

'That's so good to hear.'

During the visit Ginger had noticed that both Winifred and Janey avoided looking at her hair after the first glance and blink of surprise. Well, she was guessing that was what had made them look away. She had made a real mess of dyeing it. It was now as red as red hair could ever get, which didn't really suit her because she had a natural redhead's pale skin. Only she'd been too busy and too upset to do anything about the hair colour, what with Donny thumping her and then the interview.

Maybe she should do something now?

As they walked back through the grounds of Dennings, she took a deep breath and broached the idea of letting the dye-job grow out of her hair. 'What do you think, Nell?'

'I think that's a great idea, but I have a better plan than waiting for it to grow out, because it'd be ages before it looked good again. Why don't I phone my hairdresser and see when she can fit you in to strip out the colour? She's really good.'

'Oh. Well.' Then Ginger thought of how horrible her hair had looked in the mirror this morning and about her coming trip with Iain. Taking a deep breath, she said, 'Yes, please! It'd be wonderful if she could do it today.'

She stopped speaking abruptly, forgetting her own problems as she entered the hall of the big house for the first time. 'Oh, this is so beautiful!'

'Isn't it? I fell in love with this house as well as with Angus when I came here from Australia – he's my second husband, you know. The first one was a selfish rat. Hang on a minute. I'll just phone Penny.'

She looked up from the phone a minute later. 'She can fit you in if you go straight away, so I'll drive you into town to get you there on time.'

'I have my own car back now.'

'No time to walk down and get it, though. But that's all right. I can do some shopping while I wait to bring you back. Come on!'

Ginger was silent on the drive down Peppercorn Street

into town. She was starting to worry about what she was about to do. Was this the right thing for her? Would she look older with silver hair?

What would Iain think?

When they stopped outside the shop, Nell leant across to pat Ginger's hand as if she understood what a huge step this was for her. 'You'll look great. Penny's the best hairdresser I've ever had.'

An hour and a half later, when Penny had finished, Ginger stared at her reflection in the mirror. Her hair was now a gleaming silver and was cut differently too. It looked lovely – only it didn't *feel* like her when she looked at her face. It looked too elegant. And she wasn't the elegant type, couldn't afford to even try since she picked up a lot of her clothes in charity shops.

But it was too late now so she smiled at the hairdresser. 'Lovely. Thank you so much for fitting me in.'

The woman grinned. 'It'll feel strange at first, but you'll get used to it. Whoever did that last colour job made a right old mess of it, didn't they?'

'Um . . . yes.' She paid Penny and walked out of the shop, nearly bumping into Warren Cutler of all people on the pavement outside because he wasn't looking where he was going.

He didn't recognise her, just pushed on past with a mutter which ought to have been an apology, but sounded more like annoyance that anyone had dared to get in his way.

She stuck out her tongue in his direction as he walked

on, then smiled ruefully. She was definitely not the elegant type.

The sun was shining and she stood motionless for a few moments, enjoying its warmth. Then someone tooted a car horn and she saw that Nell had drawn up at the kerb, so got in quickly.

'Oh, my!'

She waited and when Nell didn't say anything further, had to ask, 'What does that mean?'

'It means your hair looks great, Ginger. Absolutely great. You'll wow Iain tomorrow.'

'Does it really?'

They stopped at a traffic light and Nell looked sideways. 'Are you regretting it? You shouldn't. She's done a beautiful job.'

'I'm not used to it yet. I've always had red hair, you see. Always. Whether it was my own colour or out of a packet. I don't look . . . older, do I?'

'No, of course you don't. *I* think you look younger with it silver than you looked with that garish red which took all the life out of your skin.'

Ginger let out a sigh of relief and heard Nell chuckle.

'Wasn't that Warren Cutler I saw walking down the street?'

'Yes. He bumped into me and didn't recognise me. Didn't apologise, though.'

'Hmm. He's not proving very friendly and he's an utter chauvinist, fawning over Angus and ignoring me as much as he can, though actually I'm the one who's managing the project. He doesn't seem able to accept that a female can be in charge – you'd not expect a man as young as him to have that attitude in this day and age.'

'Well, it's his carvings you want him for, not his personality, and from what Elise says, he's very clever with wood.'

Nell shot her a quick glance. 'Very generous of you to say so.'

She shrugged. 'I don't believe in holding grudges. Life's too short.'

They turned into the grounds of Dennings and at Saffron Lane, Ginger got out. She hesitated, then went into the flat rather than Elise's house. She needed to work out which furniture she was bringing and whether she had anything Nell could use.

And she needed some time alone to get used to her new hair.

It was quiet in the end house and she relished that. She went into the bathroom and stared at her reflection for a long time. 'You've done it now, girl,' she told the stranger in the mirror.

She turned and twisted, looking at herself from as many angles as she could manage, then muttered, 'Oh, don't be such a fool! It's done now.'

Pushing aside her doubts, she took out her little notebook and got to work on the lists. She could remember exactly what was in her own house and what she'd put in the storage locker, and as she walked round, she mentally placed some of them in this little flat and put them in the 'definitely' column.

She just hoped they could get the removal job done

while Donny was at work. Though that meant he'd come home to a house without furniture. Maybe she could leave him the last few bits and pieces.

And maybe not. He had no right to be in her house. He hadn't brought any furniture with him, just his sound system. She'd leave that and nothing else, to give him a nudge to get out.

Was he even living there now? She'd better phone Kerry and ask about her son. It never hurt to know what to expect.

Chapter Fourteen

'Don't forget, we're holding more interviews in a few days,' Nell told her husband that evening. 'I've been checking through the paperwork again in case I've been too optimistic, but I don't think so. That sudden late rush of applications has turned up a few artists whose work looks interesting – and is probably commercial in our sense.'

Angus gave her one of his lazy, relaxed smiles, the sort that said he'd just satisfactorily finished a tricky job and come out of his absent-minded, software-problem-solving mode. 'So you've told me. And you've got Stacy primed to join us in doing the interviews this time, which adds a new viewpoint to act as a countercheck to ours. So why are you still worrying?'

'Because I feel I chose badly with Cutler. And it was me, because I'm the one who pushed him as first choice. You two weren't as certain about him.'

'Perhaps you did make a mistake, but no one is perfect,

so don't beat yourself up over it. His application made him sound great to me too, and he was quite pleasant at the interview. Besides, whatever his personality faults, his woodcarvings *are* superb and' – he pressed one finger over her lips to stop her speaking – 'most importantly of all, it's too late to change his appointment now, anyway. He's got a contract for a residency and we have to live with that.'

Angus gave her a quick hug. 'If the worst comes to the worst, and he's horrible to have around, you can take consolation from the fact that his stay will end in six months' time and you don't have to renew the contract.'

'Six months can be a long time to live near a bad neighbour. I feel sorry for Elise and Stacy already.'

'What can he do to them? Darling, you're letting this get you off balance. Cutler's not likely to turn out to be a murderer or rapist, after all!'

She shrugged. 'I know that, of course I do, but I feel . . . well, that he could turn nasty. And Elise is in her mid seventies. She's intelligent and talented, but anyone that age is more vulnerable physically.'

'She'll have Ginger and Stacy around, and don't underestimate our Elise. She's no pushover. Stop worrying.'

'I'll try. But Angus, you will keep an eye on him as well as me being watchful, won't you?'

'Yes, darling. I promise.'

'Even if you get offered a fascinating job?'

'I'll do my best not to immerse myself completely in my work till after the interviews. More than that I can't promise. Fascinating jobs often pay fascinating amounts of money. Now, tell me more details about this new group of artists you've selected.'

'Well, one who strikes me as particularly talented is a potter, but as we discussed before we interviewed the last potter, there are a lot of hassles to getting pieces fired and I'm not prepared to install a kiln, even a small modern one, even if our venture is proved financially successful. So I discarded this woman, I'm afraid. Though I shall offer to sell her work in our shop.'

'Right thing to do.'

'Good. Glad you agree. That leaves me torn between a cartoonist, a soft-toy maker, a designer of classy costume jewellery and a weaver. All four of them stand out as having a special sort of talent, but we only have the last two houses to offer as accommodation.'

'We did expect to house two artists in Bay Tree Cottage, so that gives us housing for three out of the four – if they're suitable.'

'Yes. Number 6 divides up quite neatly into two living areas and two studios, and there's a shower room as well as a big bathroom. I'm inclined to set up a two-people arrangement with Number 5 as well. It is bigger than the first four houses, after all. It'll give them less space than having a whole house each, and they'll have to share the living area, but how much working space can a cartoonist need? Maybe two of them wouldn't mind sharing accommodation rather than missing out on a residency. We can always offer that option.'

'No other spare artists to interview?'

'No one whose work struck me as special. If these

four aren't suitable, or don't want to share, we'll have to advertise again.'

'Well, let's see what they're like. I shall hope we find our final residents this time round, so that we can get out of all that tedious reading of applications.'

She didn't let herself smile. They'd had so many applications it had been a massive chore going through them and he'd become distinctly grumpy, a rare occurrence with Angus. 'I'm glad you agree, love.'

'What about the art gallery, though? We still have to find someone to run that – and then there's the museum.' He looked at her ruefully. 'Have we bitten off more than we can chew?'

She laughed. 'Oh, definitely. But you did the same thing when you took on the renovation of the big house after you inherited and you've done wonders here. I was thinking of offering the job of running the art gallery as a part-time job locally, because now that we've given Ginger the bedsitter in Number 1, we've no accommodation to offer anyone.'

'Is this what's been keeping you awake at night?' he asked gently.

'Yes. This is so different from anything else I've ever tried to do in my life.'

'The world won't come to an end if we don't make as much money as we'd hoped from this enterprise, Nell darling. I'm still betting that we'll come out on the plus side financially after a while and lay the foundations for a steady income which will help pay for maintenance for years to come. That's the main reason we're doing it, after all. You're a born organiser, love. Don't sell yourself short.'

She reached out to clasp his hand. 'You're such a comfort, Angus. I've never had anyone to lean on and share my worries with before.'

'Then remember how you raised three sons without help and lean on me whenever you need to with this – or anything else – but don't let that prevent you from trusting in your own judgement. Above all, stop worrying. We've set it up as a long-term project, and I have enough put by to pay for the first round of residencies. And apart from that, I'm bringing in enough money for our living expenses and to cover the finishing touches to Saffron Lane. Ah, come here, my love. Don't cry.'

'They're happy tears, happy I found you.'

He put his arms round her and they stood close together for a few quiet moments, not saying anything.

Sometimes love didn't need words, she thought dreamily as she leant against him. Sometimes it was tangible, even if invisible.

Chapter Fifteen

Iain picked Ginger up at two minutes to four the following morning. She'd realised last night that they were leaving on a Saturday, and Donny might or might not be at work. She should have thought of that and planned to go on a weekday. But she couldn't chop and change when Iain was being so kind, and anyway, why should she be afraid of going into her own house?

She tiptoed outside, hoping she hadn't woken Elise. Iain took her bag of supplies, stowed it in the back of his small van and made sure she was comfortably seated. He glanced at her hair but didn't say anything.

'Ready?'

'Yes.' But she had a sick feeling in her stomach, wondering how Donny would react if he happened to come home while they were there. Kerry next door said he was still around, but out at work usually from Monday to Friday and mostly on Saturdays as well.

Ginger hadn't contacted him, was hoping desperately not to bump into him. That upset her more than anything. Fancy not wanting to see your own son!

She realised Iain hadn't started the engine and looked up to find him staring at her.

'You all right, Ginger?'

She could only shrug and admit, 'I was just thinking about Donny, hoping he won't be at home.'

Iain laid his big warm hand on hers. 'If he is, I won't let him hurt you.'

'He's big and can get violent. I don't want him to hurt you either.'

'Bless you, my work keeps me in trim and builds muscle, and I've also got a black belt in karate. I think I can hold my own, and without hurting him – unless he insists on coming back for more.'

She blinked in shock. 'I can't imagine you doing martial arts. You seem so . . . well, if you don't mind me saying so, gentle.'

'Why should I mind? I take it as a compliment. I'm not at all aggressive, but that doesn't mean I'll let anyone walk all over me. I believe people ought to be able to defend themselves whenever possible. I got mugged once, ages ago, so I took a course in karate after that, and I've kept in training, more or less, depending on work. Of course, it's not always possible to defend yourself adequately, given that some people are bigger than others, or attack by stealth. You can only do your best to be prepared.'

With that he started the engine and drove off. He didn't

talk much, didn't seem to expect her to talk either, and the peace of the early morning drive gradually settled her nerves. Her husband had always chatted, or rather, talked at her, dribbling out words non-stop whenever he was around, and expecting her to listen and reply, even if it was about sport, which she didn't enjoy. Donny was like his dad, but he would throw occasional remarks at her like darts into a board and got angry when she didn't respond.

But Iain – ah, he was different from any man she'd ever met before, so very easy to be with.

Every now and then he mentioned some point of interest on their route without seeming to need a reply. And they were always things of interest to her as if he understood that instinctively.

After two hours, he asked, 'Ready for a cup of tea yet?'

'I'd die for one.'

'Oh, good! I'm getting a bit thirsty myself. There's a service station about two miles further up the motorway. We'll stop there.'

She used the amenities then joined him at a table near the window.

'I got hungry, so I bought us something to eat.' He indicated the plates on the table as she sat down. 'I know you said you'd bring some food, but I've a dreadfully hearty appetite, I'm afraid.'

And she found she too was enjoying the crunchy buttered toast and jam. She'd been too anxious to eat any breakfast.

When she'd finished, she pushed aside her plate. 'How long till we get there? I drove down quite slowly when I was going to Wiltshire for the interview, because I'm not used to long-distance driving, and I was so het up, I didn't notice much.'

'It'll take about three and a half hours more, depending on traffic, of course. I usually stay within the speed limit. You'll have to direct me once we get near Newcastle.'

'All right.'

A couple of hours later, he said, 'We can stop and have one of your snacks before we get there or wait till we reach your house and have it then. Your choice.'

'We'll wait.' She didn't feel hungry so close to a possible confrontation with Donny but she made another excuse. 'I've brought some tea-making things in case my son has moved out, so we can have a fresh brew with it if we wait.'

From the look Iain gave her, she reckoned he'd guessed how she was feeling. He was very perceptive about other people's feelings. Or was it just about hers?

Oh, what did she know about anything? What she needed was to get today over and done with. Then she could stop worrying and get on with her lovely new life.

When they pulled up outside her old home, she was astonished at how small it looked and how run-down the whole street seemed. She hadn't been away long, but she felt completely divorced from the house and the area.

'It's not much of a place,' she muttered, feeling ashamed.

'I spent a whole year once living in a caravan. I'm not a housing snob, love.'

Love? she thought. He'd called her 'love'. When she stole a quick glance sideways, he caught her looking and winked. She didn't know what to think.

He waited and when she didn't say anything, he asked, 'Is Donny's car here?'

'Yes. That white one with the scratch down the side. I'd hoped he'd be at work. He sometimes works Saturdays. I wonder what he'll say when he sees me.'

'You're a bit nervous about going in, aren't you?'

'Yes. More than a bit.'

'I'll be right behind you – and remember, I won't let him hurt you. Not physically, anyway.'

Iain even understood that not all injuries are physical, she thought in wonderment. Him being there gave her the courage to get out of the car and walk up to the front door.

As soon as she opened it, a chair scraped back and Donny peered out of the kitchen door at the far end of the hall.

'Ah! You're back at last. Where the hell have you been, Mam?'

'Minding my own business.'

He stared beyond her. 'Looks like you're minding someone else's too. Picked up a fancy man, have you?'

She got annoyed at herself for standing there like a guilty fool, struggling for words, so began to move towards the kitchen.

Only, Donny didn't step aside to let her pass. His fist shot out and he grabbed her shoulder, holding her at arm's length, shaking her and saying in a growling voice, 'Send him away. You and I have things to talk about, Mam, an' I want some answers.'

'Speak politely to your mother,' Iain said sharply. 'And get your hand off her.'

'Oh, it can talk!' Donny mocked in a falsetto voice.

'Don't start, son!' she warned, anger starting to take over from her nervousness. Shame, too.

'You're the one who started it, running off like that to play the whore. Well, I'm not having it. Not now, not ever!'

He swung her round and slammed her back against the wall twice, so hard it took the breath from her body and made her head spin for a moment. She couldn't help crying out at the pain.

Next thing she knew, the hand left her shoulder, there was a blur of bodies and Donny went hurtling down the hall, yelling out in shock, to land sprawling on the front doormat.

Iain moved Ginger into the kitchen, so gently and yet so firmly that she was out of the way before she realised he was doing that to protect her. Then he turned to face Donny, who had struggled to his feet and was about to rush forward.

'Stop that, Donny Brunham, *this minute*!' she yelled at the top of her voice.

Her son came to a halt but the light of anger was still burning fiercely in his eyes. He had his father's temper.

Iain simply stood there in a relaxed posture that nonetheless showed confidence in every line of his body. 'I'm a black belt in karate,' he said quietly. 'Don't go any further with this, son, because I've learnt how to defend myself and to protect people like your mother, who do not deserve to be bullied and thumped around.'

The last few words were said very emphatically.

Donny stood motionless, but he was still radiating anger.

'Come into the kitchen and sit down, then we can talk,' Ginger said, hoping he'd obey her.

And he did. Thank goodness.

Iain moved out of the way, standing behind Ginger now. Once Donny had passed them, she moved towards the kettle.

But her son moved too, taking them both by surprise by picking up a chair and trying to smash it down on Iain with all the force of a big, muscular body.

But Iain didn't wait to be hit. He moved sideways and after a brief scuffle, somehow the chair fell to the ground and Donny was thrown across the room again. Only this time he fell awkwardly against the old-fashioned stove and screamed out in pain.

When he tried to move, he yelled and grabbed his left arm to hold it still.

'Oh, hell!' Iain muttered. 'He's hurt. I hope he hasn't broken that arm. He's certainly hurt it badly. Men don't scream for no reason. Call the police and the ambulance at once, Ginger.'

She picked up the phone and dialled 999, shaking with reaction as she watched Iain bend over Donny, who screeched when the older man touched him.

'I need the police and an ambulance. *Now*!' she yelled into it, giving her address. 'There was a fight and when my friend defended himself, the other man got hurt. We think he's broken his arm. That was him you heard yelling.'

Her son didn't attempt to get up, just stayed on the floor, moaning.

'Help is on its way,' the voice told her. 'Can you manage for a few more minutes?'

'Yes. He can't hurt us now.'

The minutes ticked by slowly.

Donny tried to get up and abandoned the attempt. He glared at Ginger. 'Your fancy man's broke my arm. I'll set the police – on you both. Call yourself a mother?'

'I'll join in and break the other one if you try to hurt either of us again,' she told him. Not that he could. Or that she'd even try to hit him. But it never did to try to reason with Donny when he got a fury on him. You just had to shout back.

Iain stayed near Donny but didn't attempt to touch him again.

She prayed that the police and ambulance would arrive quickly.

Chapter Sixteen

Stacy set down her little welder and looked at the new creature she'd suddenly 'seen' in her mind and made up mainly from scrap metal pieces. It was another bird. This one stood there on tall metal legs, its long beak stretching out towards her. She touched its head lightly and it bobbed at her a few times, because she'd fitted the head on a long spring. That was the only component she'd had to buy to finish it off.

She loved it, one of her best creations, she felt. She couldn't wait to show it to somebody but she knew Elise had gone out to the shops.

A few minutes later she saw her friend drive into the street and park next door, but waited till Elise had unloaded the shopping. When the older woman took out the final items, two little pots of flowers, and placed them on each side of her front door, Stacy came out to admire them.

'I might do the same thing. In fact, it'd look nice if we

all had pots of flowers at our doors, don't you think?'

'I agree, but do you think *he* would be interested in doing something like that?' Elise nodded her head in the direction of Cutler's house.

'We can mention it to him. We have to try being friendly if we're all going to live next door to one another for six months.'

'Well, good luck with that. I'm not getting involved with him beyond a nod in passing.'

'You took a real dislike to him, didn't you?'

'I take a dislike to anyone who treats me like a puddle-brained old fogey. Wait till you're my age and see how you feel about being spoken down to.'

'Does it happen often?'

'More often than you'd think but I don't let them get away with it.'

Stacy let a few seconds pass, then changed the subject. 'Have you got a minute? I want to show you something.'

'Of course. What is it?'

'Come and look at my new bird. It's one of the best things I've ever made.'

Elise had only to look at the nodding bird to chuckle. 'Oh, it's lovely!'

'How much do you think I should ask for it?'

Her friend studied it more carefully, then said thoughtfully, 'Have you thought of selling the idea instead? Make a copyright claim on the design, then offer it to a manufacturer?'

Stacy stared at her in surprise. 'That would never have occurred to me.'

'I sold a couple of my paintings to printmakers. Then I fell and broke my hip, so I didn't carry on, but I'm going to get back in touch with them now that I'm settled here and producing again.'

'What a brilliant idea!'

Warren saw the old hag drive up and fiddle around with two pots of flowers. She'd have been better saving her energy for her work at her age.

Then Stacy came out and the two women stood chatting, so he hid behind the curtain near his open window and eavesdropped. He scowled when he heard what they were suggesting. If they did things like put out flowers to beautify their houses, he'd either have to follow suit or let them gain an advantage. But he was useless at keeping pot plants alive, and anyway, who wanted to fiddle around with them?

The two women were only doing it to suck up to Angus Denning. These weren't even their own houses and they'd only be in them for six months.

Well, he wasn't going to let them show him in a poor light. He smiled as he thought of something. The pots weren't nailed down, were they? Perhaps he could do something about putting such things outside where anyone who passed by could damage them.

He'd overheard Stacy talking about finishing some object or other and wanting Elise's opinion. Ha! Another of her twee toys, probably. You couldn't call *them* art. How she'd got this residency was beyond his understanding. Denning's wife must have pushed for it. Trust a woman to favour other women, whether they deserved it or not.

He watched the two women go inside Stacy's house, which meant he couldn't hear anything. He nibbled his thumbnail. What else were they plotting, damn them?

He went outside at the rear of his house and stood in the back garden. If either of them left their French windows open, he could sometimes hear what they were saying.

This time the window next door was open and what he overheard infuriated him. Why was the old hag helping her rival? That didn't make sense. He'd never help other artists. On the contrary. He didn't intend to be outshone by anyone.

The next time they both went out, he'd see if he could check out Stacy's work through her back windows. *He* might know she wasn't all that good, but maybe her work would appeal to common types who liked novelties, and then she'd bring money into the gallery.

Well, not if he could help it. No one was going to get better sales than him. He'd make sure of it.

That was even more important than getting rid of their stupid flowers.

When Emil's phone rang, he was delighted to hear the voice of the woman from the estate agent's.

'About that flat, Mr Kinnaird, I can show you around it today, if you're free. How about this afternoon?'

'Great.'

'I'll meet you there at two.' She gave him the address.

'Happy to. Sorry to keep you waiting but there's a bit of a problem: the owner died and his daughters have inherited the flats. They're going to need one of them, so you can see them but not choose which one till the owner has made her choice.'

'Does that mean I can't move in straight away?'

'I'm afraid so. But it'll only be a day or two.'

He sighed. The hotel was all right, but there was nothing like your own home and possessions. He'd had to leave things in storage while he travelled round Australia and was looking forward to having them around him again.

The estate agent was very chatty as she drove him to a short street just outside the town centre. Emil said yes and no, almost at random, and that was all she needed to keep chatting.

This seemed like his best chance of somewhere decent to live, somewhere without the risk of electrical problems if the flats had just been refurbished. He hoped the flats would be a bit stylish.

The Quartet was a two-storey, purpose-built block of four flats, as the name suggested. Emil walked round the two vacant flats, each of which, unusually, had three bedrooms. He had a slight preference for the one on the upper floor, which had a balcony big enough to sit out on, whereas the lower ones had small courtyards.

Not wanting any delay he expressed his preference and was promised a phone call within a couple of days.

As he wanted to be ready to move in as soon as he heard, he went out to the big shopping centre to buy some bits and pieces: a bed, a small extendable table and four accompanying chairs, a recliner armchair and matching sofa. They would give him a start on furnishing the flat. He then bought a fridge/freezer and chatted to a very helpful sales assistant who promised to have the goods delivered as soon as Emil gave the word.

He went on to buy some basic crockery and kitchen stuff, which he took with him. Anything else could wait, he decided.

They were such nice flats. He'd fallen on his feet there, whichever one he got in the end.

Chapter Seventeen

There was the sound of a car stopping outside. Ginger sagged against the table in relief, still keeping a wary eye on her son. He had stopped cursing and threatening now and was looking pale.

She heard footsteps coming to the front door. That must be the police.

'Go and answer it, love,' Iain said. 'I'll keep an eye on Donny.'

She found two police officers standing at the front door. 'Thank heavens you've come.'

She didn't manage to do more than explain the bare details of what had happened, because they insisted on getting Donny to hospital.

'You two will need to stay here, sir,' they said to Iain and Ginger.

'We're not going anywhere.'

'He attacked me for nothing,' Donny said.

Ginger was furious. 'You liar! You attacked us.'

* * *

When the ambulance had taken Donny away, another police car drew up and Ginger found herself giving a statement in the front room to one pair of officers while Iain spoke to the others in the kitchen.

Now the worst of the crisis was over, reaction had set in and she couldn't stop herself from weeping as she tried to answer their questions. That somehow led to her explaining why she'd left home in the first place.

'You should have come for help when your son started hitting you,' the woman officer said in a sympathetic voice. 'There's a unit which deals with domestic violence of all sorts.'

'I couldn't. I was too ashamed.' Ginger sobbed some more.

'His shame, not yours. Um . . . your son claimed Mr Darling went for him without provocation – only he kept changing his story and the officer taking down the details didn't find what he said very credible.'

'My son grabbed me and slammed me against the wall. That's why Iain had to defend me. Iain would never start a fight and *he* hadn't had anything to drink.'

The officer smiled. 'He's already taken a breath test and registered clear, unlike your son. Um . . . is Donny a heavy drinker?'

'Yes. It's one reason I left home. He was getting violent whenever he drank. Um . . . what'll happen to him afterwards?'

'Your partner's been discussing that with the other officers. He thinks your son is an alcoholic and he's willing to drop the charges, for your sake, if Donald will agree to go into rehab – which I consider very generous of him.'

Ginger started to say that Iain wasn't her partner, but stopped because she'd heard his voice in the corridor outside, protesting about something.

'He's been trying to get in to see you,' the female officer said with a smile. 'He's more worried about you than himself.'

'I want to see him too. What will happen to my son after they've dealt with his arm?'

'He'll have to stay in hospital overnight.'

'Thank goodness. That'll give me time to pack my things.'

The officer gestured towards the door as Iain's voice was heard outside again. 'Perhaps we should let your partner in? He's very anxious to see you – unlike your son, who's threatening to break both your arms if you go near him.'

Before she could say more, the male officer went across to open the door and beckon to Iain.

He ignored the police completely and hurried across to kneel beside Ginger. 'Are you all right, love?'

'Yes. I might have a few bruises from where Donny thumped me, but—'

'Where did he hit you? Let me see the bruises.'

'Donny didn't hit me, he banged me hard against the wall, and now my arm and the back of my shoulder feel a bit sore.'

'He bumped you hard on the wall twice,' Iain put in. 'I couldn't get to you in time to stop him.'

'Yes, but they're only bruises.'

The officer frowned. 'Nonetheless, we'll have the bruises checked out and photographed. Did your son do anything else to you? Best for you to tell us the whole story before the case goes to court.'

Ginger almost protested that she didn't want her son going to court, then shut her mouth before the words could escape her. She'd been too soft before, too cowardly. Donny needed a sharp shock if he was to be saved.

If he could be saved.

She wasn't allowed to stay with Iain and rest in his arms, something she desperately craved, until after the female officer had examined her and photos had been taken of her new bruises. She refused to let them take her to a doctor. She just wanted to get her things together and go back to Wiltshire.

By the time the police got ready to leave, it was nearly teatime and she felt tired enough to fall asleep standing upright.

'Do you have somewhere to go tonight?' the policewoman asked.

Ginger hesitated. 'You're absolutely certain Donny will be staying in the hospital tonight?'

'Yes. Under guard. You do realise that what he's accused of is assault? He's already threatened the nursing staff as well.'

'If he's not being let out, I can finish packing my things and we'll leave before my son gets out of hospital tomorrow. We may even sleep here, just for tonight.' She looked at Iain. 'If that's all right with you?'

'As long as you're safe, love, I'll fit in with what you want.'

There. He'd done it again, called her 'love'. It made her feel . . . better, not so alone . . . loved.

'Keep this handy in case you need help for any reason.' The officer handed Ginger a business card. 'Do you have a mobile phone? Can you give me your number?'

Ginger gave it to her and Iain did the same with his. She almost managed to stop her voice wobbling when she said the numbers. *Just hang on*, she told herself. *They'll be gone in a minute.*

'Can you please stay in Newcastle until your son has been before the magistrate?'

Ginger looked at the woman in shock. 'You mean we can't go back to Wiltshire yet?'

'Your son will be brought up before the magistrate for a quick preliminary hearing on Monday morning, unless his health doesn't permit. Obviously, they'll want to speak to you as well. You'll probably be able to leave after that's over.'

Once the police car had left, Ginger looked round, sickened by how filthy everything was on the ground floor. 'How can he live like this?'

'Some folk do. It's not your fault, love.'

'I couldn't stand it being so dirty.'

'Nor could I. Look, I'd better phone my daughter and get her to take charge at our garden centre for a day or two longer. She loves playing boss there.'

'You own a garden centre as well?' she asked in surprise.

'Just a small one. I prefer doing the gardening to selling things, though. So you see, as I'm my own boss, I can stay here as long as you need me without you having to worry about it.'

'You always make things seem so easy.' She couldn't resist linking her arm in his for a moment's comfort. And then she didn't want to let go.

He gave her arm a quick squeeze. 'Things mostly are easy unless people try to complicate them, I find. Is there somewhere for us to sleep here or do we need to find a hotel?'

'I'll go upstairs and check what state things are in.'

'We'll both go up. I want to make sure everything is safe. And we'll bolt the front door first. No one's going to catch me by surprise again. Wait here! I'm going to be a bossy male and insist on going upstairs first, as well.'

She was nervous enough to move down from the bottom step and wait for him.

He dropped a quick kiss on her cheek. 'Stop worrying. We'll sort it all out.'

She could feel the warmth of that kiss all the way up the stairs.

Donny's bedroom was a pigsty. She shuddered at the sight and sour smell of it.

'We'll leave this for him to deal with, shall we?' Iain closed the door on it firmly.

She was surprised to find her own bedroom exactly as she'd left it.

'I'd have thought he'd have come and slept in my bed,' she exclaimed. 'It's bigger than his and he was always complaining about only having a single.'

'Have a look round but it doesn't seem to me as if anything's been messed around with, so he's not totally without respect for you.'

'It hasn't felt like that lately.'

She opened cupboards and drawers, checked the bed, even looking under it, and shook her head in bafflement. 'He hasn't been in here at all, as far as I can tell. But there's only this bedroom, apart from his and I wouldn't lodge a dog in there. I'm sorry I don't have a spare room to offer you.'

'Then we have two choices because I'm not leaving you on your own tonight or tomorrow, both for safety and because you'll start fretting again. We can both sleep in your double bed or we can find a hotel.'

'Oh.'

Iain grinned. 'If we sleep here it'd be easier, and I promise not to touch you – if that's what you want.'

And she said it out loud without thinking. 'It might not be what I want.'

He gave her an immediate cracking hug. 'Then we'll sleep here and see what happens. Do we need to change the sheets?'

'I don't think so. These are the ones I left on the bed and they'd only been on it one night.'

'Then let's go and sort out something for tea. I'm hungry again. Is there a takeaway place of some sort nearby? Remember, I'm supposed to be buying us a meal.'

She hadn't expected to be amused, not after all that had happened today, but she was. 'You're a stomach on wheels, you are.'

'I plead guilty.'

'There's a chip shop on the corner of the next street. They do really good fish and chips, too.'

'Good. We'll get some later. Now, let's start sorting out

what you want to take back to Saffron Lane. I can wait another hour or so for my meal.'

She took her lists out of her bag and as she frowned at them, her stomach rumbled. 'No, let's get the food first. I'm hungry too. I've got it all written down here, so I can go through the house quite quickly tomorrow to sort out everything I want to take. The storage place is open all weekend, so we can pick up the rest of my things when convenient.'

'That's settled, then.'

Ginger and Iain were too tired by the time they'd eaten to do anything but crawl into bed. She did get a cuddle before he fell asleep. She loved that. It had been so long since anyone had simply cuddled her.

She lay beside him, listening to his long, slow breaths. She couldn't keep her eyes open, so followed his example and let sleep take over.

Chapter Eighteen

When Ginger woke in the morning, there was no one beside her in bed, but she heard Iain whistling in the bathroom. Then the whistling stopped abruptly and he yelled, 'Ow!' and muttered a curse.

She went rushing in to see what was wrong and blushed furiously to find him naked and damp, trying to shave with the little razor she used sometimes for under her arms.

She was about to back out when she saw the blood on his face. 'You're hurt! Let me see.'

He turned with one of his cheeky smiles. 'I just failed my test in using an old-fashioned razor, that's all.'

'Let me see.'

But she found herself pressed against warm damp flesh as she started to check how deep the cut was and forgot about the blood completely when he bent his head to give her a kiss. It went on and on until they both wound up back in the bedroom.

'Not rushing you, am I?' he asked breathlessly, caressing her cheek with one hand.

'Not rushing me at all.'

It was over an hour before they got up again.

'To be continued,' he said, pressing a kiss on his fingertip and placing it on the end of her nose.

'I didn't know,' she whispered, blushing furiously but determined to tell him.

He turned at the door, frowning. 'Didn't know what?'

'That it could be so good for a woman.'

'But you're a married woman! With a child.'

She could feel the heat rising in her cheeks, but wasn't going to lie to him. 'My husband was always . . . in a hurry. And . . . he didn't do it very often. And he said that was because *I* wasn't good at it.' She'd read about it and worried, knowing it wasn't just her. But Alan had refused to seek help, so in the end, she'd just gone along with it.

She was always so tired after work it was a relief when he didn't go after her as often as some women said their husbands did.

Iain snorted in disgust. 'How selfish of him! And how short-sighted. You and I have managed better than that already. Just wait till we've had a bit more practice at being together.'

That sent a happy little shiver down her spine.

He turned to leave then stuck his head back into the room. 'I forgot to tell you how much I like your new hairdo. The silver looks very elegant.'

That made her day start even more brightly, because

she'd been wondering why he hadn't commented on such a big change and had worried that he didn't like it.

She rushed round the bedroom, piling the clothes she wanted to take with her on the bed and kicking the other stuff into a corner. They could stuff these in rubbish bin liners and drop them off at the charity shop on Monday.

'Breakfast is ready!' Iain yelled from downstairs.

She ran down the stairs to join him, not feeling shy with him now, but happy and relaxed.

'It's only the sandwiches you brought with us, toasted. But it'll hold us till we can find somewhere to buy a proper cooked breakfast. It's still only half past seven, after all.'

'Is that all?' She hadn't even thought to check the time.

After they'd eaten she guided him round the house, pointing out the furniture she wanted to keep, avoiding Donny's room.

Working together they carried the bigger things out to the van, helped by Tom from down the road, who had guessed she was leaving for good and had come to say goodbye to her. She'd helped him with his father sometimes till the old man died, and she knew what a kind chap Tom was.

It all took longer than she'd expected and she was glad of the extra day because she was terrified of forgetting something important.

When they got back from picking up her things at the storage place, she saw Kerry staring out of the window next door and stopped to say she was moving out, but didn't let Kerry start nattering.

'I like your new hairdo. Suits you, Ginger.'

'Thanks.'

Her neighbour winked and gestured towards Iain. 'I can see you fell on your feet. He looks nice. Good luck.'

'He is nice.'

She rejoined Iain and stared into the back of the van. Even after everything had been loaded, it wasn't full. She hadn't a lot to show for her life of hard work, had she?

Iain started to shut the back doors of the van, then stopped. 'Are you sure that's all you want to take with you, Ginger? We could load any other things that might come in useful and I could store them for you if you don't have room in the bedsitter.'

She pulled herself up straight. 'I'm very sure, thank you. You're sure it'll all be safe in the van?'

'I've got very good locks and an alarm system. We'll know if someone tries to break into it.'

As they sat chatting that evening, she tried to explain why she was taking so little. 'I've lived with rubbish furniture most of my life and I'm not doing it any more, if I can help it. I'm only taking enough with me to get by for a while. My sewing materials and photos are much more important to me than furniture, anyway. And maybe, if I'm lucky, I'll be able to sell an embroidery or two in the gallery. Nell says she'll let me have a go.'

'When we get you settled, I want to see all your embroideries. From what you say and what I've seen so far, you've put your heart and soul into them.'

Trust him to go straight to the core of everything. He was so perceptive.

They had another quiet evening. It was wonderful to sit with someone who really listened to what you said. He was wonderful.

In the morning Iain grinned at her. 'We've got plenty of time to grab something more substantial to eat before we have to be at the police station. Eleven o'clock, they said.'

'Oh dear! I'd forgotten how hungry you'd be. We should have bought something more substantial yesterday.'

'Much nicer to let someone else cook us breakfast.'

He pulled her to him for one of his delightful quick hugs, then set off driving. 'Tell me which way to go.'

She gave him directions.

'I can wait to eat when I have to.' He winked. 'Some things are far better than eating anyway. And loving you comes head of the list. Besides, feeding me isn't your responsibility. I'm an adult. If I get desperate, I can provide for myself.'

What a difference there was between Iain and her husband! And her son.

After they'd eaten, she looked at her watch. 'Nearly time. I'm still wondering why they phoned to tell us to go to the police station, not the magistrate's court.'

'We'll soon find out.'

When Donny was brought into the big room at the police station to join them, he was in a wheelchair. He had his arm in plaster and he looked dreadful.

He scowled across the room at his mother and mouthed the word 'bitch'.

She could have wept to see him looking grey-faced, with a fat belly and hands that kept trembling, however much he tried to hide that. He looked years older than thirty.

An older man came into the room, accompanied by a clerk. He introduced himself as the magistrate dealing with a special programme for violent alcoholics who hadn't a long record of misbehaviour. 'That's why we're seeing if we can do this more informally. It's a project I helped set up.'

'Good idea,' she said.

He turned to Iain. 'Mr Darling?'

Iain nodded across at him.

'You're still sure about waiving your right to charge Mr Brunham with assault?'

'I am, Your Honour. As long as he gets help for his problem.'

'Then if he agrees to take part in the new rehabilitation programme, we can avoid the necessity for jail completely.'

He turned to address Donny. 'Do you agree to entering this programme and staying on it for the necessary twelve weeks, Mr Brunham?'

Donny shrugged.

'I need you to answer me clearly.'

'What choice do I have but to do it?'

Ginger could have shaken him. Here they were, making things easier for him, and he couldn't even be polite.

'You can choose to go to jail instead, that's one choice. But thanks to the man you attacked agreeing not to pursue charges, you also have the choice to go on this special rehabilitation programme. There will be no jail and you'll have no criminal record if you stick it out to the end and stay out of trouble for two years afterwards. So, which do you prefer?'

'I'll do the rehab.'

The policeman standing beside him gave him a nudge and whispered something.

'Um . . . I'll do the rehab – Your Honour.'

'Good.' The magistrate turned to Ginger. 'Are you all right with that, Mrs Brunham?'

'Yes. Definitely. Thank you very much.'

'Good. Then we only have to make sure Mr Brunham gets his clothes and possessions from the council house you are, I believe, about to vacate, and we can send him on his way to the rehab centre.'

'I've removed anything I want already,' she said. 'He can have whatever he likes that's left, but I don't want to go back there with him. I'd have told the council people to clear the place but there's no one in the office on a Sunday. I'll get in touch with them by email.'

'Very well. We'll make sure your son gets a chance to collect his possessions and then we'll leave it to the local authority to clear the house. They'll want to refurbish it for the next tenant, I'm sure. And I'm sorry you've been upset by all this, Mrs Brunham.'

She glanced instinctively towards her son and for a moment she thought Donny looked shamefaced, but the scowl quickly returned to his face.

Probably just her imagination.

When the formalities were complete, the police took Donny away and Iain put his arm round her shoulders as they walked outside. 'That was hard on you, love. You did well to keep yourself together.'

She managed to hold back the tears till they were sitting in his van and then she lost it completely, sobbing against his chest, while Iain's big, capable hand patted her shoulders from time to time.

Once the tears had dried up, he said quietly, 'Let's go. You've got a new home, new life and new friends. Don't look back. You can't change the past.'

She nodded. 'I know. And Donny's future is in his own hands now, I know that too. But what he's done still hurts.'

'Of course it does, and any time I want to save on washing my clothes, you can weep all over me about it.'

That brought a smile briefly to her face and she dared to say, 'Thanks, Iain. For everything.'

'I'm glad to be here for you.'

Chapter Nineteen

Emil enjoyed shopping for furniture. He'd intended to buy only the barest necessities but was seduced by a sound system and TV, not to mention an extremely comfortable burgundy leather lounge suite which included two recliner armchairs.

He phoned the man he'd recommended to Abbie and arranged for Phil to move the various items from the bedsitter.

'Thank you very much for recommending me to the lady.'

'My pleasure. How about moving my things in tomorrow afternoon, then?'

'Fine.'

Emil gave Phil the address and arranged to have him pick up the goods and meet him at the flat.

'Second floor, did you say?' the man asked.

'Yes. But there's a lift.'

'Still sounds as if it's a two-man job, unless you can

lend a hand with the carrying? There are some quite heavy things from the sounds of it.'

'Ah. I can't do that, I'm afraid. Not at the moment. I'm recovering from an operation. Hire someone else and I'll pay the extra. In fact, if you can assemble the flat-pack stuff for me as well, I'll pay extra for your time.'

'Happy to do that. I have a friend who'll help and we can work into the evening if we have to.'

Emil dashed back to the bedsitter to pick up the few personal bits and pieces he wanted to take with him and piled the other things to one side. He'd sort out the bedsitter later.

He scowled at the bed, a cheap thing that had bounced around every time he turned over. He left the beige bedding behind too. He'd chosen sheets of a soothing eau de Nil colour, and a duvet cover with a swirling pattern of toning colours for his new flat.

It was strange. He'd never been interested in such household details before, but since his operation it seemed important to make sure every aspect of his life was in harmony, and to have a home that made him feel happy.

You could almost call what he was doing 'nesting'. It was what pregnant women were supposed to do – but perhaps it also applied to people who'd been given a new lease of life and wanted a more peaceful style of living for it.

On moving day, he arrived at the small block of flats early and started lugging his suitcase and boxes inside, dumping them near the lift. He'd made sure none of the boxes he was taking was heavy.

To his astonishment, on his second trip from his car he ran into Abbie Turrell.

He stopped dead and so did she, looking just as surprised as he felt.

'What are you doing here?' she asked in her usual blunt way.

'I'm moving in.'

Her mouth fell open. 'To the upstairs flat? You're the new tenant?'

'Yes. And you? Don't tell me you live here as well?'

'Well, actually my father left these flats to my sister and me, so Louis and I are moving into one of them. And my sister has the other ground-floor flat. I . . . um, guess that makes us your landladies.'

Fate was smiling at him for once, he decided. 'How delightful! I was wanting to invite someone to christen my flat, but my father isn't available and I don't know anyone in town yet. How about you and your sister joining me for a bottle of champagne?'

'We each have a small child.'

'Bring them with you. I'll supply lemonade and potato crisps for them as well.'

'Well . . . um, I accept. That'll be very pleasant. What time?'

'Would five o'clock be all right? What people in Australia call a sundowner. The children are too young to last far into the evening. Give me a day or two to settle in and we'll have a little celebration.'

'Yes. Right. I have to go now. I'm picking Louis up from school. See you soon.'

He watched her leave, wondering why he was attracted

to such a brusque female. Who knew what caused that sort of attraction? Scientists could talk about pheromones, but that didn't explain it nearly well enough. There was more than just hormones and chemicals to finding someone attractive. Or so he'd decided after making a few youthful errors in choosing good-looking but not so amiable or intelligent girlfriends.

He realised he was still standing next to the pile of things and hadn't taken any of it up to his flat yet, so hurried out to finish unloading his car. Phil and his helper would be here soon and could help him get these boxes up to his flat.

Emil smiled ruefully. He was going to be busy if he was to entertain guests in his new home so soon. Did he even have enough plates and glasses?

And he'd have to pace himself carefully as he unpacked. He still got tired quickly.

These were possibly rather important guests. Well, one of them was. And he hoped to make friends with the other one, too, if she was half as interesting as her older sister.

What was life without friends?

Abbie picked Louis up and then took him to choose a desk for his bedroom. She wanted to do something special to mark the big change in their lives and she'd seen a desk in the charity shop that looked as if it would just fit nicely under the window in his new bedroom. The shop had been given several of them in flat-packs, so it would be easy to take it home.

He was fizzing with excitement still about his new home and was followed outside by his teacher, who reminded

Abbie to send a note to the office changing their address and other details, if necessary.

'Did Louis drive you mad today?' Abbie asked Mr Parker ruefully.

'He was a bit more lively than usual, but we all understood how exciting it is to move to a new home, so we did a story about it.'

'Thanks. You're always so helpful.' She saw the teacher's eyes soften and become speculative as he looked at her, and said hastily, 'Now, I must hurry. We have to buy some furniture.'

Mr Parker was a lovely man but she didn't think it wise to get involved with her son's teacher, and anyway, that spark of attraction simply wasn't there, on her side at least.

Louis was standing near the car jigging about impatiently, so she clicked the door open for him and they set off for the shop.

'We've got a new neighbour upstairs. Remember Mr Kinnaird who picked you up from school the other day when it was raining? Well, it's him. We're invited round one afternoon to celebrate his new flat. Champagne for the grown-ups and lemonade for you and Susie. That'll be nice, won't it?'

Louis nodded, but was much more interested in choosing a desk then some second-hand books from the same charity shop. Now they had room to store them, they didn't need to depend solely on the library. She chose a couple of novels for herself as well, feeling very extravagant.

She knew she'd inherited quite a lot of money, which made such careful spending ridiculous, but after years of being frugal, it'd be a long time till she could bring herself to buy anything rashly.

She hadn't told Louis the details of her inheritance because he could never keep anything secret. Besides, she couldn't quite believe in the amount of money the lawyer had said was waiting for them till it was actually deposited in her bank account.

How was it possible that her father could have made so much money?

Her mother would throw a fit about it all coming to her, and another fit when she heard about the half-sister. There were definitely storms ahead from that quarter. But then her mother had always enjoyed creating storms in teacups.

When Stacy and Elise went out together, Warren seized his moment. He crept along the back garden of the houses and peered in through Stacy's window.

She'd left her creations out for anyone to see and copy, not even covering them with a dust sheet, the fool.

He got out his smartphone and took a photo of the little creature she'd made, the one Elise had raved about. The window was slightly open and the breeze was making the creation's head nod up and down slightly, and to his dismay it really was cute, even to him.

He wished he could get closer to it and smash it to pieces. 'Cute' wasn't what serious art was about, but people were so stupid it was easy to fool them. He'd studied what art critics looked for and it seemed to be about holding up a mirror to society, often satirising things. He'd worked hard to fit into that model, which suited his own feelings about the world.

He looked at the nodding bird again, really tempted to try to hook the creature out through the open window, or at least knock it off the bench and hope to damage it. But it was broad daylight and there might be someone looking out from Number 1, or that old chap might be working in the gardens of the two larger end houses again. So he didn't dare risk anything.

Not in daylight, anyway.

When he did act, he'd make sure nothing could be traced to him.

He went back inside his own house and looked out at the front. Yes, the pots were still there.

Stupid waste of time. His foot was itching to kick them and scatter their contents.

But once again, he restrained himself. He had to choose his moment with care.

To his intense annoyance when the two women came back, they unloaded shopping bags and placed two more similar plants in identical pots on either side of Stacy's front door.

Damn them!

Nell was in the upper floor of Number 1, painting the walls a soft off-white colour. She liked doing the occasional practical job and this one was not only straightforward, but her doing it would save them money. Even though they wouldn't be using this room yet, it'd be ready.

She heard a faint sound, so faint she'd normally have

ignored it. Today something made her go over to the window and look outside. She was surprised to see Warren Cutler peering into the back window of Stacy's house, so drew back a little.

What was he doing there? Surely he wasn't going to break in? She could see that the window was slightly open, so stayed where she was, trying to work out what was going on.

He got out a smartphone and took a photo of whatever was inside Stacy's studio. He was scowling, looking really sour about it.

Was he jealous of one of the other artist's pieces? Surely not?

When he went back inside Nell stood for a few moments longer watching, but he didn't reappear so she went back to work.

A little later, as she was almost finished, she heard a car draw up in Saffron Lane and nipped downstairs to see who it was from the window at the front of the gallery.

Stacy and Elise. She smiled as she saw what they were doing. The pots of flowers looked pretty outside the houses. Maybe she'd buy some for Number 1 as well. She knew Ginger was a bit short of money.

She wondered suddenly if Cutler was watching his two neighbours do this, and smiled wryly. If he was, she had no doubt he'd be scornful about the flowers. She couldn't imagine him beautifying his temporary home any more than his angry little carvings would beautify the world.

The more she saw of him, with his sour expression when he wasn't pretending to be amiable, the angrier she grew with herself for being taken in by him at the interview.

Well, that was her mistake, so she felt it her responsibility now to keep an eye on him. She didn't know why she kept mentally adding 'just in case', but she did. Just in case what happened? What could happen, for heaven's sake?

She didn't have any clear ideas about possible problems, but she'd found over the years that such uneasiness usually meant something was about to go wrong.

When she'd finished painting the walls, she rang Angus to help her carry down the painting gear and take it back to the cellar at the big house, where they stored all the tools and maintenance equipment.

As she went outside with some of the equipment, she wondered if her husband would notice the flowers and had a little bet with herself that he would.

She loved the way he was intensely aware of the world around him and the people in it.

Warren was working in his studio when he heard the car draw up and it was a few moments before he could put his tool down and go into the front room to see who it was.

Ah! Angus Denning helping his wife carry things out of the first house.

He debated going out to chat, but had started work on a piece that was going well, so left it this time. More important to produce some good carvings, ready for the art gallery opening.

He hoped they'd not take too long to finish setting it up. He was a little short of money, except for the miserable stipend they were giving him, because after some consideration he'd decided it'd be worth keeping up with his share of the mortgage payments. If his cow of a wife did sell the house, he wanted to make sure he was legally entitled to his half of the profits.

He bent over the Bengal tiger he was carving. It was just carrying off a small chital deer. If he said so himself he'd caught the last look of panic on the face of the animal the tiger had killed. He'd enjoyed doing that.

Elise came out of the house to say hello to Angus.

'You look well,' he said at once.

'I'm feeling well. I love living here.'

'The flowers are a nice touch.' He indicated the pots.

'Perhaps Mr Cutler will do the same.'

He chuckled. 'I'd bet good money that he won't.'

'How about coming up to our house for a drink before tea?' Nell suggested. 'It'll only take me a few minutes to wash and change, then I can show you round the garden at the other side of the house. It's looking at its best just now.'

'Love to.'

'Could you invite Stacy for me as well?'

'Happy to.'

They looked at one another and Elise prepared herself to refuse to pass on the invitation to Cutler, but it didn't eventuate. And they didn't knock on his door before they left, either.

Warren listened indignantly as Denning's wife invited the other two occupants of Saffron Lane round for a drink, and didn't invite him.

He watched them drive away. Elise went into Stacy's house, presumably to pass on the invitation. Kicking a cardboard box out of the way, he went to pull a ready meal out of his freezer, scowling at it. For all her faults, Michelle had been a good cook. He missed that.

Then he turned back to his tiger and lost himself in the carving, not stopping till the main carving was finished. He eased his shoulder and looked out in surprise as he heard voices and saw his two neighbours come back smiling and chatting.

Dusk was falling. Was it so late already?

He still had to work out what to do about those damned pots of flowers, but he wasn't taking care of that little problem during daylight while anybody in the houses could see him. He'd enjoy doing it.

Chapter Twenty

Iain and Ginger drove out of Newcastle after the hearing at the police station, heading south. By the time they got to Wiltshire, both were extremely tired and it was nearly midnight.

As they turned off towards Sexton Bassett, Iain said quietly, 'I've been working out what's best to do. Let's dump the things from this van in your flat, then spend the night at my house. There's a bed made up ready to fall into, food in the fridge, everything we need.'

'Can't we just go straight there and leave my things in the van till morning?'

'Unfortunately, I have to make a really early start tomorrow and I'll need to load up my van with plants first thing. There's a new load of plants arriving at my garden centre early in the morning, you see, and I need to clear the space for them. Since I'll be taking some of the plants I remove to Saffron Lane, I can drop you there then. What do you think? It won't take us long to unload the van if we simply dump your things and leave.'

'All right. I can manage one more effort.' She felt rather shy as she added, 'I may not be very good company tonight but I'd rather be with you after all the . . . the hassles with Donny. You've been such a comfort.'

'So you'll share my bed, even if it's only to sleep?'

'Yes. Happy to. After all, you've shared mine. And sleeping isn't the only thing you're good at.'

He grinned. 'I might say the same of you. In fact, it's a pity we have to get up so early tomorrow.'

'Yes. I'm sure I'm going to love living in Saffron Lane, though. The houses look good now that the modernisations are finished.'

'Angus and Nell are eager to finish the gardens as soon as possible, then they'll look good too. There's not a lot of work to do on Bay Tree Cottage now, just the planting and finishing, which I shall enjoy. Be done completely in a couple of days.'

'You're not taking out the bay tree, are you? I love its rich green colour.'

'No, of course not, but I'm going to clear round it and plant some low flowering shrubs. They'll look good against it.'

She roused herself when they arrived at Saffron Lane, got out quickly and opened up Number 1. They took the bigger furniture through to her flat and dumped it more or less in place and put the boxes and bundles along one wall.

She wasn't too tired to smile at him when they finished. 'It's been an eventful couple of days, hasn't it? I'll cook you a nice breakfast while you're loading the van in the morning.'

'Now you're talking. Something that's quick to eat but filling. We won't have time to attend to our other needs. Not then, anyway.'

She could feel herself flushing at the warmth of his gaze. Oh, he was such a lovely man!

When they got back to Iain's house, Ginger was surprised at how big it was, situated to the left of his garden centre in walled grounds of its own. And surely it was quite old?

He parked the van at the side of the car park and took her through a high gate and along a path to the house. 'How about a quick bowl of cereal then bed?'

'Good idea. You're not the only one who gets hungry.'

After they'd eaten, he took her up to his bedroom. 'Make yourself at home, love. I just want to check that the centre and house are properly locked up. It's something of a nightly ritual for me.'

She tried hard to stay awake till he got back, but could feel herself jerking in and out of consciousness, so gave up the attempt. She felt so comfortable when she was near him, awake or asleep. It was . . . miraculous and . . . he was . . . wonderful.

As Warren was getting ready for bed, there was the sound of another vehicle. He watched a big van pull up at Number 1, keeping its headlights on the front door. The old tart got out and fiddled with a key, only she didn't look as tarty without that dye job on her hair. But whatever she looked like now, her embroideries would never match his sculptures. No, he didn't need to worry about her. He'd beaten her once and would beat her every time if she tried to push herself forward.

With the outside lights of the house switched on, the driver backed the van to and fro till its rear doors were opposite the front door, then switched off the engine and began to unload, stopping a couple of times to give Mrs Tart a quick hug or a kiss.

She hadn't wasted any time giving him what a man needed from a woman.

Oh my, aren't we cosy together! Warren thought sourly. How long will that last?

He sighed as a big yawn overtook him, and made his way slowly up to bed.

He hoped the Dennings would appoint male artists to the other residency positions or he'd be outnumbered. Surely male artists would have a more businesslike attitude to their work?

Come to think of it, he didn't know many artists, male or female. He'd been too busy getting his own skills up to scratch.

That was what counted, not chit-chat and drinkie-poos, as Michelle called them.

Chapter Twenty-One

The next morning Ginger woke at dawn to see sunlight slipping past the edges of the curtains. Iain was still sleeping beside her but when she looked round, she couldn't see a clock. And where had she put her watch?

She leant across and planted a quick kiss on his cheek, then slid out of bed to go to the bathroom then nip downstairs to put the kettle on. There was a clock on the wall there and it was earlier than she'd thought.

She felt great, so happy and relaxed.

Iain came into the kitchen just as she was making him a travel mug of tea. 'Ah! Clever woman. That mug is the one I always use when I'm working outside.' He unlocked the back door and took the mug from her hands, sipping with an appreciative murmur. 'I'll be about half an hour, if you don't mind having breakfast ready. Make yourself at home.'

After a quick shower, she found her watch on the floor

beside the bed and slipped it reluctantly on her wrist. Back to checking off the time and letting it control her actions. Maybe one day she and Iain would be able to spend a lazy morning in bed.

She got everything ready for breakfast then couldn't resist wandering round his house. Parts of it were untidy but it was clean underneath the clutter, a real home, not a showplace in spite of the fact that the building seemed quite old and was very beautiful from the outside. Some of the interior was in need of renovation and there was no furniture in those rooms. But the work that had been done so far was tasteful and yet homely. How lovely it must be to live in a house as big as this and bring it back to life by your own efforts!

She went into the front room to watch for him to return, ready to start cooking the cheese on toast. She'd already put the ingredients together.

When she saw him, she hurried back to the kitchen to shove the toast under the grill. He brought the smell of fresh air and greenery in with him. She squeaked in surprise as he picked her up, whirled her round the room and kissed her thoroughly.

'If we had more time, I'd do something about how you make me feel,' he growled in her ear.

'Pity, but the toast will burn if you don't let me go.'

She handed him a banana and had a plate of cheese on toast in front of him within two minutes.

A quarter of an hour later they left. As they were getting into the van, which was now full of plants, a smaller van with his logo on it drew up and a young woman got out of it. He introduced his daughter, who had come in early to receive the delivery of new seedlings.

To Ginger's surprise, Katie greeted her cheerfully, not seeming in the least put out to find her father entertaining a woman. That made her wonder with a sudden jab of fear how often he'd done this before.

'I told Katie when I phoned last night that you'd be here,' he said as they got into the little van. 'She's been nagging me to find a partner for a while.'

'No wonder she didn't mind me being here.' Partner? What did he mean by that?

He shrugged. 'Why should she mind? Katie's got a life of her own. She doesn't need to live through me.'

That gave Ginger something to think about as they drove through the early morning streets. Would his life continue to include her from now on? Oh, she did hope so.

Iain parked in Saffron Lane. 'Need any help moving the bigger pieces of furniture around?'

'No, thanks. We put them more or less in place last night. I'm stronger than I look and can easily tug them about on the wooden floor if I have to. Get off to your work now.'

She watched him move the van to the other end of the little street then realised she was staring like an idiot and hurriedly unlocked the front door of Number 1.

It wasn't till then that it occurred to her that Iain hadn't said anything about seeing her again. They could easily have made arrangements. Why hadn't they? Surely he wanted to?

All her uncertainties about men came crashing down for a few moments, then she shook her head and muttered,

'Just get on with it, girl! You can't waste your life worrying about what might go wrong.'

But she couldn't help hoping desperately that he would want to keep seeing her. He wouldn't call her 'love' and 'partner' if he didn't want them to be together, surely?

The inside of Number 1 smelt of fresh paint and Ginger couldn't resist taking a quick walk round the rest of the building before she started sorting out her flat. She could picture clearly how best to fit a small café into one side of the back room and use part of the storeroom between the front and the back areas for the big, ugly boxes of supplies. She hoped the place wouldn't be difficult to work in when it was fitted out.

When Nell arrived just before nine o'clock, Ginger came out of the flat. 'I'm here. We brought my furniture down from Newcastle yesterday and I've now moved in.'

'Oh, good. You'll be able to help keep an eye on the place, make sure no one comes in who shouldn't.'

Ginger stared at her. 'Why are you worried about that? Is something wrong?'

'That stupid official at the council, who is the ultimate caricature of the worst kind of bureaucrat, keeps finding more paperwork and insisting we fill in forms. She won't take no for an answer and is still insisting she has the right to poke her nose into everything we're doing. Angus won't let her. He thinks she's a weirdo and a control freak.'

'She does sound a bit strange.'

'Tell me about it. She rang again yesterday afternoon, *demanding* to view this house, saying she couldn't sign it off for use as a café without checking it in person.'

'Is she from the catering department? I thought when you mentioned her before you said she was the acting head of planning or something like that.'

'She is in temporary charge of planning, I think. But they're about to appoint someone permanent to the position and I doubt it'll be her. She's very good at getting on your nerves and no one has a good word for her.'

'Why is she interfering in catering affairs, then? Perhaps you should get in touch with the food services department and ask them what's going on, or I can do that if you like. My former employer always left the paperwork and permissions to me so I'm used to dealing with that sort of thing. I can tell them I'm new here and I'm going to be in charge of the café, so want to get everything right. They usually prefer it when you ask their advice and keep them informed, and actually they can be very helpful.'

Nell gaped at her. 'You are a constant surprise to me, Ginger Brunham! You have so many skills, yet you never mentioned any of them at the interview, only your embroideries.'

'Oh. Well, I'd never done an interview like yours, so I didn't know you'd want me to talk about the rest of what I'd done. Before that I'd only applied in person for jobs at cafés which had signs saying *Help Wanted* in their windows, and not even that for the last ten years. But I've worked in catering most of my life so I know about a lot of the details of how it's run.'

She couldn't help smiling. 'Working as a waitress can be

quite a window on the world if you're interested in people. And even though I've only been in lowly roles officially, I've got eyes in my head, haven't I? As well as having had a lazy boss for the past ten years who dumped everything he could on me.'

'What you did can't have been all that lowly if you did the liaison for permissions and inspections and so on.'

Ginger shrugged. 'I preferred to do it. Heaven help whoever has taken my place if they're not used to the paperwork because Joe will let things slide till the very last minute. He's hopeless. When I was working there I didn't want the authorities closing down the café, did I, so I took over. It was convenient to work within walking distance of home when my husband wasn't well and I simply stayed on afterwards, I don't know why.'

'Well, if you don't mind taking that over here from now on, I'll leave everything that concerns running the café to you. Will you be all right with that? I'll give you a raise for doing more, of course.'

'Fine by me.' She hadn't even had to ask for this raise in wages. Ooh, she wished Joe could have heard that offer.

'Good. I'll bring the latest letter from Charlene Brody to show you after lunch, but just ignore it and do what you said: contact the catering department. How's it going in your new home? Did we forget anything when we set it up?' She gestured towards the little flat.

'I'm getting settled in nicely. Come and see it.' She was rather pleased with her rapid progress. She hated living surrounded by mess.

Nell stared round, then, at Ginger's handwave in that

direction, peeped into the bedroom. 'Wow! You've got it incredibly neat and tidy already. Do you need any more furniture? We have all sorts of bits and pieces at the big house in the attics. You'd be quite welcome to pick through them.'

'Thanks, but for the first time in my life I'm going to take my time choosing how I live. I can manage with what I've got here for the time being. The only thing I still need for certain is storage for my sewing materials and equipment. For that, I'll probably go to a second-hand office supplies place and get one of those old-fashioned cabinets full of pigeon holes and little drawers.' She'd been wishing she had somewhere to put one for a while.

'You know, you're amazingly well organised.'

'I've had to be, Nell.'

'I do understand. I brought my three children up mostly without my ex's help, except for the financial payments. At least he kept up with those.'

'You haven't always been rich, then?'

Nell laughed. 'We're not rich financially now, because we don't have a lot of spare money. Though I must admit, I do consider it wonderful to have the big house and the special gardens. Believe me, I know what it's like to count every penny and I still try not to waste anything. If everyone had to cope with a period of being poor when they were young, I doubt there'd be so much debt in the so-called advanced world. Those adverts on TV about borrowing money make me furious. So irresponsible to encourage that.'

'I hate them too. I shout at them when they come on sometimes.'

After a few moments of companionable silence, Nell changed the subject. 'Another thing: I'll be bringing Emil Kinnaird here tomorrow morning to discuss the little museum his father is funding in the secret room. We won't need to disturb you. From now on, your flat is your home and isn't in any way public territory, which is why we put a proper lock on the entrance. I just thought I'd emphasise that.'

'Thanks.'

'Now, there's another thing I'll need your expert help with and we need to do it quickly: the shopfitters want to finalise the design for the café and the art gallery side of things, so I'll need your input. Could we get together with them, maybe on Thursday afternoon, about the final details? Here are their contact details.'

'I'll look forward to that. I have all sorts of ideas about how cafés should be set out, having had to work in inefficiently designed and unorganised places for most of my life.'

'Don't hesitate to change the design, then, if you know a better way. What do I know about cafés? And finally, on Friday, we'll be holding the interviews for the rest of the residencies in the art gallery space. I know the café won't be in place, but do you think you could supply us with tea and coffee? I'll bring down some crockery and Angus will install a couple of garden tables and some chairs in the front room for us to use. I'll pay you for doing the refreshments. Just something simple.'

She snapped her fingers as an idea occurred to her. 'Maybe you could check with Winifred about her making us a cake for Friday?' She fumbled in her handbag. 'I've been writing down phone numbers that might be useful to you. Hers is on this list. It's nowhere near complete, I'm sure, but it'll give you a start.'

'Happy to. Thanks.'

'What a blessing it is to have you here! Now, I have to dash.'

Ginger hadn't seen Nell when she wasn't in a hurry to do something. Talk about busy! Angus and his wife might have inherited a huge old house, but they weren't living a life of luxury and ease. They seemed to be very hard workers and if there was one quality Ginger respected in people, it was that. Well, maybe that and kindness were equally important.

She went to Number 3 to retrieve the rest of her personal possessions and thank Elise for giving her shelter. Then she came back and began to organise her sewing materials. For once she'd be able to leave them lying about openly, instead of having to put them away to keep them safe. Neither her husband nor Donny had thought twice about plonking mugs of tea or coffee down on them if they were left on the table.

But as she pottered round, she couldn't help listening for her phone. Only it didn't ring and Iain's van had left. Surely she hadn't been mistaken in his feelings about her? Surely he'd want to see her again?

Why hadn't he *said* something about next time, then?

Whenever he heard noises outside Warren nipped into the front room to keep an eye on the comings and goings in the street, staying at the back in the shadows. He scowled to see the tart settling in at Number 1. Such a stupid accent she had, all sing-song. You couldn't take her seriously.

He scowled out at the pots of flowers a few times. He was surrounded by idiots.

And when Mrs Denning went into Number 1 carrying some papers and left without them, he couldn't help wondering what the hell was going on there.

They hadn't invited him up to the big house for drinks as they had Elise and Stacy, nor had either of the owners come to see him today to ask how he was.

When he went to get his lunch, he discovered he'd nearly run out of food again, so would have to go shopping before the end of the day. He ought to be putting the tiny details of the tiger's coat on to his carving not playing housekeeper, but he couldn't settle to it knowing he had to go shopping soon.

Some residency this was turning out to be! He'd expected much more free time now he didn't have to go out and earn a living, he had indeed. But the shopping and housework ate into it and he kept forgetting to buy things. He'd have to start making lists.

Oh, hell! He might as well get the shopping over and done with for a few days at least, then settle into his work again. He'd make sure to buy a lot of frozen stuff for when he didn't want to stop work. You could put bread into the freezer as well, couldn't you? Yes, of course you could. He'd buy several loaves.

He stuffed his wallet into the back pocket of his jeans and went out to his car.

* * *

The shopping centre was as horrible as he'd remembered, with its glaring lights and echoing noises. He kept having to avoid women pushing little children in buggies or old people tottering along with their walking sticks or little children running about heedless of other people.

It was the final straw when he realised he'd forgotten to bring shopping bags with him and would have to pay for plastic ones. He muttered a curse.

The checkout operator stiffened and glared at him. 'I'll thank you not to use language like that in front of me, *sir*, or I'll refuse to serve you.'

'They don't care what they say these days,' the old man behind him said loudly. 'You tell him, lass. Don't put up with rudeness from anyone.'

Rage boiled up in Warren, as it did sometimes, but he managed to control it. He had to shop here, because he didn't know where else to go, so he couldn't afford to make a scene. At least here he was beginning to know where to find things. Who'd think they'd have so many different types of each item on the shelves?

As he unloaded the plastic bags from the trolley into his car, he admitted to himself that he was missing Michelle's help and support on the domestic front more than he'd expected to. He wasn't missing her company, though, or her inane chatter about what she'd done at work and who had said what.

Just before six that evening Ginger realised she hadn't phoned Winifred to ask about a cake for the interviews. 'Sorry to be giving you short notice, but I've been so busy I've been spinning like a top.'

After chatting they arranged for cupcakes instead, as being much easier for Angus and Nell to hand round.

She'd just put the phone down when someone rang the doorbell of Number 1. She saw who it was through the fluted glass panels in the door and her heart started to beat more quickly.

Iain stood there, hands held up with palms outwards as if to protect himself. 'I'm sorry, really sorry, love. I meant to phone you, but there was trouble at the garden centre, some youths trying to nick plants, and in the scuffle my phone fell out of my pocket and got trodden on. I was going to call you on the landline at the centre once things had settled down, but we were so busy I didn't have a minute to myself because my daughter had to pick up my grandson from school and I couldn't leave the till unattended.'

He waited, head on one side, eyes crinkled with laughter. 'Am I forgiven?'

'Of course you are. Come in, you fool! You look as if you're expecting me to slam the door in your face.'

'Not exactly. But I'm glad you haven't taken umbrage and I will try harder to keep in touch from now on, I promise. Well, I will once I've bought myself a new phone tomorrow.'

He followed her into the flat. 'Good heavens! It looks all neat and tidy. Except for those boxes.'

'I'm neat by nature and when you don't have many possessions, it's easy to keep them tidy. But the other boxes can't be unpacked till I've found some sort of big cabinet for my sewing things. An old commercial storage thingo – I don't know what they're called.' She described her needs.

'I know an old converted barn that calls itself "Bassett Barn Antiques", though it's more junk than antiques. They have an old office furniture section and I bet we can find you something suitable there. Unless you want to buy new flat-pack units from somewhere online.'

'I want to buy the cheapest thing I can find. I don't care what it looks like, just that it must have a lot of different compartments.'

'It'll take up a lot of the space in your living room.'

'I don't care about that, either. I want my materials to be properly sorted out, for once, and stored so that I don't have to pack and unpack them every time I start work, to hunt for threads and so on. As long as I have room to sit down and entertain a friend, I'm all right for the time being.'

'All right, love. I understand. I'm like that with my tools, too. How about I take you shopping tomorrow morning? If we take the big van, we can bring what you buy back in that. After having to manage on her own for a couple of days, my daughter's hired a new woman part-time. She says this Linda knows what she's doing so I'll leave them to it. I've been meaning to find someone for a while. It'll let me spend more time with you.'

'Sounds like your Katie is on the ball about the centre. And tomorrow morning would be great as long as we don't take too long about it.'

'Now, what about tonight? I'll take you out for a meal then we can go back to your place or mine. Don't feel you have to go out, mind, if you're too tired. I can go and fetch a takeaway.'

'I'm only a bit tired. Let's go to your place.' She was a bit shy of letting Elise and the others see that she was sleeping with Iain, though they must have guessed by now.

Chapter Twenty-Two

Nell was glad to see Emil arrive on time early the next morning because she had a busy day ahead of her. The front door of Number 1 was propped open, presumably to air the place out, because it still smelt of paint, so she and Emil went straight in.

Ginger immediately popped her head out of her flat to see who it was, which was good. 'I'm just grabbing a few things and going out.'

Nell introduced them, then saw Iain's van draw up outside. 'Can I leave you for a few minutes while I speak to someone, Emil? You know your way upstairs, don't you?' She gave him the access number for the new lock on the door of the secret room, which was now more visible.

'Yes. And I love looking at the things there so take as long as you want.'

'I'll come straight back if I see the guy from heritage arrive.' She ran lightly down the stairs and to her relief, Iain was still outside. He gave her one of his broad smiles.

'Hi, Iain. It's all looking great. I just wanted to check how things were going and see if there's anything else you need.'

'No. I'll finish the back later this morning and return tomorrow to start on the front gardens of these two houses. I have to go out and get something first.'

'Great. It's going to look lovely, don't you think?'

'Yes. Just one thing I'm worried about. There's a patch of ground near the wall of Number 6 that doesn't seem happy to grow anything. I wonder if we should get the soil tested?'

'Ah.' She hesitated, then decided he could be trusted. 'That's where the secret passage from the communications room leads into the cellar of Number 6 and the soil isn't as deep there.'

'Oh, I see. Of course, they'd need more than one way of escaping if the communications room was discovered.'

'Yes. The other end of the passages comes out under an electricity substation in the next street. So to answer your question, it's not the soil.'

'That's all right, then. I'll just put in a few annuals, and not bother with shrubs.'

She looked along the street at the area he was talking about. 'It does stand out rather, doesn't it, when the rest of the plants are so lush?'

'It won't look different when I've finished. We could maybe put a little lion's head on the wall, so that the flowers seem to be kept low on purpose.'

'That's a great idea. I probably don't need to tell you, but please don't mention this to anyone, especially that

Brody woman.' She knew he'd had trouble with her too.

'Of course not. Is that stupid female still bothering you as well?'

'Unfortunately, yes.'

'She's been pestering us about another greenhouse I want to put up. She's a pain in the backside, that one.'

When Nell had nipped out, Emil went into the secret communications room and let out a long, happy sigh. He loved coming here. It was wonderful that it had been preserved untouched. No wonder his father was over the moon about being able to set up a little museum here in honour of his father's distinguished war service.

He was almost sorry when Nell came pounding back up the stairs and they discussed how soon the museum could be open.

When they'd finished, he raised the other matter. 'I hope you don't mind, but the regional heritage group have put me in touch with an expert on this sort of thing. He's coming shortly, but couldn't give me an exact time. Dad showed him round a while ago and he wants to check a few details before he finalises his suggestions. Is it all right if I hang around here till he comes?'

'Of course. Look, Angus and I thought you should have a key so that you can get in whenever you need. But you must promise not to give a copy to anyone or to leave anyone alone in here. And you must lock the front door after yourself, even if you're only going upstairs for a few moments.'

He looked surprised so she added, 'The gallery will hold some valuable artwork soon and besides, part of the downstairs is Ginger's home. Even though there's a lock on the door of her flat, we can't be too careful about her safety.'

'It'll be great to have a key and I promise I'll be careful. Pity the café isn't open now, eh, or I could grab a coffee while I wait. And would it be all right if I brought some friends and showed them round upstairs another day? One of them has a little boy who'll love seeing it.'

'With the usual proviso.' She held out the key. 'Anything else you need to know?'

'Not at the moment. Thank you. Dad is getting quite excited about it all. So am I.'

Fraser Jarman arrived a few minutes later and made up for his tardiness by his enthusiasm for the project and the clever plans he had worked out for displaying the many small artefacts in the little museum as if they had only just been put down by those working there.

They went over these in detail, and Fraser asked Emil if he could walk the tunnels again. 'I want to do something special with them. We have to let people see that such places exist so they won't forget how much ordinary people were prepared to do to save their country.'

Emil frowned. 'Last time I spoke to Angus, he told me he didn't want to disturb the other entrances. Well, we can't get to the one near the electricity substation without official permission from the council. Look, I'll phone Nell and see if we can go inside the other passage so that *you* can see the far end under Number 6.'

To his relief Nell answered at once, but she was reluctant for Fraser to open up the connection to Number

6 and definitely didn't want it to show from outside.

'Sorry, Emil, but it's a balancing act between history and intruding on the daily lives of the people who live in Saffron Lane.'

Fraser took over from Emil, insisting gently that the project wouldn't be finished off properly if the visitors being shown round couldn't see at least part of the tunnels too.

'We'll have people staying in Number 6 soon, though,' she said. 'They won't want strangers tramping through their living quarters, interrupting their work.'

'Oh, hell. Can't we come to some compromise about it?'

'I'll have to discuss it with my husband. Perhaps you can put any suggestions you come up with in writing?'

'If we could only get access to the other end of the tunnels,' Fraser said regretfully, then looked thoughtful. 'I can see why people living there wouldn't want strangers popping up into their cellar, or wherever it leads. How about . . .'

'What?'

'A glass barrier of some sort at that end, one that shows the stairs going upwards?'

'Might be possible. As long as the other end is locked.'

'I'll check our records, see if anything similar has been done elsewhere so that I can show you what it'd be like.' He handed the phone back to Emil.

Emil locked up carefully and drove to the office, but everything was fine there so he left the staff to deal with anything that came up. They both seemed very efficient and pleasant to deal with.

He had to finish preparing for his little house-warming

party so he went back to his flat. He was looking forward to seeing Abbie again and hoping that the presence of her sister and the children would make her feel more relaxed.

He felt Abbie was attracted to him. You could usually tell. But she didn't seem prepared to act on it. Had her experiences with Louis' father been so bad that she'd sworn off men completely? Or was he mistaken about the strength of the attraction?

When he got back he sat down for a minute or two and woke an hour later. That was what came of having such comfortable armchairs. He smiled at himself for still taking involuntary naps, something he'd never done in his life before. But they did seem to refresh him. And he was feeling a lot better these days.

Iain drove Ginger to a big barn on the outskirts of the town. 'This place used to be part of a farm, but when the farm was sold and the land built on, the farmer kept a couple of acres with the barn on, hoping for further profit in the future. But this is a small town and the council hasn't allowed a lot of development, so he didn't manage to get planning permission for building houses. And then his daughter got into antiques big time and this place is ideal for that, so he let her have it. She'd trained as a lawyer, so he was rather disappointed.'

'You can't choose for your children once they've grown up,' she said sadly.

'You did your best, I'm sure.'

'Sometimes it's not enough. Anyway, never mind Donny. He's got his chance now and I just pray he won't waste it.'

'He has your good genes. There's bound to be a chance of him sorting himself out.'

She laid her hand lightly on his arm for a moment. 'You always manage to say something positive. I love being with you.'

'That pleasure is mutual.'

She didn't pretend. 'It's happened so quickly.'

'When someone is right for you, you just know.'

She wasn't as sure about that as he was. After all, she'd married Alan, hadn't she? And a lacklustre relationship that had been.

Iain parked the car and escorted her inside a big echoing building where furniture and objects of all sorts were dumped roughly into aisles, with the more expensive items like silver pieces or jewellery in locked glass display cases near the counter. A youngish woman was talking animatedly on the phone and merely gestured them to look round.

'It's all right,' Iain whispered. 'I know where the sort of furniture you're looking for has been dumped. They don't take a lot of care of such stock here, because Ebony wants to be known as an antiques seller, not the owner of a junk shop.' He rolled his eyes to indicate what he thought of that.

'Ebony? That's an unusual name.'

'She was christened Elizabeth and changed the name herself.'

'Ah. Arty type, eh?'

'Tries to be.' He chuckled. 'I can remember her as a tomboy with skinned knees. She used to play with my daughter. A right old pair they were, always into mischief.'

There were various cabinets in one of the far corners

and he stopped talking to say, 'You look here and I'll look over there.' He wandered away, leaving Ginger to study the cabinets intently.

He came back about a quarter of an hour later as she was wondering whether some metal cupboards would do, and whether she could live with their battered external greyness.

'Come and look at what I've found,' he said. 'It's perfect for you.'

He took her to the other rear corner, where a good many huge pieces of furniture were standing close together. 'This is Victorian and Edwardian stuff mostly. Dark-brown furniture is well out of fashion these days unless it's very special. It's this piece I wanted to show you.'

'Oh!' She stared in delight at what must once have been shop fittings, perhaps in a haberdasher's. There were a series of pieces, with lots of drawers of all sizes, cupboards and one section lower than the others, forming a sort of counter. All were made of gleaming mahogany, at least it would have been gleaming if it had been dusted. She took out a tissue and wiped one corner, admiring the beautiful wood.

'I could live with this, but will it fit my room?'

He pulled a measure out of his pocket. 'I reckon it will. Let's see.'

She took the end of the measure and held it while Iain pulled it out as he walked to the other end of the row of pieces.

When they'd finished measuring the various dimensions and noting them down on a rough sketch, he showed her them.

'You're right, Iain. If I pull one piece out, it'll fit. It's perfect for my purpose and it'd look so much nicer than gunmetal grey. Only, it must be expensive.'

He grinned. 'Not if I buy it for my garden centre to put in a shed. I'm good at bargaining. How about you play the disapproving wife who doesn't want the piece at all? Are you a good actress?'

'Iain, you fraud.'

'Shall we play it that way? Could save you a lot of money.'

She nodded and as they walked back to the counter, she got into the mood, saying loudly, 'I'm still not sure, love. It's going to look ever so dark.'

Quarter of an hour later, they carried the first of the pieces that made up the display out to his van.

'Don't let Ebony see how elated you are,' he whispered, 'or I'll never dare come back.'

When it was all loaded into the van, Ginger dragged him round to the other side of the vehicle, where Ebony couldn't see them, and flung her arms round him. 'Thank you, thank you, thank you. I can't believe we got all that for only fifty pounds.'

He spoke like a mock gangster from an old movie. 'Stick around, babe. You ain't seen nothin' yet.'

Chapter Twenty-Three

The next morning, Ginger slipped out of bed early and woke Iain with a mug of tea.

He blinked at her for a few seconds then beamed and sat up, taking the mug. 'I don't insist on five-star service but I must say this is a great way to be woken. Are you coming back to bed with a drink for yourself?'

'No, I can't. That's why I wanted to stay here last night, remember? The shopfitter is coming today and I want to go over my ideas first.' Her voice became diffident as she asked, 'Do you think Nell meant it when she said I could change what she'd talked about with him – the design of the café, I mean?'

'I'm sure she meant it. Do you have some better ideas?'

'Yes. And I think they'll allow the café to work much more efficiently. Come and see.'

'Give me a couple of minutes.' He took a sip of tea and headed for the bathroom, joining her in the shop area clad only in jeans.

She walked up and down, gesturing and explaining, and somehow he could see exactly what she meant and how well it'd work for moving around to serve customers and prepare food. In that sense the two of them had similar skills, he decided, because he too had to manipulate spaces mentally when designing gardens.

'Well?' She looked at him anxiously.

'It's brilliant, absolutely right.'

'You think so?'

'Yes. I can see how well it'd work and it'd certainly make the most of the small space.'

She let out her breath in a big whoosh of relief.

'Have confidence in yourself, love,' he chided. 'You've a lot of skills.'

'But no formal education to prove it.'

'Neither have I. I had to go into the family business when I was sixteen because my father wasn't well. He could tell me what to do and teach me about commercial gardening but he got breathless if he tried to work. The important thing here isn't a piece of paper qualification, but that you've got a good brain and know how to use it.'

He nearly fell over as she flung herself at him, hugging him and kissing him. He was coming to understand how life had battered her and how she had had to fight for every single thing she had. If that son of hers didn't pull himself together, Iain would personally stand between them and protect her from more bullying.

Oh, he was a goner, had been almost as soon as he met Ginger. She was so *right*.

'You know what,' he said suddenly. 'We should get

married. Would you do that – marry me, love?'

She froze and her eyes seemed to go huge as she goggled at him. '*Marry you*? Isn't it, well, a bit soon?'

'Nope. I was sure almost as soon as I met my first wife and we were truly happy together, and I feel just as sure with you, love. I know this is quick, but hey, I'm not a bad bet.'

'You're the most wonderful bet that I've ever met.'

'Is that a yes?'

He saw the fear in her eyes and then it seemed to ebb away and be replaced by a sparkling happiness.

'Yes. Yes, *please*. I'd love to marry you.'

So he had to whirl her round the room, laughing aloud for sheer joy.

When they came to a breathless halt, she looked up at him. 'Could we . . . get engaged first, with a ring and everything? It doesn't need to be an expensive ring, but I never got engaged last time, never had time to relish the situation, or . . . or grow into the relationship. Alan and I just got married, had a drink at the pub with our two witnesses, and then we went home and I cooked tea. We were as poor as church mice. I don't know why church mice are supposed to be so poor, do you? We managed but he was never a good earner.'

'I'd love to get engaged to you, Ginger. We'll go and choose a ring as soon as we can find time. New or antique ring?'

'Antique, please.'

There was a knock on the shop door.

'Oh dear, he's even earlier than planned.' She gave him another quick hug and moved towards the door.

'I'll come back for lunch. I'll go and finish getting dressed. And Ginger, when you talk to him, don't give way unless his ideas are very much better than yours – which I doubt they could be, because he won't have worked in a café.'

She tried to switch to business mode in her head but was still a bit too happy for that to be completely successful. The smile would keep creeping back.

She opened the door. 'Mr Jimson?'

'Um, no. My name's Taylor. I'm from the local council, the planning department. I need to come in and check—'

He was daring to push her backwards. She stiffened, but he was clearly stronger, so she shoved him back good and hard.

His expression suddenly grew angry and she felt afraid of him, so yelled, 'Iain. Help!'

But no one came and there was the sound of water flushing, so when the man grabbed her, she squirmed till she could bring her knee up into a tender part of his anatomy, still yelling for Iain at the top of her voice.

Why hadn't he heard her?

Suddenly the door to her flat crashed open and Iain came running across the shop towards them.

The man had folded up in agony when she kneed him, but hadn't let go of her and didn't seem to have noticed Iain. 'You bitch. You'll pay for that and—'

With a growl of anger, Iain grabbed the man's hand and yanked it away from her shoulder. 'What the hell's going on?'

'This man's trying to push his way inside.'

Taylor stopped shoving at her and stood in a way that protected himself from further attack. 'I could . . . sue you for that,' he gasped out.

'Well, go ahead and sue, because I'm going to report *you* to the police. You thought I was on my own and you could break in, didn't you?' she demanded.

'It wasn't meant like that. I was just . . . eager to see the secret room.'

'Do you have your council ID?' she asked.

'Um . . . yes.'

'Then can I see it?'

He hesitated, then took out an ID card with his photo on it. He tried to cover the name with his thumb but she saw that it was Clarke, not Taylor.

'This is a driving licence not a council ID. And you were giving me the wrong name too, weren't you?'

He took a hasty step backwards as if to leave, but Iain grabbed his arm and swung him round, standing between him and the doorway. 'I can bear witness that you were pushing your way into the shop and manhandling Ms Brunham.' Iain frowned, studying the man. 'I don't recognise you and I've dealt with most of the council officials.'

'I'm new, temporary. Look, please don't tell anyone I was using a false name or I'll never get a job. Only I was told that the person here at this hour was just a cleaning lady who hadn't a clue about the value of the room and didn't like to let people in. They're desperate to check that room out, want to keep it safe.'

'Who are "they"?'

'I don't know. They phoned and asked me to get some photos.'

Iain looked at Ginger, a question in his eyes. She answered it by saying firmly, 'Then you'd better tell the person you're dealing with that I'm in charge of the café and even if I were "just" a cleaning woman, I'd not let an intruder in, whoever he said he was. Let him go, Iain.'

'You sure?'

'Yes. But I'll be reporting this to Nell and Angus.'

Iain stood beside her watching the man get into a shabby little car and drive off, then he turned to Ginger. 'I was terrified when I heard you yelling for help. Are you sure you're all right?'

'Yes. But I'm glad you were here. He really was intending to force his way in and he seemed so confident, as if he enjoyed violence.'

'You did an excellent job of holding him at bay.'

'Yes, but what if you hadn't been here? He was much bigger and stronger than me, wouldn't let go of me even when I hurt him.'

'You're going to need an emergency button or pendant, because I can't be here all day. It's the sort of thing Angus can fit. And I'll make damn sure either I'm here at night or you're over at my place.'

Another car pulled up outside and she sighed. 'Oh dear. I suppose this is the real Mr Jimson. I could have done with a few minutes to pull myself together.' She straightened her shoulders, gave Iain a wry look and said, 'Onwards and upwards.'

'That's my girl.'

He walked back into her flat to finish getting ready for work, filled with admiration for her plucky attitude. What a woman!

He knew where they could buy an engagement ring. He'd come back this afternoon if she was free and take her out to do it.

He liked the idea of their being officially recognised as together even before they got married.

Falling in love with her might have happened quickly, but he was quite sure of his feelings – and just as importantly, of hers.

Mr Jimson came in only at Ginger's invitation and his manner was very different from the other guy's. 'I hope I'm not too early. The traffic was so light today and it seemed silly to sit outside in my car when I could see that someone was up and about.'

He looked outside and frowned. 'I passed someone I recognised driving away from here.'

'I think his name was Clarke. He was trying to push his way in. Do you know him?'

'Yes. He's a bit of a bad egg, hires himself out to bully people, from what my son tells me – my son's in the police in Swindon. Was Clarke trying to bully you? If so, you should report him to the police.'

She turned as Iain came out of the flat. 'Did you hear that, love? Mr Jimson knows that fellow who was pretending to be from the council, says he hires out to bully people.'

'Good thing I was here, then.'

She introduced the two men and Jimson said at once, 'Do call me Dan.'

'And I'm Iain. Ginger and I have just got engaged.'

She was surprised that Iain would announce this to a stranger, but a quick glance showed him looking proudly at her, and her heart gave a happy little skip at that.

'Oh, congratulations! I've been happily married for years and I love to see people falling in love. Well, your affection shines out of you two, if you don't mind me saying so.'

'I don't mind at all,' Ginger said. 'I'm still a bit surprised by it all, though. We've only known one another for a few days.'

'It was just the same with my wife and me. We knew instantly.' He beamed at them.

The warmth of such happy feelings was still lingering when Ginger and Dan got down to business and she felt comfortable enough with him to share her ideas. He listened with what seemed like genuine interest, then walked to and fro, eyes narrowed as if seeing something.

When he turned to Ginger he said, 'Well done! I'd never have thought of that way of arranging the flow of work. You're in the wrong trade, if you ask me, should be working in my area.'

She could feel herself blushing and saw by his grin that he'd noticed.

'I mean it, Ginger. In fact, I'll pay you a fee to look at any problem shops with me.'

Words failed her for a moment. 'I-I'd be happy to do that.'

He held out his hand and they shook on it. Then he started taking measurements, discussing shelving and display cases, and didn't leave until nearly midday.

She locked the gallery door and wandered into her flat, feeling as if she was floating.

When Iain phoned and asked her to come and choose an engagement ring that very afternoon, her emotions overflowed and she was mopping her eyes as she agreed to be ready at two o'clock.

Angus arrived soon afterwards, with some plastic garden furniture in a trailer. He saw the traces of tears on Ginger's face and asked if she was all right.

'I've never been better. I just got engaged.'

His mouth really did fall open. 'Who to?'

'Iain Darling.'

'Good heavens! That was quick. But he's a lovely fellow. You couldn't find a nicer chap to hitch up with. My Nell thinks the world of him.'

Ginger insisted on helping him unload the plastic furniture, which was light and easy to carry, and they set out the front room for the interviews.

When that was done, she told him about the morning's incident and he immediately said he'd fit a panic button. 'And I've got one with a pendant to go with it. I'll set them up tomorrow after the interviews. You must promise to wear it all the time you're here on your own, and to be especially careful till the gallery is up and running, and the other artists are in residence.'

'I suppose so.' She didn't like the idea of it, though. It seemed so – melodramatic. But then she hadn't liked fighting off that oaf, either.

Angus left and she went to get something to eat then prepare for her afternoon's outing. Only it took longer than usual, because she kept stopping to smile and stare down at her left hand, which had been bare of rings for a few years.

Who would have thought her visit to Saffron Lane would lead to this?

Who would have thought her life could become so interesting?

When Angus got home he went to find Nell, who was stealing an hour to work on her beloved garden, which was in itself a historically listed feature of Dennings.

'Guess what?'

She sat back on her heels. 'What?'

He explained about the would-be intruder. 'My guess is he was hired by that Brody woman.'

'We'd have difficulty proving it.'

'I'm beginning to think she's mentally ill. Why is she making such a fuss about our activities, for heaven's sake?'

'To show off, perhaps, in order to prove she can do the job permanently?'

'Well, I doubt she's convincing anyone. I heard a whisper that someone else was the front runner to get the job.'

'Where did you hear that?'

He touched the side of his nose and gave her a sly smile. 'From a friend. He ran into her in town and she brought up the subject of Dennings. He said she ranted on and became rather incoherent. Ah, never mind her. She has no real power over what we do here.' He looked round, changing the subject. 'You're making good progress.'

'Iain lends me a hand now and then. He loves this garden too. Though at this rate, by the time we get it all cleared, the part we started with will need doing again.

It's a never-ending task.' She gave the garden a fond smile.

'Good thing you love doing it, then. Everything ready for tomorrow's interviews?'

'Yes. You'd better go and read through the summaries. They're on my desk.'

'OK. Still only the same four people?'

'Yes.' She waved one dirty hand at him. 'Go on! Do it! And I don't care who calls you with a job. You can't take anything on till after the interviews.'

He turned, then remembered the news. 'Oh, and by the way, Ginger and Iain just got engaged.'

She gaped at him. '*What*? But they've only just met.'

'Yes, but it's great news, isn't it?'

'The best. I like to see people happy. Why didn't you tell me about it first? That's much more important than the interviews.'

'I forgot.'

'Men!'

'Yes, my lady!' He gave her a mock bow and walked back into the house. He'd go through the applications, and then prepare a panic button system for Ginger. He had enough small components on hand to do that.

When Iain arrived to pick Ginger up that afternoon, he was dressed more smartly than she had ever seen him before.

He turned round in a circle, gesturing to himself. 'Will I do?'

'You scrub up very nicely.'

'You've Katie to thank for that. When I told her about us and where we were going this afternoon, she wouldn't let me come out on such an important errand "dressed like a scarecrow" to quote her exact words. Oh, and I'm to take you round to her place for drinks in a day or two so that you can get better acquainted.'

'She's not annoyed about you marrying someone else?'

'No, love. Not my Katie. And in case you're wondering, nor would my wife have been. We always told one another if anything happened, the other was free to marry again. Only it's not so easy to find someone. You and she would have got on well, I know it.'

Oh, how she envied him his loving daughter! And his wife sounded to have been a lovely woman. Could she live up to Mary? Would he feel she was second best?

He squeezed her hand. 'You're different. I'm not comparing you with her, except in niceness, if there is such a thing.'

'Oh, Iain.'

Ginger's family was just Donny now and she wished she knew how he was going on.

She banished that sad thought resolutely but of course Iain had caught her mood.

'We can only hope your Donny will come good,' he said gently.

She brought his hand to her cheek for a moment and they stood smiling at one another for a moment or two before they set off.

She carried the warmth of that moment in her heart as they drove to the shops. She hadn't smiled so much for years.

* * *

Half an hour later they found the ring, a beautiful sapphire set in a circle of tiny diamonds. Ginger fell in love with it on the spot and it fitted perfectly. Then she caught sight of the price and took it off hastily. 'Too fancy for me.'

Iain slipped it back on her finger. 'You're trying to save me money, but don't. This is too important and I can afford it.'

She stared down at the ring. 'Oh, Iain, I don't know what to say.'

'Say that you love it and will wear it always, even if you have to put it on a chain round your neck when you're working.'

'I love it and I'll wear it always. But I love you most of all.'

He took her back to his house and opened a bottle of champagne with a flourish, after which they didn't answer the phone but spent the evening together, making love then making plans for the future.

Chapter Twenty-Four

Emil decided that his flat was now as tidy as he could get it so invited the sisters to come and help him celebrate that evening. He set out the nibblies, hoping the crisps, grapes and cheese would tempt children and adults alike. He had prosecco chilling in the fridge and now had time, he hoped, for a few minutes' rest before they came.

He was more tired than he'd expected to be after all the exertions of settling into the small town. It was taking him longer to recover fully than he'd hoped – taking as long as the doctors had told him, in fact. He should have listened to them about pacing himself, but he hadn't wanted to upset his family and he still didn't want anyone to know about his medical problems. As far as the rest of the world was concerned, it was a ruptured appendix that had caused his trouble.

He managed ten minutes of fidgeting around in an armchair before the doorbell rang. Relieved, he hurried to open it. 'Keziah! How lovely to see you.' He smiled down at the child. 'Hello.'

'This is Susie. Say hello to Mr Kinnaird, darling.'

But the little girl clung obstinately to her mother's leg and wouldn't even raise her eyes to him.

'Just ignore her and she'll come round. We haven't been to a lot of social events involving other grown-ups. Abbie will be up in a minute. Louis delayed her.' She looked round. 'Your flat is exactly the same layout as my place, isn't it? Well, it's on top of mine, so it would be. Abbie's is a mirror image. But you get the views.'

'Didn't either of you two want to claim those?'

'We wanted to be together. The other tenant on the top side has been there for years and she's quite elderly, doesn't want to move, so we left her.' She shuddered. 'As for me taking an upper flat, not with this young demon to keep an eye on. Susie's into everything and they have no sense of self-preservation at that age. I'd worry myself sick about having a balcony. The door to it is locked now, isn't it?'

He hurried across and turned the key, then took it out and slipped it into his pocket for extra security. 'It is now. That hadn't even occurred to me.' He indicated the bowl of crisps. 'Am I allowed to offer her one and a drink of lemonade?'

'Yes. You make the offer. That might tempt her out of the shyness.'

He bent down. 'Susie, would you like a drink of lemonade? And a crisp?' He held out the bowl.

The child hesitated, looked at her mother for permission, then took a crisp and said, 'Nemonade?' hopefully.

'Just half-full,' Keziah said hastily. 'And you haven't said thank you, Susie.'

'Fank you.'

He put the glass on the plastic box he was using as a side table temporarily. The doorbell rang just then and he said apologetically, 'I'll get your drink in a minute, Keziah.'

'That's all right.'

He opened the door and Abbie was there, looking flustered with a sulky little boy standing behind her.

'Sorry we're late. Louis wanted to finish arranging his possessions in his new room.'

'I'm here if you need help with anything.'

'Thank you, but I'm sure I'll manage. I usually do.'

She always tried to be so independent. Did she never accept anyone's help? He looked at her son. 'Would you like a glass of lemonade, Louis? And there are some crisps and other nibblies. Help yourself.'

But Louis' attention had been caught by two of Emil's favourite tinplate toys, something he'd been collecting for years and had now got out of storage. One was a 1930s car, complete with driver. The other was a World War I soldier who shouldered his rifle and marched up and down when wound up. He came to a standstill, his rifle back in its original position by his side, the butt on the ground.

The lad was across the room in a minute, staring at them in delight.

Emil smiled. 'I'll show you how to wind them up later, Louis, but first, I must get your lemonade and a drink for your mother and aunt. Prosecco all right, ladies?'

'Yes, please. That'd be lovely.'

The conversation limped on for a few moments. Louis drank his lemonade and ate a few crisps, but continued to eye the tinplate toys longingly.

'Let me show you how to get them working, Louis.'

Abbie looked at him anxiously. 'Perhaps you shouldn't do that.'

'They were made for children to play with and that's what I like to see.' Emil went across and lifted the toys down. As he demonstrated how they worked, he kept a wary eye on the little girl in case she tried to grab them. She was just that bit too young to trust. But at her mother's command she sat obediently down on the floor and watched them perform, clapping her hands in glee.

'She's very well behaved about touching them,' Emil commented.

'She's no angel, but I've had to teach her not to grab things that don't belong to her,' Keziah said. 'My father was rather fussy about her touching his possessions.'

'Louis didn't have many things to touch, the flat was so small,' Abbie said. 'We're still getting used to having all the space. What about you, Emil? Did you grow up in a big house?'

'Well, we did have a largish detached house. My parents still live there. But I've been living quite rough at times in Australia. It's a great country.'

'Why did you come back? Didn't you consider settling there? So many people do these days.'

'I did think about it, but England is still home and my father needed me.'

'You're going to manage and expand the Wiltshire branch of his company, I gather?'

'That's the idea.' He shrugged. 'It's a job.'

'What would you do with your life if you had a free choice?' Abbie asked.

'I don't know. That's the trouble. I started off playing soccer, rather well but not top flight. Then I went overseas to play for a club in Sydney. When I got injured, that career was off the table, so I wandered away to see the country, then came back here. Who knows where I'll end up? In the meantime Dad needs help.'

He hoped he sounded convincing. His prognosis was good. But you never knew, so he wasn't making long-term plans yet.

He caught Abbie looking at him as if she'd guessed he wasn't telling the whole story, so he asked about her plans instead.

Her wary expression softened. 'Thanks to Dad's money I can take my time to find something. But I'd never want to be idle. I love history, may study it for my own pleasure. I've given up the job I was doing, though. They didn't treat their lowly staff members gently.'

And that's when it occurred to him. 'You wouldn't like a part-time job in my father's museum when it opens, would you? We're looking for someone to show people round, preferably someone who loves history.'

She leant forward as if eager to hear more, so he told her about the secret room and the small museum his father wanted to open in his own father's memory.

'I'd love to see it.'

'I'll take you round, if you like. What about you, Keziah? Are you interested in history?'

'Not as much as Abbie, though I would like to see a secret room. I'm still trying to sort my life out. I'll let you know when I think I'm getting there.'

When they left, he lay down on the bed. He'd enjoyed having guests, but he'd just have a little rest before he finished clearing up.

He woke around midnight, not knowing where he was for a moment or two, then visited the bathroom and went back to bed, still feeling drowsy.

When he woke again, it was morning and he'd had the most restful sleep in ages. Usually he tossed and turned, waking two or three times during the night.

He smiled as he remembered Louis' bright alert face as he was allowed to examine the vintage toys, and the fond way Abbie watched her son.

Then something occurred to him about the picture in his mind. That's what he really wanted. A family! Would his health allow him time to acquire and enjoy one?

Did Abbie want the same things he did?

She was certainly a good mother.

He had to get to know her better, break down those barriers in her head.

Chapter Twenty-Five

Late on Friday morning, Winifred walked down to Saffron Lane from her home on Peppercorn Street carrying the cupcakes carefully in a tin.

When she opened it in the gallery, she smiled happily when Ginger oohed and aahed over them.

'I like decorating cakes. I've saved a broken one for you to try.'

Ginger nibbled it and rolled her eyes in bliss. 'This is wonderful. Now, how much do I owe you?'

'Just the cost of the ingredients.'

'No, Winifred. Double the cost of the ingredients plus the cost of cooking, and that's what I'll pay you.'

'I can't ask you to do that!'

'You didn't ask me. But I do have an ulterior motive. I want to be able to order more supplies from you. If it's not too much work?'

'I'm happy to bake for you a couple of times a week.'

'And since you don't drive, I'll pick them up from you.'

Winifred suddenly realised what the ring on her companion's left hand meant and touched it gently. 'Is that what I think it is?'

Ginger could feel herself blushing. 'Yes. An engagement ring.'

'Iain?'

'Does everyone know about us?'

'Everyone connected with Dennings and the top end of Peppercorn Street, perhaps. We're a gossipy lot and we knew you were seeing him. Just as they all know about me calling Janey a relative. We're more like a small village than part of a town.'

'That's nice. I like being part of it. Now, let me drive you back. I'm nipping into town to do a bit of shopping.'

Winifred hesitated. 'Well. All right. If you could let me pick up my library books from home on the way, I'd be most grateful. I'll get a taxi back. I usually do that, walk down the hill, ride back up it.'

It only took a few minutes to help Winifred and get back, because Ginger didn't really have any shopping to do. She set out the cakes on the surface of a display plate with a cover. This was one of the treasured items she'd left in the storage unit, because it was one of the few things her mother had left her. She set out the plain white plates Nell had brought down from the big house and filled the kettle.

When all was ready she decided to spend a little time sewing. She was in the middle of a rather nice figure of a young child.

She looked round and sighed happily. Much as she loved Iain, she didn't want to rush into marriage, needed some time to live peacefully on her own first and 'get her balance', as she thought of it. That'd give her a better foundation for settling into her new life – or so it felt to her at the moment.

She needed to shake off the shadow of several bleak years, and there was the ongoing worry about Donny.

And Iain, bless him, understood that. Oh, she was so lucky to have met him!

Nell and Angus came down to Number 1 together and admired the way Ginger had set out the shop space for the interviews, then she went back into her flat till refreshments were needed.

Stacy joined them almost immediately and the three of them discussed what they hoped for from the applicants.

'No formal questions,' Nell said firmly. 'We want to follow their lead and find out what they're really like.'

The first candidate arrived early, a cheerful young man with a twinkle in his eye: the cartoonist.

Nell took to Rashid at once, because he had such a lovely smile.

He seemed completely at ease as he answered their questions, adding information and confessing that he'd been in trouble a lot at school because of his irreverence and ability to see humour in most situations.

'It suits me to be a cartoonist, but I want to do some bigger cartoon pictures as well, a bit like Heath

Robinson's only covering the vagaries of today's society and technology.'

Stacy beamed at him. 'I love Heath Robinson. I have some books of his cartoons. I do steam punk gadgets myself sometimes.'

'I'd love to see them.'

On Nell's signal, they took Rashid for a quick tour of the houses at the end of Saffron Lane while Ginger made a pot of tea.

When they came back, they fed him one of the cupcakes and he ate it hungrily. Nell only poured half-cups of tea for the panel or they'd be awash by the end of the morning.

After they'd explained the potential living arrangements, Rashid shrugged. 'I don't mind sharing the smaller house, if I get a residency. I enjoy company. In fact, I don't think I'd work as well if I were living on my own.'

After he'd gone, Angus said at once. 'He'd be great.'

Nell and Stacy agreed unconditionally.

By mid afternoon, they'd interviewed the three others.

One was a woman who made soft toys, such cute little creatures Nell immediately wanted to buy one. In the nicest possible way, Debbie was just like her toys, small and plump, with a perky face.

The third person was a weaver, who'd need space for his loom and was less outgoing than the first two candidates, though pleasant and positive. He seemed another very acceptable person for a residency.

It came out in the interview that he volunteered at a local care home for people with Alzheimer's and when Nell asked about it, he flushed and said his grandmother had had it and he liked to make the old people happy. 'I sing a bit but I don't like to perform in public except at the home. I just enjoy singing. Anyone I shared a house with wouldn't have to mind, because I don't even know I'm singing half the time when I'm on my own.'

The fourth person was a man who made costume jewellery and he too needed space for his various bits of apparatus. He was older than the others, nearly sixty and had turned a hobby into an income for his retirement. He made a point of telling them that he was gay, not in a challenging way just as an aside. But he looked at them very carefully as he said it, Nell thought.

'That's none of our business,' she said at once. 'It's your art that matters to us here.'

His face cleared, he gave her a little nod and let the matter drop. He pulled out an example of a new venture, making small items that were a cross between jewellery and ornaments.

When he showed a sample to them, Nell immediately reached out to touch it and set the small dangling 'jewels' quivering.

'That's just the effect I want,' he said. 'Make people want to touch it and enjoy the glitter. Bling with a heart.'

When the fourth interview was over, they discussed the candidates, but it didn't take long.

'Any problems that you see?' Nell asked the other two.

'No. They're all good as far as I'm concerned,' Angus said.

'I agree. And I want one of those little toys to stand on my windowsill. Aren't they cute?'

'The only thing to decide is who gets which accommodation.' Nell looked from one to the other. 'Though even there, it seems obvious that the weaver and jeweller are the ones who particularly need more space.'

'We're good to go, then,' Angus said. 'Do you agree, Stacy?'

'Definitely.'

'I'll contact them,' Nell said. 'If only the first group of applicants had been as easy. We were all right with you and Elise, Stacy, but we made a mistake with Cutler. While I think of it, any more trouble with him, Stacy?'

She hesitated.

'Go on.'

'I don't know whether you noticed but the plants we put outside our houses are dying, all four of them.'

They went out to look at them and exchanged angry glances.

'That's not natural,' Nell said. 'One might die – it happens – but not all four equally.'

'Smell them,' Stacy said.

Angus picked one up. 'Bleach.'

They all looked towards Number 4 then went back into Number 1.

'He was watching us again,' Stacy said. 'He seems to think we can't see him if he stands at the back of the room, but we can either see him or his shadow.'

'Damn the man!' Angus said. 'I doubt we can prove

anything, but I'm going to reinstate the CCTV cameras. We didn't think you'd want to feel spied on, Stacy, but I think we need to keep an eye on things.'

'Wait till he goes out to do it,' Stacy said. 'I can phone you when the coast is clear. He does go shopping now and then, but doesn't leave the street otherwise. He seems to want to live completely alone.'

They stood there thoughtfully for a moment, and she added, 'I'll tell Elise you agree with us about the vandalism, if you like, and warn her about the CCTV. She'll be glad about having that, I'm sure, because she's furious about him killing her plants.'

'She hasn't accused him openly?'

'She was going to, but I persuaded her not to because I think this is only a small sample of how nasty he could get.'

Nell was startled. 'Do you feel unsafe?'

'Let's say I'll feel better when the newcomers move in.'

'Well then, we'll get everything going as quickly as possible, including finishing off and opening the café.' Her face took on a determined look. 'I'm a demon when I want something to happen.'

Nell wanted the shopfitters to start work on both the café and the art gallery the very next week and thanks to a job cancellation and her offer to pay as much overtime as needed, the owner was able to oblige her.

Though the gallery didn't need a lot of fixtures, Nell felt they needed some flexible shelving that could be erected, changed or removed at will. It was a big, light room and always felt welcoming to her.

She discussed this with Ginger, who took her to the antiques shop Iain had shown her. The shop fittings they'd seen were still languishing at the back and contained a couple of screens, the sort characters used to change behind on the stage and which Ginger promised to brighten up.

When they got back she walked up and down the gallery, then suggested using narrow protruding columns on the long wall, ones which only jutted out about thirty centimetres, to which shelves or screens could be attached. 'If we used mirror tiles on them, they'd enhance the exhibits.'

Nell stared at her in surprise. 'You're brilliant at this sort of thing, Ginger.'

'Oh. Well. I've always changed houses and places inside my head because I could never afford to do it for real. I can often see how to improve places. I used to do it while I was doing boring jobs in cafés which were set out inefficiently.'

'You're a real treasure. I'm so glad we found you a niche here.'

'She's sucking up to you,' a voice exclaimed. '*Just – sucking – up*! Her ideas won't work. Can't you see that?'

They turned in shock to see Cutler standing in the doorway glaring at them.

How long had he been there eavesdropping? Nell wondered. And why?

He didn't wait for her response. 'It'd be better to discuss the needs of people who will require shelving for their exhibits. You should deal with the artists not the café attendant who hasn't an original idea in her head.'

He strode forward suddenly, bumping into Ginger as he passed and knocking her to one side. He said, 'Oh, sorry!' but didn't even look at her. 'What you need here, Nell, is a wall across the back, to separate the overflow art from the eatery, if you must have a café, and—'

Nell didn't intend to stand and be harangued. 'This building isn't open to the public yet, Mr Cutler, so I'm afraid I must ask you to leave. Nor have I asked for your opinion about the design.'

His jaw dropped in shock at this direct command. 'But I need to tell you about what I—'

'You don't need to tell me anything. This is my project and you're a temporary participant only in our artists' group, so I'll finish it my way.' She walked towards the door, gestured at it with one hand and waited for him to leave.

With a dirty look at Ginger that somehow managed to threaten future retribution, he walked slowly out of the building.

Nell shut the door and locked it, then went across to Ginger. 'Is that man mentally unbalanced, do you think? He always acts so abruptly. I don't think he knows the meaning of polite.'

'I think he has a personality disorder.'

'He makes me feel uncomfortable just to be in the same room with him. And the way he went out so slowly was the act of a sulky child, not an adult.'

'I agree.'

'Look, Ginger, I don't care how hot it gets, will you

please keep all the doors locked when you're on your own?'

'I can't always do that. There will be men working here soon doing the fitting out. But I'll be very careful, I promise you.'

Chapter Twenty-Six

Emil had arranged to take Abbie, her sister and the children to see the secret room the following Sunday. When he went to pick her up, he found that Keziah couldn't come because little Susie was running a temperature and Louis had gone to play at his friend's house for the afternoon.

'We can go another time, if you prefer it,' Abbie said in her usual abrupt manner.

'Why wait? It's you who's truly interested in history, you I'd be offering a job to. It'll probably be better with just the two of us the first time. We won't be boring other people with what we consider to be interesting historical information, which they might not care about. And I can take the time to answer your questions about what my father is planning as fully as you wish.'

'Oh. Right. I must say, I'd been looking forward to seeing it. I'll have to pick Louis up at four-thirty, though.'

'Where is he?'

'Just outside the town. His friend's parents are taking them to a lake which has recently had a children's play area created at one end and there's a little bay that's very shallow. There are barriers between the play area and the deeper water, and they have someone on duty to keep everything safe at weekends. They charge an entrance fee but it's very reasonable and my Louis loves it there.'

He could hear how her voice softened when she spoke of her son. She was a strange mixture of affection and stiffness. 'I'll drive you to see the secret room and then we'll go and pick up Louis. No need for us to trail to and fro when we're partway to the lake at Saffron Lane.'

She studied her feet carefully. 'Um . . . all right.'

Once again, he wondered whether it was him she was cautious of or whether it was men in general. And he didn't know why he found her so interesting, but every now and then, like when they talked about history, she seemed to come alive and almost sparkle with intelligence. That was so attractive, lighting up her whole face.

On the way to Saffron Lane he told her that the tenant of the flat below the hidden room had had a little trouble from someone, so he'd have to lock the door of the art gallery carefully behind them.

'I'd prefer that, anyway.'

He nodded and waited for her to say why but she didn't. She was, as usual, sparing with both words and information.

As he was letting them in, a man hurried along the street, one of the artists, if Emil remembered correctly.

'Don't lock it! I need to get in.'

Emil frowned. 'Don't you have a key of your own?'

'I left it upstairs and saw you going in so didn't bother to get it.'

The door at the far end of the big space opened suddenly and Ginger came through from the café area.

'Is it all right if I let this—' Emil began, but when he turned the artist had gone.

'Was Cutler trying to get in?' she asked.

'Yes. If that's his name.'

'Don't let him in. He's not—' She broke off and didn't finish what she'd started to say. 'Um . . . I mean, if Nell had wanted him to be able to get in and out, she'd have given him a key.'

'He's creepy,' Abbie said suddenly. 'I'd not want him prowling around on his own in our building.'

Emil realised he hadn't introduced them and did so, then locked the front door and took Abbie up to the first floor, where he showed her how to get into the hidden communications room.

She lost her inhibitions almost at once and followed him around, asking questions, even explaining a couple of items she recognised and he didn't. She looked vibrant and alive.

'Is it me?' he asked suddenly, unable to bear it any longer.

'What?'

'Is it being with me that makes you go stiff and uncommunicative? You've been a different person up here.'

'Oh.' She hesitated, and looked down at the display. 'It's not you. It's – I don't want to get involved with a man again, so I keep my distance. Keziah says it's a bad habit and I've got stuck in a rut, just because my partner was difficult. She may be right, but it's helped keep me going for the past eight years.'

'What did he do? Hurt you?'

'No. Well, not physically. But he was unfaithful and when I got pregnant by mistake, he hated being a father, being tied to a "brat", as he called Louis. And then he left one day while I was out, taking some of my things with him, and I haven't been able to trace him to get them back, let alone get maintenance out of him. I was told he's gone somewhere in the EU, Spain or wherever. They're welcome to him. Only it's been . . . hard going – financially, I mean. I don't miss him.'

'Didn't your father help you?'

'Yes. But I wouldn't take more than the bare minimum from him. I'd vowed not to be dependent on anyone ever again, you see. And then we quarrelled, because my father kept letting Louis down, promising to attend something like a sports day, then not turning up.'

'I see. That must have been hard for the lad.'

'Yes. But at least I'd never married Louis' father, so I've not had the hassles of getting a divorce. Have you ever been married?'

'No. I've been in relationships that lasted a while, but I've never wanted to settle down until now. I think I've got the wanderlust out of my system and I'm really enjoying being back in England. What I want more than anything now is a proper home of my own. I'll start looking at houses to buy next year, when I've got a little more time.'

Silence fell and it was a more comfortable one as they moved on round the exhibits.

'It must be this place,' he said suddenly.

She didn't pretend not to understand. 'Us talking like this, you mean?'

'Yes.'

'I don't usually confide in people.'

'Nor do I. But I'd like to make a few friends now I'm back.'

She looked at him warily.

He held up his hands in a surrender gesture. 'Is that too much to ask? I like you. I like your son and he even seems to share my interest in tin toys. Most people stare at me as if I'm mad, a grown man collecting them.'

'I don't see why you shouldn't collect anything you can afford. You're not doing any harm. We haven't had enough money to collect anything for the past few years, or space to put it in, but we might be able to now.'

'The prospect of being financially independent must take a lot of the strain off you.'

She smiled at him, really smiled. 'Yes. And I'd like to be friends with you, but only friends. Let's be clear about that from the start. Not friends "with benefits", as they call it these days.'

'I'm recovering from an operation. I'm not in a highly active mode sexually yet.' He pretended to twirl an imaginary moustache. 'So you're safe from me, my proud beauty.'

She ignored his joke, frowning at him. 'I thought I saw you wince once or twice when you were crawling around showing Louis how the toys worked.'

She waited but when he didn't volunteer any more information, she turned back to the displays.

He stole a glance at her. Should he have told her? No. He didn't even want to think about the problem himself, let alone face other people bringing it into a conversation.

Before they had to leave to pick up Louis, Emil took her down the secret staircase and into the tunnels, which she seemed to enjoy in her usual quiet way. It was nice to be with a woman who didn't go in for idle gossip.

'I don't suppose you'd show Louis round here sometime?' she asked as they came out of the house and he locked the door.

'I'd be happy to.'

'Thank you. He'll be thrilled, and I'd like to come again too, if you don't mind. This place fascinates me.'

'Then you'll consider taking a job here?'

She nodded. 'It might be interesting. Only part-time, though. I need to be there for Louis after school. I think I'd enjoy it. I'm normal enough to need and enjoy some contact with other people, even if I don't want . . . more.'

'I couldn't just stay at home on my own, either.'

He kept it to himself, but this afternoon had gone well enough to give him hope that one day he might pursue more than a mere friendship with her. The better he got to know her, the more he liked her quiet steadiness, as well as finding her physically attractive. He'd been thinking seriously about marriage recently, even before he met Abbie. He didn't want to marry a 'show pony' of a woman who needed attention, clothes and possessions to be happy. He wanted a friend, lover, soulmate.

Could he find that sort of relationship with Abbie? He was thinking it might be worth giving it a try.

Was he tilting at the moon, expecting women to fall into his arms?

Abbie's ex seemed to have made her mistrust men. Would she continue to refuse to consider any long-term relationship? That would be such a waste.

Chapter Twenty-Seven

When the shopfitters started work, the whole building was filled with the buzzing of saws and the whirring of drills. The noise echoed round the empty rooms and through the nearby flat, too, and nearly drove Ginger mad.

At first she kept the front door of her flat closed and looked out regularly to keep an eye on things, strolling past the storeroom that divided the area so that she could see the gallery at the front properly. Then she noticed a man peering into the window.

When she looked out a few minutes later, he was still there and had edged right into the shop. What was he doing? The place was clearly not open for business.

He didn't notice her watching him till she went out and accosted him.

'Can I help you?'

He shook his head. 'Just watching them work. I'm

thinking of hiring that company to do a job for me. You pleased with them?'

'They haven't finished yet.'

'I'd better come back another day, then.' He walked out quickly, got into a little van and drove off.

Automatically she memorised the registration number and noted it down when she went back into her flat. You couldn't be too careful with strangers who loitered for no obvious reason.

After that she stayed in the gallery, taking out a chair, sitting to one side and doing some patchwork while the men worked.

The van came back but drove away again, presumably because the driver had seen her. So she was right to keep watch. Hmm. She arranged for Stacy to come and sit in there while she nipped to the shops the second afternoon. She was running out of tea and instant coffee. Those fitters were always thirsty.

The three people working on the shop and café fittings seemed a pleasant trio but she'd seen Cutler talking to one of them a couple of times when he went out into the back garden, and was wondering why.

In the end curiosity got the better of her. 'Did my neighbour want something?' she asked the young guy.

'He wanted to know how long we'd be. Said the noise was disturbing him.'

'He said that both times?'

The guy shrugged. 'No. The second time he wanted a piece of wood we'd thrown away. I didn't see any harm. He says he's a woodcarver.'

'He is.' But Nell said Cutler was very particular about the type of wood he used. Throwaway pieces of pine didn't sound right for him.

Ginger didn't know why him poking his nose in worried her, but it did. And if she was being paranoid, too bad. That young fitter could have given away a lot during even a short chat. Cutler was cunning enough to wangle information without the person realising it.

Well, he still didn't have a key and Nell had told him very firmly to stay out of Number 1, so Ginger would have to rely on that and keep her eyes open where he was concerned. She couldn't trust him. Not one bit.

When the shopfitters finished after three days of hard work, Ginger walked round the gallery and café, really pleased with how well they had done things.

She swept up more carefully than they had and gave the floor a quick mopping over before Nell came to check.

The rear part was starting to look like a café now. It'd look even better the next day, because the various electrical gadgets were supposed to be delivered.

After they were installed, she'd be able to set out the furniture, stock the café with crockery and food basics, and open for business.

She was looking forward to that, nearly always enjoyed her interactions with customers.

Iain was as busy as ever during the daytime, but he slept at Ginger's flat every night except for the one where he was going to visit an old uncle who lived down in Cornwall. It was too far to do the journey there and back in one day, and besides, his uncle loved to be taken out to a restaurant and treated to whatever he fancied on his birthday.

The trouble was, on the night Iain wasn't there, Ginger was sure she heard someone prowling round outside the house and when the security lights that overlooked the rear garden suddenly came on, it proved she hadn't been mistaken.

She peered out of her bedroom window, but couldn't see anyone and after the lights had switched themselves off, she waited, watching. Nothing else triggered them so she told herself she was worrying about nothing. She had the CCTV system and its allied alarms, neighbours close at hand and Angus could be down from the big house in minutes.

It couldn't have been an animal going past, could it? No, of course not. How would an animal big enough to do that get into the back gardens, which were fully fenced?

After that she slept only fitfully. There had been someone prowling round, she was sure, but who could it have been? Not Cutler this time. She'd seen a light in his workshop when she'd looked out, and his shadow as he sat working on a carving. He couldn't be in two places at once, so the prowler couldn't possibly have been him.

Who else was interested in the Saffron Lane development, though? Or was it the little museum and its contents they were targeting? No, that didn't seem right, either. The things in the secret room might be of interest to a museum, but Nell said Mr Kinnaird had told her they wouldn't be worth a lot on the open market, were worth more *in situ*, bringing history to life for a new generation.

It was a relief when dawn brightened the sky. It was

strange how much safer one felt in daylight, and yet a friend of Ginger's in Newcastle had been mugged in broad daylight.

Never mind. Iain would be back that night and she'd catch up on her sleep then. She smiled. She was surprised at how much she'd missed him.

It was nice being engaged, but she didn't seem to need the thinking time she'd asked for. Should she suggest setting a wedding date? It'd be nice to have something to look forward to. Or should she leave that to him?

And they hadn't really talked about where they would live when they did get married. She loved this job and was looking forward to setting up the café and running it properly. But though the flat was too small for a permanent home, it'd be harder to run things if she was living elsewhere.

Was anything in life ever straightforward?

Well, she wasn't going to make even minor decisions about anything important now. You didn't think nearly as clearly when you were tired.

Someone knocked on the front door of Number 1 soon after dawn. Ginger nipped out of her flat and peered through the door next to the storeroom. She saw Angus standing outside and waved. He waved back and unlocked the front door to let himself in.

How thoughtful of him not to walk in and startle her. She pulled her dressing gown belt tight and asked, 'Is everything all right?'

'I'd like to check the security system, if you don't mind. It came on once or twice during the night, but when I checked the monitors I couldn't see anyone. After a couple of alerts, nothing more happened, and I didn't realise till this morning that someone had disabled the system.'

She gaped at him, feeling a chill run up and down her spine. And she'd been relying on it to keep her safe! 'I'd be glad if you did sort it out! Something, or rather someone disturbed me as well.'

'Right-ho.' Angus took a ladder out of his little van and fiddled around with the cameras.

When he got down, he was looking grim. 'Someone knew exactly what to do to disable a standard CCTV system. I just want to check something.'

He walked round the side of the house and then across to the shrubbery between it and the boundary wall of the grounds of the big house.

She went to scramble into some clothes, then went to watch what he was doing.

He returned, still frowning. 'I shall make some modifications to upgrade the CCTV system today and program in a few little tricks of my own. The intruder has been trampling round the house and poking something down into the soil at the side of the house where the secret passage connects your house to the cellars, as well as further along where it leaves my land. I suppose they were testing to see where the roof of the passage is, but how did they know the passage leaves my grounds at exactly that spot?'

'Who knows? Why would they do it, Angus? What benefit can an underground passage be to a burglar, for heaven's sake?'

'All I can think of is that it's a fanatic who wants to get hold of some WWII equipment by fair means or foul, a collector. You do get the odd one who'll break the law to get something. Well, they're not going to get into *my* houses or damage *my* property. I'll make sure of that.'

He took out his smartphone and began fiddling around, ready to do some shopping online. After a few moments and more fiddling, he clicked his tongue in annoyance. 'I can't get hold of a couple of the essential parts till tomorrow. I'll have to come and sleep down here till then. I'm not leaving you in danger.'

'Iain will be back tonight, so he'll be here to keep watch on me as well as the museum. I'll press the alarm button if the intruder comes back, even if he doesn't trigger the alarm system.'

'Whoever it is seems well prepared. Must be pretty determined.' Angus stood frowning, then said, 'I'll have a word with Iain, if you could get him to phone me when he arrives.'

'Yes, all right.' Ginger had a sudden thought. 'Perhaps you should let Emil Kinnaird know what's going on as well? The more people we have keeping an eye on things, the better, surely? He comes here regularly.'

'Good idea. I'll contact him. You're sure you'll be all right till tonight, Ginger?'

'Of course I will. There will be people delivering stuff all day and I don't need to go out. Besides, one of the other artists is usually around, and I think even Cutler would come to my aid if he saw someone trying to murder me.'

Or would he? No, of course he would.

'You can't be sure who these people delivering goods are.'

'If they come in an unmarked van, I'll ask for ID.' She was a bit annoyed at herself for letting what had happened spook her.

'All right. But don't hesitate to sound the alarm. I'll make one little modification and reinstate the standard systems before I leave. They won't know what I've done to it and it'll look as if it's still disabled.'

The day was as busy as she'd expected, with people coming and going, delivering various electrical goods and supplies for the café. All were, of course, in vans with signs and names on them.

Ginger was thrilled at how good the café was looking but worried that she couldn't keep an eye on everyone who came into the shop for every single minute they were there, because the phone would ring and of course she had her own personal needs. And the storeroom made it difficult to keep everything in view, even though she left the door between the two areas open.

She saw Cutler saunter along the back of the houses and peer in. Let him peer! He wasn't coming in till the café was open and there were other people around to help her if he became awkward.

He had a face like one of his nasty sculptures, she decided, after staring out at him for a while. Malicious was the word that came to mind.

He noticed her suddenly and scowled. You'd think he hated her. What reason could he have for that? Or perhaps he just hated the whole world.

Iain rang in the middle of the afternoon to say he'd be

back around eight o'clock and would come straight to her place, if she didn't mind.

'I'll have a meal waiting for you,' she said at once, beaming at her phone.

'Good. I love your cooking. It's as honest as you are and as wholesome.'

'That's a strange sort of compliment.'

He chuckled. 'I took my uncle to a fancy restaurant last night and who knew what they'd put into the various dishes? My uncle loved all the fussing, but the portions were tiny so I came away still feeling unsatisfied. As for the sauces, they were such little dabs that you could hardly taste them.'

After the call ended, she checked her fridge and freezer, planning what to make for him, only she'd need to go out and buy a few things. She'd have to see if Elise or Stacy could keep an eye on things while she was gone.

Then she realised there was no noise from the shop and hurried outside, just in time to see the last delivery van pull away.

Of course, then she had to go upstairs to check the upper room and make sure no one had slipped in. But it was empty. Mr Kinnaird was going to put displays up here and run tours of the secret room and passages every hour or so, by which time the gallery downstairs would have plenty of items for sale.

At least that was the general plan.

When she'd gone downstairs again, the man hidden in the secret room smiled to himself, then went down the narrow stairway that led to the tunnels and along the one that connected with the electricity substation.

Piece of cake, he thought with a smile. And lady luck on his side for once. What amused him most of all was that he wasn't breaking any law by coming here, but was acting on the orders of someone with the official right to do this. Money for old rope.

He set about opening the padlocks on the metal grille that barred the way from the tunnel on Denning's land to the part passing under land belonging to the council and substation.

Idiots who had no idea how to make things secure must have set this barrier up. They were relying on the law-abiding folk not to damage things set up to keep them out.

Pity there weren't valuable items stored in the secret room or he might have been able to pinch one or two. He still couldn't work out what the person paying him wanted to break in for. Oh well, money was money and he was being paid generously to do this little job.

He found the door on the other side of the padlocked grille unlocked, as promised. So he opened it and slipped through, closing the padlocks on the metal grille to look as if they were locked, and making sure he hadn't left any footprints in the soft earth nearby.

The doors in the electrical substation were all unlocked too, as promised

First stage completed.

First payment due.

Easy-peasy.

*   *   *

It being a weekday, Emil brought Abbie and Louis to see the secret room and the tunnels after school ended.

The boy was fascinated, spending a long time looking at the various displays and asking a series of intelligent questions. Amazing questions for one his age, Emil thought, enjoying sharing his knowledge with the lad.

After that he took the two of them down the narrow staircase into the tunnels, stopping at the exit linked to Number 6, then, at Louis' pleading, going along the tunnel in the other direction, to where the grille prevented visitors to the museum from trying to get to the very end.

'There are footprints along the edge here,' Louis commented as he shone his torch around on the way back.

'I daresay we'll have left footprints too,' Abbie said.

'These are right at the edge and they don't seem to be from heavy boots like the others. Have a look, Mr Kinnaird.'

Emil did so and was puzzled by what he saw. These footprints seemed to have been made by ordinary shoes, not boots or trainers, and recently too, because they were fresh and undisturbed. 'It must have been someone Mr or Mrs Denning were showing round. I doubt it was anyone working on the tunnels.'

But Louis still frowned. 'There aren't any others like them and they're on top of all the other footprints.'

Emil and Abbie stared down at where the beam from the boy's torch was pointing.

'He's right,' Emil said. 'Easy to solve the mystery. I'll ask the Dennings who's been down here lately. Come on. We'll go back now. I'm going to buy us all ice creams.'

'You'll spoil his tea,' Abbie protested.

'From what I've seen, he could eat for Britain. It just means eating the dessert before the main course.'

Louis nodded vigorously and Emil's remark brought one of those rare, sweet smiles to Abbie's face. 'Oh, why not? I'm rather fond of ice creams too.'

'I'll get Dad to talk to you both about the museum he's planning next time he comes to visit. He knows so much more than I do. And I've got some books if you want to read more about the era.'

'Good.'

'I'll bring them down from my flat after tea. Some of them have a lot of pictorial information and I think Louis would find them interesting.'

'Thanks.'

But later, as he left them and went upstairs to his own flat, Emil couldn't help wondering about the footprints. Next time he saw Angus he was definitely going to ask who had been in the tunnels.

He got his chance an hour later, when Angus rang and told him about the prowler and the damage to the CCTV.

'I don't like the sound of that,' Emil said. 'Ginger could be very vulnerable in that flat if thieves have targeted the secret room and found a way to get through to it. I think we should call the police in.'

'Let's give it a day or two, see if they return. Iain will be staying with Ginger tonight, so she'll be OK, and my new components are supposed to arrive tomorrow, after which it'll be a lot harder for them to get into Number 1, I can assure you.'

'What about the footprints in the tunnel?'

'We'll have to keep our eyes open. It's probably someone from the council, because they have the key to that end of the tunnels. Maybe that Brody woman is sneaking around. I'll make sure she can't get into the houses, though.'

'She sounds weird.'

'She is. Which is why she's never got a promotion, apparently. No one likes her, but unless she seriously misbehaves, they can't get rid of her. See you soon.'

Chapter Twenty-Eight

Iain arrived back early, swinging Ginger round in his arms before she could say a word and then kissing her soundly. 'Traffic was a dream, for once.'

'Good. I can get tea ready in a few minutes if you're hungry because I made a casserole in my trusty crockpot this morning.' The gadget was well used, one of her favourite ways of cooking when she was facing a busy day, and also providing extra portions to put in her freezer.

'Let's have a drink first while I unwind. Wine or beer? I brought both.'

'Wine, please.'

He began opening the bottle. 'My uncle sends his congratulations and is very pleased that I've found someone. I've promised we'll FaceTime him in a day or two so that I can introduce you. I'll have to phone first to check that he's got his tablet switched on, though. He's like me, prefers real people to images.'

He poured two glasses of wine then fumbled in his pocket. 'Nearly forgot. He sent this, says it's a little engagement present for you to buy something for the house.'

The envelope had her name scrawled on it in shaky handwriting and when she opened it she found a voucher for so much money she could only gasp and look at Iain in shock. 'It's too much.'

'He's not short of a few pennies. I'll take you down to meet him next time I go. He's eighty-six and doing very well for his age.'

'He'll be the second of your relatives I'll be meeting. I wish—' She didn't finish her sentence and when he gave her hand a squeeze she knew he understood she was thinking of her son. For all the good that did.

After a couple more sips, he said, 'I'd better warn you now: there will be plenty more meetings with my relatives. I've got all sorts of cousins scattered around the south-west and we keep in touch.'

He set his glass down and took hold of her hand again, such a loving look on his face that she was sure her heart really did skip a few beats.

'How long do you want to be engaged for, Ginger? I'll wait till you're ready to marry, of course I will, but for me, the sooner we're properly together the better. I shall be proud to call you my wife.'

Tears of joy welled in her eyes. 'We'd better decide on a date and do the deed, then, though let's have a quiet wedding, eh, not a big fuss?' She was glad he'd brought it up first.

'Good girl. I don't care *how* we get married as long as we do the deed.' He raised his glass at her and winked, then kissed away a happy tear that had escaped her control.

After the meal, he said, 'Look, I'll bring more plants tomorrow evening, two for each house, to replace those that have been killed, even for Cutler's house. That'll flummox him, because if it's me doing it, he won't be sure whether it's at Angus's bidding or not.'

'That'd be great.'

'But I don't at all like the idea of someone prowling around when I'm away. Will you please promise me you'll go and sleep at my house if I have to stay overnight anywhere in future?'

She nodded. When you didn't know what you were facing, it was better to play safe. But it upset her that this had blown up just as she was settling in.

'And if you don't mind, we'll sleep at my house tomorrow night, because I want to show you a few things and discuss any changes you might like to make.'

'What things?'

He grinned. 'Wait and see.'

The outside lights came on suddenly around one o'clock in the morning and Iain woke as the light shone through the window into his eyes. He sat up in bed, glad he'd drawn the curtains back in case this happened as well as annoyed at being disturbed.

'Oh, hell. Can't a man have one night in peace?' he muttered.

He didn't switch the bedroom light on but looked out of the window and scanned the back garden. Nothing to be seen.

He slipped through into the shop and keeping to one side, stared out of the window at the front of the houses. There was a figure edging past. Surely it was . . . yes, Cutler. What was he doing out at this hour? Was he the prowler?

Iain watched as their neighbour moved past. He waited as the scrawny little weasel stood watching something. He looked in that direction too. Was it his imagination or could he see another figure in the shadows of the little grove at the end of the street?

No, it wasn't his imagination. There was definitely a figure there, moving away now, slipping from one dark shadow to another, but in places moonlight fell on some part of his body so it was possible to tell he was there, moving. Well, Iain assumed it was a fellow, but you couldn't tell for sure at that distance.

He waited till there were no more signs of the figure. Whoever it was must have left now.

As Cutler came back, Iain moved even deeper into the shadows at the side of the big room.

'Who was it?' Ginger whispered from behind him.

'That was Cutler, but I saw another fellow too. Cutler seemed to be watching him.'

'Were they together?'

'I didn't see them together or even signalling to one another. I don't think the one in the distance knew he was being followed.'

'Let's go back to bed. I don't know if I can get to sleep, though.'

But she did, cuddled in his arms.

In the morning someone knocked on the front door of the gallery and Iain went to answer it.

'Cutler, isn't it?'

'Yes. I thought I saw movement near the end house. Did you see the security lights go on last night?'

'Yes. And I saw you creeping down the street.'

'That's because there was a prowler. Fine caretaker Ginger is. She should have been on to that.'

'She isn't the caretaker, as you've been told before, and I don't like your tone. If you speak about my future wife like that again in my hearing, I'll take great offence.' He raised one clenched fist and slapped it into his other hand for emphasis, letting that unspoken threat sink in before continuing, 'But since I was here, I came out of the flat to see what was going on. All I saw was you creeping around, then going back into your house, and another figure in the distance.'

'The other figure was the prowler. I happen to live here. And if *she* has no responsibility for this sort of thing, I'm calling Denning about it. He should have better security set up for us than this. The carvings I produce are valuable.'

'Why didn't you call Angus last night?'

'The prowler went away. I stayed up to check, but he didn't come back.' Cutler's scowl deepened. 'Have you moved in with her permanently? Does Denning know? I thought this place was for artists, not gardeners!'

Without waiting for an answer he went back inside his house.

Nasty little oik, Iain thought, using his old uncle's favourite word for a person he disliked and distrusted.

He'd make sure Ginger spent tonight with him at his house. She'd looked tired yesterday and now she'd had another broken night. It wouldn't do. He'd tell Angus himself that she needed a rest and someone else should be found to keep watch on Saffron Lane, if he felt it was needed.

In fact, he'd do it straight away.

Angus answered the phone and listened to what Iain said. He agreed to look into it and try to do something about the problem permanently.

When the call was over, Angus was about to explain what had happened to Nell but another call came in. This time it was Cutler, telling him the same thing as Iain in a much less polite way, and complaining about the lack of security, as if he expected his every wish to be granted.

Angus had heard people refer to this as 'the entitled generation'. He wasn't sure he agreed for everyone, but the description certainly fitted Cutler.

After he'd tried to reassure the fellow and failed, Cutler put the phone down with a bang. Damn him! Could he not even be polite?

After a few moments' thought, Angus decided to discuss the situation with Emil, because he could only think it must be something about the secret room that was attracting attention. What else could it be? He phoned him to explain what had happened, invited Kinnaird to drop in for a coffee to discuss what they could do, and went to warn Nell that a visitor was on the way.

It took Emil only ten minutes to get there. He frowned when Angus explained in more detail about the prowler. 'We can't have that. Apart from anything else, I'd hate to see anything happen to Ginger. I really like her.'

'We do, too,' Nell said. 'So what are we going to do about this? Set a trap?'

Emil said at once, 'Well, we can't let this person continue to upset her. We or the police do have to catch him at it.'

'And the police are not going to waste officers on the mere possibility of such a minor incident,' Nell said.

'Exactly.' Angus eyed Emil in an assessing way. 'You look as if you could stand up for yourself in a fight.'

'Ah. Well, I could before I had this health problem and I will be able to again. But at the moment—'

Emil saw them looking puzzled and knew he couldn't hide his reasons if he was to retain their respect. 'I'm just recovering from major surgery.' It was hard to say the word, because he didn't like telling people, but he forced it out. 'Cancer. They think they caught it all, but I have to take things a bit easy physically for a few months.'

'Then of course we won't involve you in anything dangerous. I'll ask Iain to keep watch with me. He's a strong fellow and he'll want to make sure Ginger is safe.'

'I could help with the watching, at least. I could occupy Ginger's flat, if she doesn't mind, and keep watch at the back while you watch the front.' Emil nodded decisively. 'Yes, I could at least do that.'

'And you're not leaving me out of this, Angus Denning,' Nell put in.

'Look, love—'

'I mean it.'

He gave her a quick hug. 'OK. I'll contact Iain and ask him to come round for a chat, see if he'd like to be involved. I'm not having whoever it is upsetting my tenants.'

That afternoon Ginger worked hard with Nell to finish setting out and stocking the café. There were still some things to buy, but they were getting there.

She had been going to raise the matter of the prowler with Nell, but they got engrossed in what they were doing and what other supplies they'd need to think about, so she didn't get round to it.

Nell had originally suggested using interesting old chairs and tables for the café, but Ginger had managed to persuade her that they'd be too hard for staff to lug around. Thank goodness for that. It seemed obvious to her that they might want to use this space for gallery overflow when serving refreshments at events, or even for small groups to meet. This was another reason for having modern light furniture they could stack easily. And they could also use the chairs for audience seating at talks in the gallery.

'You were right about the furnishings,' Nell said studying the room. 'You certainly know your stuff about cafés. These chairs and tables are easy to move and they look good.'

Ginger tried not to smile smugly but knew she'd failed. 'Matching furniture always looks better, believe me.'

'Did Iain tell you he's meeting me here this afternoon to measure up and give me a quote for installing a patio with roof?'

'Yes, he did mention it.' He'd also told Ginger to pack an overnight bag so that he could take her back to his place afterwards. For once he hadn't asked, he'd insisted, said he was worried about her safety and wanted to get a good night's sleep.

Nell went to stroll up and down in the back garden, studying the corner formed by the L-shape of Number 1. 'He doesn't think it'll be all that expensive to do a simple patio roof and it'll certainly add to our seating area. Even in winter, some people like to sit outside. I can just imagine how it'll look.'

She hesitated as they studied the café, then the outside area. 'What do you think about allowing smoking out here?'

Ginger was comfortable enough with Nell to say, 'Oh, please, no! Apart from it being a hazard to people's health, it makes for a lot of clearing up and the smell lingers, whatever you do, which upsets the non-smokers. I think the stink it leaves behind would affect my flat, too, and it'd waft into the gallery and affect the soft toys and embroideries.'

'I never thought of that. I should have done, but we've

been busy and anyway, you know so much more about cafés than I do, I've been happy to leave some things to you. Um . . . has Angus spoken to you about tonight yet? He was going to phone.'

'No. Is something wrong?'

'He wants to set a trap for the prowler, and wondered if you'd let Emil keep watch from your flat. And he's going to ask Iain to join him in the nearby grounds.'

'Of course Emil can use my flat to keep watch, but why do they need Iain's help? There was only one prowler.'

'We have to keep Emil out of things, in case there's any fighting and—' She broke off as Iain came into the café to join them.

'What's that about fighting?' he asked at once.

'Hasn't Angus spoken to you yet?'

'No. He phoned and I've arranged to nip up to see him once I've finished here. He didn't say exactly what he wanted.'

'Well, don't tell anyone but Angus wants to try to catch the prowler, only Emil is recovering from an operation and he hasn't got to do anything strenuous, let alone get into fights. So Angus needs backup from someone else.'

Iain said at once, 'I'm happy to help catch the prowler. I don't like someone upsetting my Ginger.'

The two women exchanged long-suffering glances. 'And you want to keep us both out of it because we're such delicate blossoms?' Ginger asked with an edge to her voice.

'Are you any good in a fight, love?'

'Not exactly, but—'

'No buts, lass.' He looked at Nell. 'Ginger here is a slip of a thing, and you're not a power figure, either.'

'I suppose you're right. But how about we both camp out at the big house tonight?' Nell suggested. 'Then we can feed our heroes after they've caught the prowler. OK with you, Ginger?'

'Fine by me.'

They left Iain to measure up outside and Nell said in a low voice, 'What's the betting no one turns up tonight down here?'

'They have done the last two nights.'

'But they didn't try to break in, did they? I bet you five pounds they won't even turn up.'

'I don't normally gamble money, but I will bet you a box of chocolates on it.'

'You're on. Mind you, Angus will be disappointed if nothing happens, but I hope it doesn't because I don't want him risking himself. There's such a possessive streak in him about Dennings, talk about being prepared to defend his own. Anyway, it's settled. You and I will have a girls' night up at the big house.'

She frowned then added, 'How about we invite Elise and Stacy as well? That'll get them out of the way in case things turn nasty.'

'Great idea. They're good company, anyway.'

'The men are going to get in place before dark.'

'They could be seen going there if it's still light.'

'No. Angus says they'll use the tunnel entrance at Number 6 to get in. It leads to Number 1 via the secret room. He unlocked the door to the tunnel today.'

'It's like something in a crime novel. I can't believe it's happening. Surely it's just vandals?'

'I hope so. Angus is very angry underneath it all at someone daring to target his houses for any reason. Heaven help them if they do turn up. He says he'll make sure they don't want to try it again.'

'He can get a very determined look on his face.'

'Oh my, yes! Anyway, we'll be ready to tend any wounded *if* something does happen.'

'You've had experience of tending the wounded?' Ginger asked with a grin.

'After raising three sons? What do you think? My three got into scraps at the drop of a hat, especially when they were in their mid teens. Talk about needing to prove their manhood.'

'I only have one son and he's been in a few scraps in his time so I've had some practice, but probably not as much as you.'

She'd give Iain a good talking-to, though, about not asking for trouble and calling in the police if trouble turned up. She was glad he'd have Angus with him.

And Emil, too, and since *he* had to be careful, surely he'd be a calming influence?

When she'd first come to Saffron Lane, she'd expected it to be so peaceful here. But now, who could tell what was going to happen? All she knew was that she'd made friends with people who stood by one another, and it felt so very different to face things with such support.

* * *

The man kept watch on the houses from behind a fallen tree near the gate to the Denning estate. He didn't intend to take any risks about this.

There was a car parked outside Number 1. He'd seen Mrs Denning get out and go into the gallery earlier. By using his binoculars he'd managed to catch glimpses through the connecting doorway of the two women setting things out in the back room, then walking all round the place, gesturing. So her presence didn't seem anything to worry about, just normal work on the new café.

When he saw the van arrive, however, he stiffened. If that gardener fellow was going to stay the night with the woman who lived in the flat, things could become a little more difficult.

Mrs Denning came out and drove away. Good. One down.

Now what about the gardener and the woman who lived there?

But to his relief, when they came out some time later, the woman was carrying what looked like an overnight bag. As he watched them get into the van and drive off, he thumped his fist down on the soft earth in triumph. Yeah! That was one problem solved.

He'd continue to keep watch, though, to make sure no one came back to Number 1. And he'd keep an eye on the occupants of the other houses in the street, as well. The two female artists seemed to be early to bed types, but the guy at Number 4 could be a problem. The stupid fellow was up working at all hours of the day and night, or at least he had been the past two nights.

As afternoon turned into evening, the two women

came out of the other houses. They seemed to be going out together because they both got into the younger one's car and she drove off. Women didn't usually stay out all that late, so it'd probably be better to do the job before they got back, or at least get in position ready to go for it.

He took out his phone and let the person who'd hired him know they were going to start earlier than planned.

'Come and meet me in about an hour,' he suggested.

'Wouldn't it be better to do this after it's fully dark?'

'No, it damned well wouldn't. They're all out now, except for that little twerp who carves wooden animals, and if necessary, I'll deal with him.' And he was fed up of lying here behind the fallen tree trunk, not to mention damp and stiff.

'Ah. Well, remember, I don't want anyone hurt.'

'I know. You've said that several times already. I do understand English. Now, are we going to do the job or not?'

'Um . . . yes. I must have that information.'

'Then don't forget to bring some cash. I want payment in advance and we're not talking about bank transfers here.'

'I won't forget.'

'See that you get here without being noticed. Pretend you're using your phone as you walk, wear a scruffy hat and keep your head down.'

'No need to repeat yourself. You already suggested that.'

'I'll be waiting for you where we agreed in an hour, then. Remember to stop and check that there's no one around before you go into that area.'

'Yeah, yeah!'

'Get back to me if you see anything – anything at all – to suggest you're being followed or observed.'

He scowled as he switched his phone to vibrate. He hated working with amateurs!

Chapter Twenty-Nine

Angus, Emil and Iain met at the big house, drove round to the other side of the small estate and parked there. Angus knew a way into the back gardens of the two end houses.

'I found out about this hidden gate from my uncle's diaries,' he said, brandishing a big old key.

'I found it too, when I was clearing the undergrowth,' Iain said. 'I was going to mention it, but something came up.'

Angus led the way round the edge of the garden, hurrying across the final open stretch with the house key at the ready. Once they were inside Number 6, he couldn't resist teasing Iain. 'Not "something", it was Ginger who came up and everything else went out of the window.'

'Yes. I've been lucky. Meeting her and getting on so well has lit up my life. We're going to plan our wedding after this bit of trouble is over. And you're both invited, of course.'

Emil listened to him with a sudden rush of envy. Both of his companions had met women they not only loved but seemed to be best friends with. Would Abbie gradually soften her attitude to men and let him court her? He could only hope. He had never met anyone who interested him as she did.

There was another thing about it: if he could make no further headway with her, he'd lose the excuse to enjoy young Louis' company as well. He enjoyed being around small children but you had to be so careful how you interacted with them these days. He didn't want his feelings to be misconstrued, so normally kept his distance. He didn't want to be seen as the sort of person to prey on young children.

Finally, there was his cancer – his *ex*-cancer, he hoped. Would it be fair to court anyone now, knowing it could come back? You couldn't help wondering about that in your darker moments, even after being given the all-clear.

He realised Iain was looking at him as if waiting for an answer. 'Sorry. My thoughts strayed for a few moments.'

'You've just been invited to his wedding,' Angus said. 'Say yes, for heaven's sake. I think he wants the whole world to come.'

Iain flushed slightly and shrugged.

'I'd love to come,' Emil said.

'Right. That's settled. Now let's get another thing straight while I've got your full attention. Emil!' Angus gave him a stern look. 'If there's any fighting, you're not to join in, not under any circumstances.'

'Only in the direst necessity,' Emil corrected.

'Hmm. Well, we'll do our best to make sure that doesn't happen. If we're outnumbered by these people, we'll call the police, barricade ourselves into the flat and wait for them to arrive. Now, let's go into Number 6 and I'll show you how to get into the tunnels. I oiled the lock and tested it earlier because that entrance isn't often used, so it's perfect for our purposes today.'

'What if they've found a way into the tunnels, as well?' Iain asked.

'They'll find it difficult to get into them from the other end, because the council erected a metal grille across the other entrance with a heavy-duty lock on it, to keep people out.'

'Any questions? No? Then we'll start and try to move really quietly from now on.' He led them down into the cellar, using a keyhole that was well hidden to unlock a hidden door. When they were through, he whispered, 'There's a similar keyhole on this side.' He pointed to it and locked the door again.

'They went to a lot of trouble with these emergency resources,' Emil murmured admiringly. 'It was most definitely an all-out war, you understand that so much more clearly when you see places like this tucked under ordinary streets. And there are all sorts of tunnels and emergency centres under London. Amazing.'

They followed him along the tunnel, each having provided himself with a torch.

It was the strangest feeling, Emil thought, to know that you were walking underneath Saffron Lane. He shone his torch upwards for a few seconds and saw curving corrugated iron, only a bit rusty in parts.

When Angus stopped moving, Emil followed suit.

'We go inside and up those narrow stairs I showed you last time, Emil. It'll be better to access the house from up there. Be ready to switch off your torches when I tell you. We don't want even a flicker of light showing to any watcher. We'll wait for a few moments before we move out of the secret room to give our eyes time to adjust to the dimness. Count to 100 for that.'

Angus unlocked another door and they moved through into the cellar below Number 1, then climbed up the steep, narrow stairs that were little more than a ladder.

When Angus switched his torch off, the others followed suit.

Emil recognised exactly where he was now. He looked round the room, feeling as if ghostly figures might come and sit at the desks to send messages across the country. What must it have been like?

Once their eyes had adjusted, the door into the house was opened and they made their way down the normal stairs to the gallery area on the ground floor.

When Angus touched his shoulder and gestured towards the rear of the building, Emil went into Ginger's flat. His eyes were accustomed to the semi-darkness now. Was there any such thing as complete darkness in a modern house, anyway, with little green or red lights on gadgets winking here and there? Even the secret room had them now.

He sat down on an armchair, but it was too comfortable and he could see himself dozing off, so chose an upright dining chair instead. It seemed bizarre to be sitting in someone's house in darkness waiting for who knew what.

Maybe nothing would happen. That'd be a disappointment after all their efforts.

Time seemed to pass very slowly. Every now and then he got up and walked round the open plan living area and kitchen, checking the time by the clocks on kitchen equipment. He moved into the bedroom, then came back, taking great care not to go near to the window.

Let's face it, this is boring, he thought as he sat down. He'd be glad when something happened. He hated hanging around.

Cutler put the finishing touches to a new carving of a nobbly old man and stood back, pleased with what he'd done. He went to stand by the window that looked out on to the back gardens. No lights shone from the two female artists' houses. That just showed how dedicated they were, going out socialising instead of working every minute they could.

He looked round the room, then decided to get a breath of fresh air before having his evening meal. It'd clear his brain. He felt tired and muddy-minded now that he'd finished another carving. There was always this let-down period when one was completed.

He opened the door and felt a gentle breeze on his face. Ah, that felt good. He hadn't wanted to stop to eat at teatime, but now he was hungry for both fresh air and food, in that order.

Letting himself out, he strolled along the street and into the little wood. Then he stopped in shock, because two people wearing hoodies were standing with heads close together as if talking. He hadn't heard a sound, but he saw one give the other something small enough to be slipped into a pocket.

He jerked back behind a big bush and to his relief they didn't shout or show any sign of having noticed him.

But as he was turning to creep back to his house, someone grabbed him from behind, someone very strong, who covered his mouth when he opened it to yell for help.

When the hand was removed the second person stuffed something into his mouth before he could make a noise and fastened it there. The larger assailant yanked his hands behind him, and tied them there.

Terrified, Cutler tried to kick out but they swept his feet from under him and as he was lying on the ground, they tied his feet together.

Then the large chap slung him over his shoulder, doing it so easily, Cutler's fear increased. They could murder him and he'd be utterly helpless to stop them now.

Who were they? What were they going to do with him?

From inside the gallery, Angus and Iain saw the whole thing, but stayed where they were, pressed back against the wall.

'Hell, that prowler chap's quick off the mark!' Angus muttered. 'Should we try to rescue Cutler?'

'Let's see what they do first,' Iain said. 'I doubt they're intending to kill him.'

'I'll tell Emil what's happened.' Angus was gone before Iain could say anything, so he continued to watch the two people. He expected them to move towards the houses and leave Cutler lying helpless on the ground while they carried on with whatever they'd planned, at which point he'd have tried to rescue the poor fool.

But they didn't do that. Instead, the bigger guy slung Cutler's bound body over his shoulder and led the way back out into the street that ran from behind the estate.

Angus returned and whispered, 'I've told Emil and he's going to keep watch from the gallery now. What the hell is going on?'

'Damned if I know. Should we follow them?'

'I'll do that. You come as far as the gateway, Iain. Stand there and come after me if I yell for help.'

'Is this wise? Shouldn't we just call the police? It's gone beyond burglary now. And I think we should try to rescue Cutler.'

'Emil will call the police if he thinks we can't handle this. I intend to find out what these two are after and make sure this is the last time they ever trespass on my property.'

Even at a whisper his voice sounded furiously angry.

He set off without waiting for further agreement and Iain shrugged and followed him outside.

Nell and the other women were having a pleasant get-together at the big house. She'd bumped into Abbie at the shops, and on impulse had invited her to join them. She liked Abbie and her sister, and the two of them seemed to need a few friends. She'd also heard the way Emil talked about Abbie and guessed he was smitten.

The gathering went well, with lots of laughter at first, then they grew quieter.

'I hope they're all right,' Ginger said suddenly. 'I don't

like the thought of Iain tangling with whoever's prowling around. I can't bear to think of him getting hurt and—don't laugh at me, but I've had one of my feelings about this.'

'I've got an uneasy feeling too,' Abbie said.

'I'm going to creep down to Saffron Lane and check that everything's OK,' Ginger told Nell. 'I have an uneasy feeling about tonight.'

Her hostess frowned at her. 'We told the men we'd stay out of it.'

'No, *they* told us to stay out of it and we put up with it. You did that because you didn't really think anything was going to happen and I—well, I didn't realise how much I'd worry about Iain's safety.'

The others stared at her so doubtfully, she added, 'Anyway, if I move quietly, the men won't know I've been to check on them, will they? It'll only take me a few minutes.'

Nell stood up. 'I'll come with you.' She looked at the others. 'Will you stay here?'

'We three will stand just inside the front door and if anything happens, you must yell at the top of your voices and we'll call the police,' Elise said.

'Sounds carry well at night,' Stacy said.

'I don't think the men are taking much of a risk, but still, better safe than sorry, so one of you should have a phone ready as well, in case there really is a prowler,' Elise added. 'There are three men there, so they should be able to protect themselves, but there may be several people trying to burgle Number 1. Not so much for the contents of the secret room, but perhaps for the brand-new equipment in the café, which cost quite a bit.'

'I never thought of that,' Ginger exclaimed. 'I was thinking the historical things might be valuable. Ooh, I'm definitely going to go and check things out now you've put the idea into my head. No one's going to burgle my café before it's even open.'

'We'll go together, then. But just in case there's someone around, we'll be quiet and you should wear something dark, Ginger.'

'I'll wait partway down the slope,' Abbie said abruptly.

Nell lent Ginger a navy jacket and headscarf, and the three women set off from the big house via the front door, leaving Elise and Stacy standing just inside the doorway, with no lights on in the hall.

The women moved very carefully along the softer ground at the verges, not talking.

'You stay here,' Nell told Abbie. 'We'll have a laugh about this afterwards. I'm sure they'll be all right.'

Iain will think I'm mad, Ginger decided as she and Nell continued. But her feeling of him being in danger was too strong to be ignored. Once, when she stumbled, Nell reached out to steady her.

They stopped before they got to the small wood between Saffron Lane and the entrance to the grounds, just in time to see Cutler come out of his house. He began stretching and easing his shoulders, then stopped abruptly just inside the wood.

When two figures who'd been out of sight from the drive pounced on him, Ginger clutched her companion's arm in dismay.

Nell leant close to her and whispered, 'Don't move yet.

We're not strong enough to stop them, so all we can do is see what they do.'

'Where are our men?' Ginger whispered back.

'Probably waiting to take action.' She kept one hand on Ginger's as it lay on her arm. There was a comfort to its warmth.

She couldn't believe this was happening. She'd been so wrong to find all this amusing. If anything happened to Angus, she didn't know what she'd do.

She just hoped Abbie would stay back, hoped Angus would be all right.

Chapter Thirty

Even though Cutler was very slight in build and his captor big and muscular, the man carrying him was panting by the time they'd gone the short distance along the street to the electrical substation.

I'm out of condition, he thought in disgust, *getting slack. Have to pull my socks up.*

His companion said nothing, just walked along beside him wearing the permanent scowl that was getting on his nerves. From time to time a quick glance would be thrown in his direction from a face showing pale against the darkness. But the scowl never lightened.

'Get the bloody door open, then,' he growled as they reached the entrance. He dumped Cutler on the ground in the outer room of the electrical substation and kicked him in annoyance.

Bending down he said slowly and clearly, 'If you ever mention what's happened tonight to anyone or attempt to identify us, I'll come back and kill you, if it's the last thing I ever do. I know who you are and if you become famous, I shall expect to take my share . . . in return for sparing your life tonight.'

He watched with satisfaction as the bound man cringed away as far as he could, then he glanced towards his accomplice, who was still fiddling with the door. 'Nod if you understand what I just told you.'

The bound figure nodded vigorously just as the heavy door swung open.

The man picked Cutler up and carried him inside, amused by his terrified reaction. As if he'd ever bother to chase after anyone like this wimp! Revenge didn't pay well and it was money he liked most in the world. People let you down; money sat in the bank ready to serve you when and where you pleased.

Once again he dumped Cutler on the ground with more force than was necessary. 'We'll leave him there for the time being.'

'What if he gets away?'

'Do you think he's suddenly going to turn into Harry Houdini? He won't get out of those ropes, believe me. I know what I'm doing.' Good thing he'd brought them, too. It had been a last-minute precaution based on this contractor's ignorance about breaking and entering, plus worries that they might run into some nosey parker – which they had done.

With a nudge he added, 'But if you're keen to take him along, you're welcome to carry him yourself.'

'I couldn't manage it.'

'Then shut up and leave me to handle that side of things. Got your camera?'

'Yes, of course. It's the whole point of this exercise.'

'Well, it's doing no good in your pocket. Get it out and ready. And remember, do *not* film my face, because if you do, I'll come back and make *you* sorry as well as him.'

'I'm not stupid.'

'I think this whole venture is stupid, but you're paying me well, so I'll go along with it. Now, lock this outside door.'

'It's not supposed to be locked when people are working inside.'

He rolled his eyes. 'Give me strength! You're worried about occ. health and safety rules when we're breaking and entering? You *are* crazy.'

There was silence for a moment, then he said thoughtfully, 'Probably better to leave that door unlocked, though. No one will be able to see whether it's locked or unlocked, and I doubt anyone will try it. If we have to make a run for it, we can get out of here more quickly and no one's likely to be exploring in the middle of the night. But remember, if we *do* have to escape quickly, you'll be on your own. I'm not your babysitter. Now, give me the keys so that you can get on with the filming.'

'It's this one that opens the inner door and that one for the metal grille.'

He took the small bunch of keys, holding it by the one he needed to use first, checking that his balaclava was in place and his back mostly to the camera, then switching on a powerful torch to light what he was doing.

He waited but nothing happened. 'Start the damned filming.'

'It's going.'

The inner door was stiff and it took him a minute or two to open it. 'Needs oiling,' he commented and ran lightly down the curved metal staircase to the grille.

At the bottom he waited till the camera was again at the ready, then walked along the corridor to the grille and opened that, propping it open for convenience in case they had to escape by scraping up a pile of earth from the tunnel floor with the heel of his heavy boot. This was too easy. Money for old rope.

He waited again. 'Still filming?'

'Yes.'

'You were right about one thing: this is a pitiful attempt at security.'

'I know. I'll find that very helpful when I use this material to get what I want. OK. I'll stop filming now till we get somewhere significant.'

It took some time for his companion to fiddle with the controls before a nod told him the camera was switched off. Amateurs! Didn't even have the wit to practise beforehand.

He began tramping along the underground tunnel, letting his companion go first and light the way. He wished he were out in the open air. These damned tunnels gave him the shivers.

It felt as if someone was right behind him, but when he glanced over his shoulder there was no sign of anyone else. Had he heard something? He listened carefully. No, no sound. Probably just his imagination.

They didn't have a long way to go, he'd been told, but it felt a long way to him.

Angus listened carefully but heard nothing moving inside, so crept into the substation, surprised that the intruders had left the outer door open. He fell over something soft, no some*one* soft, and flashed his torch down. Cutler. It would be.

Oh, hell, he couldn't leave the fellow lying here. He got out his penknife and began slicing at the ropes. It was surprising how often this little knife came in useful.

The minute his hand was free, Cutler tugged at the gag, but Angus grabbed his hand and said in a low voice, 'If you make one sound, I'll gag and bind you again.'

Cutler stiffened and seemed to be trying to see who it was.

'It's me. Angus.'

Cutler kept silent as Angus finished cutting the bonds and yanked him to his feet.

He whimpered then, as if something hurt.

'Shh! Do you want them to hear you?' He gave Cutler a shove. 'Get going while you can – and quietly. Knock on the door of the nearest house and ask the people there to call the police. *Hurry*!'

Cutler stumbled out of the substation and of course the fool moved noisily.

Grunting in annoyance, Angus turned to study the gaping inner doorway. Should he follow them or not? Releasing Cutler had delayed him. The prowlers might be on their way back by now.

He shrugged. He had to risk that, because he needed to see what they were doing. Besides, they'd find it hard to gang up on him in a narrow tunnel. Hard to move silently in the darkness, though. He'd have warning of their approach, hear something. Wouldn't he?

He set off down the metal stairs, moving silently in the increasing darkness. At the bottom he risked using his torch and moved along. When he reached the grille he used the torch again, whistling softly in surprise when he saw that the grille had been propped open. A quick examination showed the lock to be undamaged.

So, they must have had a key. How had they got hold of that? Even he, owner of the other end of the tunnels, hadn't been able to obtain a key to this grille from the council, thanks to that busybody Brody.

When the two intruders stopped, the man waited while his companion checked the door that led into Number 1.

There was a gasp and then, 'It's unlocked. Does that mean they've come into the tunnels?'

'Shh. Let's see if we can hear anything.' He listened for a few moments and shook his head. But at that point he almost turned and left via the tunnel. Only his pride at always completing the job he'd been paid for kept him standing there, because he was beginning to feel more than uneasy. He usually paid attention to that kind of feeling.

The trouble was, if he *had* heard someone following them, he'd be better leaving through the house than the tunnels, assuming there was no one waiting for them there. Oh hell, why had he got himself into this idiotic situation?

'Can you lock the door to the tunnel behind us?'

'I don't have a key to it.'

There it was again. Amateurs! Never prepared properly. 'Hurry, then, damn you.'

They went up into the secret room he'd been told about. He wasn't impressed by the old rubbish lying around and was tempted to relieve his feelings by sweeping it off the desks, he was so on edge now.

Why did people bother to save such stuff, anyway? If there was ever another war, it'd not be won by ancient communication methods like these.

He turned to see her still using the camera. 'How the hell long are you going to be? I've had enough. Open the door and let us out through the house.'

'I don't know where the secret door is from inside this room.'

He breathed in deeply, then stiffened. Had he heard a sound?

He held one finger to his lips.

They both stood very still.

He could hear nothing, so took a careful look round the room. He was good at figuring layouts and opening locks. There seemed only one place possible for a door and he shone his torch round that area saying, 'Ahhh!' very softly as he found this assumption to be correct. The door hadn't been locked from this side at all.

Within a couple of minutes he had it open, easily working out the simple procedure, which he'd guess hadn't been designed to conceal the way the door opened, but to prevent it being opened accidentally.

When his companion moved forward, he grabbed her jacket and hauled the idiot backwards, moving to go first. He wasn't having anything blocking his way forward now. If this was the way out, he was legging it as soon as he could.

This was turning into a farce and he'd had enough. After all, he'd been paid most of the money. His freedom was more important than getting the final payment at the end of the job.

He found himself in a big empty room, shone his torch round and saw some bare shelves to one side. That was all. Nothing to steal here.

He turned towards the stairs and began to go down them slowly.

Of course, the idiot following him had to stumble and gasp and the noise echoed round the empty room.

The man froze again, putting one arm out to stop the idiot continuing.

Angus followed the intruders along the passage, risking using his torch to check the way a couple of times. He switched off the torch and continued to fumble his way along the tunnel. There were no turnings, after all. But he stumbled on some uneven ground at one stage and made a faint noise as he steadied himself against the corrugated iron wall. Once again he froze, afraid that they might have heard the slight sound he'd made.

He debated for a few moments whether to continue, realising that he couldn't make out exactly what lay ahead of him in the darkness, had no idea how far along they were and didn't want to risk using his torch.

Worst of all, he didn't know how many intruders he might have to face. He was still angry about all this, but not to the extent of risking his life. With great reluctance he decided to go back and consult Iain. Better if there were two of them to face whoever had broken in.

Emil would surely have the sense to stay inside the flat.

And by now Cutler must have found someone to call the police to their aid?

You could never guarantee that people would do the sensible thing, though. That thought made him turn and hurry back towards the substation.

Emil heard a sound from the gallery at the front of the ground floor, stood up and tiptoed to the door of the flat. Another faint sound, undoubtedly a footstep, proved that there was definitely someone there.

He'd hoped it was Angus, could see the outline of someone staring towards him and realised it was definitely not his friend. This man was much burlier.

Hastily, Emil moved backwards into the flat and tried to lock the door. But in his haste, he fumbled and that gave the intruder time to hurtle across the dark echoing space and jam a foot in the opening.

The man must have been strong, because Emil was no weakling. But even had he expected such a vicious attack, he'd have been no match for this brute.

With a roar of anger, the man kicked and punched him, sending him hurtling across the living room of the flat. From somewhere in the gallery a woman screamed. Then, as his opponent smashed a chair down on him, Emil heard another scream from closer at hand and a plea to stop.

He struggled to roll away but the room seemed to waver round him and pain exploded in his side, sending him spinning into darkness.

Nell and Ginger heard the screams from just outside the street, where they were still keeping watch, and instinctively started running towards the first house in Saffron Lane. Someone sounded to be in trouble.

Another scream rang out.

Make that big trouble.

The door was open and they could see a figure standing just inside the gallery. It could have been either a man or a woman, but the screams had come from there and had sounded more like those of a woman.

They were close enough to see a big man appear in the doorway of the flat. Ginger dragged Nell out of sight to one side as he ran across the gallery towards the outer door.

He sent the person who'd screamed tumbling backwards like a human skittle when she tried to bar his way.

As the man ran away down Saffron Lane, the woman struggled to her feet, sobbing.

'The two of us can cope with one woman,' Ginger said grimly. 'Lock that outer door once we're in, so he can't return.'

As Nell used the catch to do this, the woman saw them, shrieked and ran towards the stairs.

Ginger pounded after her, catching hold of her leg before she'd got halfway up them and keeping hold in spite of being kicked. The woman's struggles made them both roll down the last few stairs again, by which time

Nell was waiting at the bottom to help hold the stranger.

From the distance came the welcome sound of a police siren and they could hear someone running down the street towards them.

'Open the door!' the person yelled. 'It's me.'

'That's Abbie. What's she doing here?'

They dragged their prisoner to the door and let Abbie in.

'I was worried about Emil,' she gasped. 'Where is he?'

Nell shouted, 'Leave this one to us and check inside the flat. I think Emil's been hurt.'

Abbie was off across the room at once.

Turning back, Nell yanked away the balaclava from the woman, who was still struggling violently to get away from them. 'It's Charlene Brody from the council!'

'I don't care who it is,' Ginger panted. 'She just bit me. If she does it again, I'll slap her face good and hard.'

Nell managed to grasp one flailing arm and twist it behind Charlene's back. She'd seen that done on TV in police shows, and was surprised when it worked. Charlene yelled in pain and stopped struggling. But she continued to sob.

'What do we do with her?' Ginger panted. 'I daren't leave you on your own with her or I'd go and fetch something to tie her up with from my flat.'

'We'll have to wait till the police arrive.'

They heard a groan from the flat.

'It sounds as if Emil's been hurt,' Nell worried. 'Who was that brute? Hey, you! What was he looking for?'

Their captive erupted into hysterics at that, weeping and yelling incoherently. Nell still kept tight hold of the arm. She wasn't letting the woman get away.

Charlene Brody might work for the council but that didn't give her the right to be breaking into people's houses in the middle of the night. And the guy who'd presumably attacked Emil must have come with her. How had they got in?

She'd have to trust Abbie to cope with Emil, could only hope he'd be all right.

Iain and Angus saw the running figure before he saw them. A police car came into view and when he tried to change direction to avoid it, that gave them the opportunity to grab him.

The car screeched to a halt beside them and a voice ordered them to stop fighting.

Relieved, they obeyed orders but when they did, their captive rolled to one side and tried to run away. He only got a few yards before a police officer tackled him.

Shrill screams could be heard faintly in the distance.

'I think there's another intruder in Number 1,' Angus said. 'Can we go and help, Officer?'

'No, sir. I don't want you getting injured. And you might just run away like he tried to do.'

'I shan't run away. I'm the owner of Dennings.'

'Ah. So you say.'

'There's a man recovering from a serious operation in Number 1. We have to check that he's all right.'

'It sounded like a woman screaming, not a man.'

'Sorry. I'm going to find out.' Angus took off, afraid Nell might have gone against his wishes and got involved. He found one of the police officers running beside him.

'Go back,' yelled the officer.

'Not if someone's hurting my wife.'

Fear for Nell seemed to add speed to Angus's feet and he took the lead.

When Abbie ran into the flat, she found Emil lying on the floor, groaning and clutching his side. She didn't wait to ask what was wrong, could see that he was in severe pain, so pulled out her phone and rang for an emergency ambulance. Then she knelt beside him, all the time keeping an eye on the door in case another intruder came in.

'What can I do to help you, Emil?'

'Nothing. He hit old wound. Going to be sick. Pain bad.'

She managed to hold him in a position to vomit on the floor, then pulled him gently to one side and dived towards the kitchen sink to moisten some sheets of kitchen roll and bring them back to help him wipe his mouth.

After that she could only hold him in her arms till a police officer walked in and knelt beside them.

Emil explained in halting phrases that he'd been hit in a place where he had a weakness from a recent major operation.

And all the time Abbie cradled him against her, willing him to be all right, praying that the damage wasn't serious.

Chapter Thirty-One

Angus saw Nell as soon as he entered Number 1. She was keeping a wary watch on a woman who seemed to be having hysterics. It took him only a minute to realise who the woman was, and by that time the police officer was insisting on his attention, asking what the hell was going on.

It was Nell who answered. 'This is Charlene Brody, who works for the council. She and a man broke into this house tonight. She doesn't have a key or permission to come here, but she's been trying to get in for a while, even though the heritage specialists are dealing with our finds.'

Someone called from the flat, 'We have an injured man here, sir. An ambulance has been called but I'm checking that it's on its way.'

The officer moved across the room to the door of the flat.

Angus followed him and saw Abbie holding Emil. 'That's Emil Kinnaird,' he told the officer. 'He and his father are involved in opening a museum upstairs in what used to be a secret communications room in the war. He does have a key to this house and permission to come and go here.'

Ginger had let go of Charlene, who tried to get to her feet, but the police officer was the only one who reached out to help her.

She flinched away from him so violently she fell backwards, lying on the ground again and wailing even more loudly.

'I think she's having a total mental breakdown,' Ginger told him softly. 'She probably needs medical attention, too.'

An ambulance pulled into the street and Ginger went to the door to beckon to the paramedics.

They came inside and were about to go towards Charlene when the officer pointed to the door of the flat. 'I think the man in the back room needs checking first.'

Within minutes they'd fetched a stretcher and lifted Emil on to it, and were wheeling him out to the ambulance. One paused to run a quick check on Charlene and nodded to the police officer. 'You were right. Hysterics. She can wait for attention.'

That set off more incoherent shouts and rolling about.

Abbie followed the paramedics outside. 'I'm going with him to the hospital.'

'You can follow in your car.'

'I don't have a car here,' she lied. 'Can't I come in the ambulance?'

He hesitated. 'Only close relatives are allowed to do that.'

She didn't even hesitate. 'Well, I'm his fiancée. That's surely close enough.'

Emil managed a faint smile and didn't contradict her, sighing and closing his eyes.

She sat on a little pull-down seat at the rear of the ambulance, watching him.

He reached out his hand and she took it, holding it all the way to the hospital.

Only when they had wheeled him away to be seen by a doctor did she think to pull out her phone and ring her sister to tell Keziah what was happening and ask her to keep Louis with her.

Then she sat and worried. And wondered about herself. Why had she been so reluctant to let a relationship start between her and Emil? Because she was a fool, that's why. Emil was . . . special. Yes, that was the word. He even got on with Louis, who kept talking about him and asking when they were going to see him and the toys again.

She wasn't going to keep being a fool, though, Abbie decided. Her heart had literally lurched in her chest when she saw Emil curled up on the floor, badly injured.

Not all men were like her rotten ex. Emil definitely wasn't.

One police car stayed at the scene to take statements, while the other took Charlene away.

After they'd explained what had happened – to the best of their knowledge, anyway – Angus took a police officer out of the house via the secret room and tunnel. At the other end of the tunnel the officer used the keys taken from the male intruder to lock the grille and outer door of the electricity substation. The other officer had driven to meet them there.

'Who'd have thought this was all underneath the road?' the officer marvelled.

'There's going to be a small museum in the secret room.'

'I'll be bringing my kids to see it, then. I served in the army for a while and I take *Lest we forget* very seriously. I'm making sure they know what they owe to our ancestors. My father lost an uncle in the Second World War. We were lucky. He was our only family casualty.'

'I'm glad for you.'

Nell was looking exhausted and the officers kindly drove her and Angus back to the big house before going back on duty.

Angus brought Elise and Stacy up to date on what they knew about this puzzle, after which the two artists got into Stacy's car and returned to their own houses.

'I never expected this sort of thing to happen here,' Elise said.

'You won't be too nervous to sleep from now on?'

'Nah. Too excited tonight, perhaps. And I always keep a poker near my bed. There's something very reassuring about a poker. I'd better have some hot milk, though, to relax me.'

'You're amazing.'

'For a woman of my age?' Elise teased.

'Well, you must admit most women in their seventies don't take intruders in their stride.'

'Most women in their seventies have had to cope with far worse than intruders, my dear. People forget that and often treat them like children. It makes me and my friends furious.'

'You're such a good role model for me.'

Elise chuckled. 'Nice to be useful still.'

Iain stayed on at Number 1 with Ginger after everyone else had left, standing at the door to watch them go and staying there looking up at the sky as dawn started to gild the shadowy greyness that still shrouded the grounds. 'What a night!'

'We came safely through it. I hope Emil is all right.'

'I do too. If anyone had hurt you I wouldn't have been answerable.'

'I'd have felt the same if anyone had hurt you. But I couldn't help feeling sorry for that poor woman who had a breakdown, even if she has been a pain in the neck for Angus and Nell.'

'The police were surprisingly gentle with her, weren't they? Kind, even.'

'Yes. I was glad about that. Whatever it was she'd been trying to do tonight must have been an act of desperation.'

They heard a car approaching.

'What now?' she asked.

'It's only Stacy bringing Elise back. I recognise the sound of her engine.'

They waved to the two women, who were yawning as they went into their houses.

As silence fell once more on the little street, Iain said, 'I shall always look at this street and Bay Tree Cottage with fondness. Wasn't it lucky we met here?'

'Yes. Very lucky. Do I hear a "but" in what you're saying?'

'Yes. I'd rather we live in my house once we're married, though, if you don't mind, Ginger, love. This flat is a bit small for two.'

'I agree. But I've had a happy respite here, found myself, as some might say.' She reached up to kiss his cheek. 'As well as finding you.'

He gave another huge yawn. 'Let's go and get some sleep. I've no doubt we'll discover what this was all about later today.'

Nell rang round in the early afternoon to invite all the occupants of Saffron Lane to tea. 'We've got some explanations for what went on,' she said. 'The police have been in touch with Angus, asking questions and supplying some answers. It helps sometimes to be a landowner, even of a small chunk of land like ours, and to come from a noble family, even if you are, as Angus says, just a twig on a lower branch of the family tree.'

She let that sink in, then asked, 'Have you seen Cutler today? I can't get through to him.'

'No. Do you want me to knock on his door and give him a message?' Ginger asked.

'Would you? You'd better ask him to join us. We can hardly leave him out and he hasn't answered his phone.'

But as Ginger opened her door to go and see if she could find him, he came out of his house, looking haggard.

'Hey! Just a moment!' she called.

He turned to scowl at her. 'What do *you* want?'

'You're not answering your phone. Nell wants us all to go up to tea at the big house so that she can explain what's been going on.'

He didn't even hesitate. 'Tell her no. I've had enough of the Dennings and this damned place. I have an appointment today that's much more important than listening to them rabbit on about this stupid place. I know what happened to me and I don't care about what happened to the rest of you. I'm going to find another job somewhere safe.'

'Tell her yourself.'

He opened the door of his van. 'Can't. I don't have time.'

She watched open-mouthed as his car pulled away, narrowly missing Iain's vehicle.

Iain was standing in the doorway keeping an eye on her and listening. 'What's that fool doing now?'

'Who knows? We're all invited to tea and explanations at the big house but he's not even taking the time to refuse. He has something much more important to do, apparently.'

'Important to him. He believes the universe revolves around him.' He tapped his forehead. 'I think he's a very strange man.'

'Tell me about it. Good riddance to him, as far as I'm concerned. I hope he does find somewhere else to live. Today's gathering will be more pleasant without him, that's for sure. We'll stroll up, eh?'

He plonked a kiss on her cheek, as he often did. 'On condition you hold my hand all the way.'

Emil woke in hospital a few hours after he'd been carted away in an ambulance to find Abbie sitting beside his bed staring at him.

'How do you feel?' she asked at once.

He lay considering this and a faint, floaty feeling suggested they'd given him painkillers. He felt his side and touched only flesh. 'They didn't have to operate?'

'No. They checked things out and they think you'll be all right when the bruising goes. It's not bleeding inside, apparently. What was it caused by originally?'

'Cancer. The surgeon thought he'd got it all, but said I had to go carefully, because it'd involved quite a major bit of work in that area.'

'It's wonderful what they can do these days. Aren't you glad you weren't born a hundred years ago?'

'Yes. Very.' He reached out and she put her hand in his willingly. 'It doesn't seem to worry you that I've had cancer. Some people shrink away from me, as if it's catching.'

She shrugged. 'Life gives and takes away. You just have to do your best with what lands on your plate.' She flushed and added, 'I've been stupid, though, trying to avoid men because one rat hurt me.'

'Understandable. But perhaps you'll let me get to know you better so that I can prove I'm not a rat. You *and* Louis. He's a great little lad.'

'He thinks a lot of you, too.'

Emil closed his eyes but kept hold of her hand. 'Where is he?'

'With Keziah.'

'Then can you stay with me a little longer? Till I know when I'm going to be released.' His smile vanished. 'That can't happen soon enough for me. I've had enough of hospitals, more than enough.'

The door to his room opened just then and a nurse came in.

'Oh, good. You're awake, Mr Kinnaird. How are you feeling?'

'A lot better,' he said firmly.

'Perhaps you could leave us for a few minutes so that we can check that, Ms Turrell? But don't go away. We may be able to release Mr Kinnaird if there's someone at home to keep an eye on him.'

'Fine.' Abbie left them to it and took the opportunity to phone her sister. 'Sorry not to have got back to you. I fell asleep.'

'Doesn't matter. Louis helped me with Susie and then slept in her room on an air mattress. They had a great time bouncing on it when they thought I didn't know. How's Emil?'

Abbie explained, and had to explain all over again as Louis took over the phone.

The doctor came out just then, looking a bit tight-lipped.

'I've got to go.' She switched off her phone and looked anxiously at the nurse who followed him.

The nurse waited till the doctor had turned into another room and grinned at her. 'It's all right. Your fiancé is fine. It's just that he's determined to leave today and the doctor wanted him to stay. Mr Kinnaird was rather emphatic about it.'

'He's had enough of hospitals.'

'So he said, and in no uncertain terms. Anyway, if you can arrange to take him home and stay with him today and tonight, he should be all right.'

'I'll look after him very carefully indeed, I assure you.'

Abbie went into the room and found Emil sitting on the edge of the bed, smiling at her. He was still pale, but looked much more cheerful.

She smiled back. 'So, you've refused to obey orders and want me to take you home?'

'If you don't mind.'

'I don't mind at all. But you'll be careful, eh?'

'Yes. Very careful indeed. I'm not stupid.'

The nurse came back with some paperwork and pills, plus several sheets of printed instructions and then at last they were free to leave.

'I don't have my car,' she told him, 'but we can take a taxi. There's a stand for them at the main door, apparently.'

He took her hand. 'Thank you, Abbie.'

His gaze was warm and something inside her responded to it. This time she didn't try to stop herself and plonked a quick kiss on his cheek. She wouldn't, couldn't rush into anything, but oh, she did like this man. And so did Louis.

That was a good start, surely?

When they got back to the flats, she took Emil up in the lift to his flat, then ran down to Keziah's flat to collect her son. But Louis must have heard them come into the building because he came rushing to greet her in the hall and flung his arms round her.

Keziah came to join them. 'Better leave my nephew here with me after you've finished cuddling him, Abbie love.'

'Oh? Why?'

'Nell and Angus have invited everyone involved round to their place for afternoon tea, to explain what it was all about. About four o'clock. Is Emil well enough to go? What do you think?'

'That's up to him.'

'Can I go and see him, just for a minute?' Louis begged.

'Of course. And thanks, Keziah. I'll bring this young rascal back to you when we leave.'

She went into the flat to find Emil sitting on his new recliner chair with his feet up, listening to Louis and answering questions.

She explained about the afternoon tea and Emil said at once that he would certainly be well enough to go, but perhaps he'd better change his clothes first.

'If you're sure.'

Emil smiled at her. 'I'm sure.'

Louis looked from one to the other and grinned. His expression was rather knowing for a boy his age. She hadn't expected him to be aware of the attraction between her and Emil.

She left Emil in his flat and hurried down to hers to take a quick shower and change her clothes.

Louis waited for her in the living room. 'Auntie Kez said not to bother you about it, but she thinks you and Mr Kinnaird might be getting very friendly. I'm not bothering you but I just want you to know that it's all right by me.'

She blinked at him in surprise.

'One of the boys at school has a mother who got married again. He says it's made her happier and he gets on well with his stepfather, so he said I should look out for a man for you. Only you found one yourself. And I like Mr Kinnaird, as well as his mechanical toys.'

He left it at that, but her son's concern for her warmed her heart. He was nearly eight now, growing up fast and starting to become more aware of other people's needs. Keziah must have explained the situation to him. She owed her sister for that.

'Let's go up and see if Emil needs help with anything. He and I don't have to leave quite yet, but I want to make sure he's not overdoing things.'

Angus looked round the main drawing room at Dennings, filled now with everyone from the street who'd been invited except for Cutler. He felt happy that these people who had once been strangers had now become good friends.

There were others in Peppercorn Street who'd become friends too, but they hadn't been involved in this recent series of events so he hadn't invited them today. All of them seemed to be at a happy stage in their lives now, though, thank goodness.

He and Nell made sure all their guests had a drink of some sort, then he stood up. 'If you'll give me your attention for a few moments, I'll explain more or less what that was all about. The police only gave me a broad outline, not the details, of course.'

He allowed them time to settle, then began. 'It seems that Charlene Brody had become paranoid about being bypassed for promotion. She's always been a strange one, but no one realised how bad she had become. She was counselled about her attitudes generally but nothing anyone said or did could change her view that she always knew best what was right, and she was utterly determined to get the next promotion.'

He paused, watching them shake their heads and exchange glances. He knew what they were thinking: a more unsuitable person to manage others would be hard to find.

'The latest problem blew up because she knew the council's management were going to restructure the area in which she worked and appoint a new person to head the revamped section. And when she wasn't even called for interview, she hired a criminal to break in and prove that she knew better than anyone about security for our local heritage site.'

'But surely her job was only incidentally about heritage?' Iain said.

'Yes. But she didn't see it that way. She was obsessed

by the thought of that secret room, heaven knows why. I'm afraid the poor woman has now been committed to a mental hospital and will receive appropriate treatment there. Let's hope it works.'

'What about the fellow she hired?'

'He's claiming she told him this was council business, and says she had the keys to prove it, so he was unaware that he was committing a crime.'

There were soft, cynical sounds in response to this from those gathered.

'He's out on bail at the moment. He may or may not get away with helping her. I hope he doesn't.'

There were murmurs of agreement.

'Anyway, Emil, you should now be able to take your time setting up your father's pet project and the woman appointed as the head of that new section assures me that the council will do all it can to facilitate the preservation of such a valuable historical resource.'

'That's good. And the regional heritage people are being a huge help, too.'

They discussed it a little more, then Nell brought out some champagne. 'I think it's time to celebrate something, don't you?'

They looked at her in puzzlement.

She waited till they all had a full glass and raised her own. 'Here's to Iain and Ginger's engagement.'

There was a chorus of approval and glasses were raised and clinked with wholehearted pleasure at this news.

Angus nudged her. 'The letter.'

'I nearly forgot. Ginger, this came for you.'

Ginger took it, gulped and looked at Iain.

'What is it, love?'

'It's from Donny. Oh, no. He must have wangled my address from my neighbour.'

He put an arm round her shoulders. 'We'll read it when we get outside, eh?' He looked at Nell and Angus. 'Thank you for your kind wishes. I'm quite sure Ginger is going to lead me a merry dance. But I'm looking forward to it. If you don't mind, I'll take her home now. She's exhausted.'

When they got outside, Ginger couldn't wait a minute longer and tore open the letter.

Iain stood next to her, waiting patiently.

Tears formed in her eyes and ran down her cheeks but when she looked at him, she was smiling. 'Donny says sorry for how he treated me. He says he's doing well in rehab. And he's met someone there.' She handed him the letter. 'And he says he's given up smoking, too. Oh, I do hope he has!'

Iain read it quickly. 'He hasn't written much.'

She smiled. 'Donny hates writing. He likes to *do* things or make things.' She waited a moment then looked at him pleadingly, 'It sounds promising, doesn't it?'

'It sounds very promising, my love.'

'I'll write back straight away and tell him our news.'

'Um . . . better just concentrate on his news. Tell him about us another time you write.'

'You think?'

'I'm sure of it.'

'But it's a good start, isn't it?'

'Yes, my love. A very good start.' He hesitated, then added, 'And if he really is sincere about making a new start, I'll give him a try with a job in the nursery garden.'

She flung herself into his arms, sobbing even more happily and he prayed he wouldn't regret this offer.

Epilogue

Six weeks later

Ginger got dressed, her stomach full of butterflies. But when she looked at herself in the mirror, the butterflies began to subside. It was the nicest dress she'd ever owned, a soft floral material, with lots of lilac in it, with a plain lilac jacket. And Elise had been right when they went shopping: the small fascinator went perfectly with it. Such a lot of money she'd paid for such a small hat!

When she went outside, Iain was waiting for her next to a limo.

She gaped in surprise. 'I thought we said no fuss.'

'Just a little bit of fuss,' he pleaded.

Elise and Stacy came out to join them in the limo so that they could act as witnesses. The new guy who'd taken Cutler's place peeped out of Number 4 to wave and wish them well.

'Isn't Jack a big improvement on the former occupant?' Elise said. 'The people who've got Cutler as their artist in residence must be regretting it deeply by now.'

They went to the town hall where, in spite of Ginger wishing it to be just the four of them, several members of Iain's family were also waiting for them.

She turned to frown at him.

'My family would have killed me if I'd tried to stop them coming. And I'd better warn you, there's another surprise waiting for you inside. If you don't like it, I'll eat that hat of yours. That's a promise.'

She shot him a quick look, then they went into the section reserved for marriages. There Donny was standing, holding the hand of a rather scrawny woman who must have had a very hard life from the look of her face but who was smiling broadly at Ginger now.

She ran across to hug her son and be introduced to his new girlfriend, then they sat down to wait for their turn to enter the inner sanctum, where she and Iain could get married. Her nervousness had vanished now and she held his hand, quietly content to become his wife, even reconciled to having a group of people watch it happen.

When they came out after the brief ceremony, which she'd found surprisingly moving, a photographer was waiting to record the occasion.

'We said no fancy photos!' she exclaimed because she never liked photos of herself.

Iain grinned at her. 'So shoot me!'

'I want a photo of you, Mum,' Donny said. 'Iain's right.' He held out his hand to his stepfather. 'Congratulations. She's a treasure.'

Which brought a lump to Ginger's throat.

On the way back, she and Iain sat in solitary state in the limo, holding hands. He asked the driver to stop at the park and brought out his own camera. 'Will you take our photo?'

'Happy to, sir.'

Then Iain took several of her, so she did the same for him.

'Why more photos?' she asked as they got back into the car.

'These are our own photos in every way.'

As the driver started off again, she raised Iain's hand to her lips and kissed it.

He leant forward to kiss her gently on the lips and murmur, 'Well, Mrs Darling, how does it feel to be married?'

'Wonderful, Mr Darling.'

When they got to Saffron Lane everything was quiet and in spite of their stop they seemed to be the first to get there. 'I hope I've provided enough refreshments,' Ginger worried. 'There are going to be more people than I'd planned for.'

'I hid some extra champagne so we'll get them tiddly, at least.'

He offered her his arm and when they got to the house, he picked her up and carried her over the threshold.

'Stop it, you fool, I—' She broke off as she saw that the café at the rear was filled with people. The other artists, Nell and Angus, everyone she'd met here and others who seemed to be some more of Iain's friends.

'You didn't think we'd let you get away with a skimped wedding, did you?' Nell asked.

Everyone erupted into cheers and shouts of 'Congratulations!'

Ginger clutched Iain's hand tightly and whispered, 'I'm no good at making speeches. If they want one, you can do it, because I'm quite sure you were in on this.'

'Of course I was. I wanted to show off my lovely new wife.'

'You'll pay for that tonight.'

'Goody, goody!'

She couldn't hold back another smile. She doubted she'd ever be able to stay mad at Iain – even if she ever had a reason to be mad at him.

Then she saw the cake sitting on the table full of food at the back of the café. It was such a beautiful creation, more happy tears rolled down her cheeks.

'Time to stop snuffling,' Iain whispered.

'I will. It's just . . . I never had any of this last time, not even a cake.'

'All this and me, too,' he teased.

Very seriously she took his face in both her hands and said, 'And you are the best thing of all, Iain Darling, Iain – my – darling!'

ANNA JACOBS is the author of over eighty novels and is addicted to storytelling. She grew up in Lancashire, emigrated to Australia in the 1970s and writes stories set in both countries. She loves to return to England regularly to visit her family and soak up the history. She has two grown-up daughters and a grandson, and lives with her husband in a spacious home near the Swan Valley, the earliest wine-growing area in Western Australia. Her house is crammed with thousands of books.

annajacobs.com

To discover more great books and to
place an order visit our website at
allisonandbusby.com

Don't forget to sign up to our free newsletter at
allisonandbusby.com/newsletter
for latest releases, events and exclusive offers

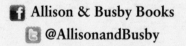 **Allison & Busby Books**
@AllisonandBusby

You can also call us on
020 7580 1080
for orders, queries
and reading recommendations